John Collingwood Bruce

Bruce Roman Wall Handbook

Third Edition

John Collingwood Bruce

Bruce Roman Wall Handbook
Third Edition

ISBN/EAN: 9783337736590

Printed in Europe, USA, Canada, Australia, Japan

Cover: Foto ©Andreas Hilbeck / pixelio.de

More available books at **www.hansebooks.com**

TO THE

ROMAN WALL:

A GUIDE TO TOURISTS TRAVERSING THE

BARRIER OF THE LOWER ISTHMUS,

BY

J. COLLINGWOOD BRUCE, LL.D., D.C.L., F.S.A.,

HONORARY MEMBER OF THE SOCIETY OF ANTIQUARIES OF SCOTLAND,
AND OF CAMBRIDGE,
CORRESPONDING MEMBER OF THE ROYAL ARCHÆOLOGICAL INSTITUTE OF ROME,
ETC., ETC.

THIRD EDITION.

LONDON: LONGMANS, GREEN, & CO.
NEWCASTLE-UPON-TYNE: ANDREW REID, AKENSIDE HILL.

———

1885.

PREFACE TO THE SECOND EDITION.

THE former edition of this little work was called "The Wallet Book of the Roman Wall." This designation not being generally understood, the more common one of "Hand-book" has now been adopted.

The Romans were not only great Conquerors but they were wise and politic Governors. They brought all the nations of the then known world into unity, and spread the blessings of order and civilization to the very ends of the earth. The people of England are in this respect, the successors of the Romans. Through their instrumentality vast continents, of the existence of which Cæsar never dreamt, have obtained the advantage of a well organized government; their rude inhabitants have been induced to engage in the pursuits of peaceful industry; and the blessings of Christianity have been pressed upon their attention.

As Englishmen we cannot but feel an interest in the history of our great predecessors, and have special pleasure in tracing those memorials of their presence and power which they have left in this and other lands. There is, besides, much advantage in doing so. We can hardly hold fellowship with the mighty men of the past without imbibing some of their courage and some of their lofty aspirations.

The grandest monument of the daring, the power, and the determination of the Romans which is to be found in the dominions of our most gracious Sovereign Lady, Victoria—dominions on which the sun never sets—is to be found in the Northern Counties of England. Educated Englishmen cannot but wish to visit the Wall of Hadrian, which stretches from the estuary of the Tyne to the waters of the Solway Firth. To assist them in doing so this Hand-book has been prepared.

Whilst substantially the same as when first published, care has been taken in this new edition to bring up the information to the present period. A new map has been prepared, and several plates depicting various scenes met with on the Wall have been introduced, for which the writer is indebted to the artistic skill and kindness of his friend Mr. C. J. Spence.

Newcastle-upon-Tyne,
        12th July, 1884.

PREFACE TO THE THIRD EDITION. .

In a few weeks after its issue, the second edition of this Hand-book was exhausted, and for a third time the writer has found himself engaged in preparing it for the press. Under the impression that he was doing so for the last time, he has spared no pains in making the present issue as complete as possible. Some of the newest discoveries on the Wall have perhaps been described with a minuteness scarcely fitting a work of this character. The writer's object in doing so has been to render the little volume, in some measure, supplemental to the last edition of his larger work, "The Roman Wall."

An Appendix is added, in which an account is given of a diploma of Roman citizenship found at Chesters, and some suggestions are made as to how the Wall may be visited. Some additional plans and illustrations have also been given.

In traversing the Wall from time to time, the writer notices with regret that those portions of the great structure which have, in recent times,

been divested of the covering which has protected
them for centuries, are beginning to yield to
adverse influences. Should the tourist, half-a-
century hence, find the descriptions in the Hand-
book more glowing than the reality, let him
charitably consider that we have written of things
as they are, not as they may eventually be.

J. COLLINGWOOD BRUCE.

June 10*th*, 1885.

CONTENTS.

CHAPTER I.

PLANS, ETCHINGS, AND MAP.

TOGETHER WITH 137 WOODCUTS.

THE HAND-BOOK

TO

THE ROMAN WALL.

CHAPTER I.

INTRODUCTORY.

HE who contemplates a pilgrimage *per lineam Valli*, if he be imbued with a thorough love of antiquity, and duly appreciate the importance of the great structure which invites his attention, will not lightly enter upon the enterprise. Before adopting the "scallop-shell" and adjusting his "wallet," he will probably wish to renew his acquaintance with the earliest chapter of our English history, and glance at the authors who have written upon the subject of his inquiry. Perchance, too, he may wish to carry with him upon his journey, in the form of *memoranda*, some of the results of his reading. To direct him in his earlier inquiries, and to supply him with some materials for subsequent reference, the following sections of this chapter are set before him.

I.—WORKS UPON THE SUBJECT.

Camden, in his *Britannia*, besides describing the inscriptions under the various localities where they were found, has a short chapter headed *Vallum, sive Murus Picticus*. The last edition printed in the author's lifetime is that of 1607. The *Britannia* was translated in 1610 by Dr. Philemon

Holland under, as is understood, the supervision of the author. The edition of 1637 is illustrated with the wood-cuts and plates of the last Latin edition. Bishop Gibson published in 1695 a new translation of Camden's *Britannia*, with "additions and improvements." New editions appeared in 1722, 1753, and 1772. The Bishop's additions unhappily are not always improvements. The later editions contain a chapter on the Wall, written by a person who surveyed it in 1708. This writer is probably the earliest, who, having traversed the whole length of the structure, has given us an account of it. The editions of Camden most in vogue at present, are those of Richard Gough, the one published in 3 vols., fol., 1798; the other in 4 vols., fol., 1806.

The *Itinerarium Septentrionale or a Journey through most of the Counties of Scotland*, and those in the North of England, was published by Alexander Gordon, 1727. He is the "Sandy Gordon" of the *Antiquary*. Gordon traversed portions of the Wall in company with Horsley.

Horsley's *Britannia Romana*, published in 1732, is still the great storehouse of information on the Roman Antiquities of Britain. He has treated of the Wall and its inscriptions largely and lucidly. Unfortunately his engravings, for the most part, do great injustice to the altars and sculptures which they are intended to represent. The lettering of the inscriptions is good. I fancy that he was his own artist. As an epigraphist he knew the importance of representing the letters with absolute fidelity, while perhaps he cared less about the exact form of the stones on which they were inscribed. Besides it is easier to draw letters than artistic figures.

Warburton's *Vallum Romanum*, published in 1753, consists of those portions of Horsley's work which bear directly upon the Wall, transferred to his own book, with the smallest possible acknowledgment. It has the advantage of being portable.

In 1776, some years after the death of its author, Stukeley's *Iter Boreale* was published. It contains the memoranda of a journey taken in 1725, in the company of Mr. Roger Gale, over the western and northern parts of England. His account of the Wall is interesting—many of his remarks being as original as they are just.

Brand, in an Appendix to the first volume of his *History of Newcastle*, published in 1789, gives a brief account of the Wall.

William Hutton, of Birmingham, in the year 1801, at the age of 78, traversed the great Barrier on foot, and gave to the world the result of his observations in a work entitled *The History of the Roman Wall*. Though the work betrays some weak points, a fine vein of enthusiasm runs through it. In his preface, he says, "Perhaps I am the first man that ever travelled the whole length of the Wall, and probably the last that will ever attempt it."

The Rev. John Hodgson, who was at the time incumbent of Jarrow and Heworth, published, in *The Picture of Newcastle-upon-Tyne* (1812), a comprehensive and useful account of the Wall.

The fourth volume of the *Magna Britannia* of the Messrs. Lysons (1816), contains an article on the Roman Wall, and a good account of the Roman Inscriptions of Cumberland.

The Rev. John Hodgson, M.R.S.L., devoted nearly the whole of the last volume which he lived to publish of his *History of Northumberland* to the Walls of Hadrian and Antoninus. This volume was also published separately, under the title of *The Roman Wall and South Tindale, in the Counties of Northumberland and Cumberland*, 1841. To this work, as well as to Horsley's *Britannia Romana*, the present writer is largely indebted.

Bruce's *Roman Wall*, first edition, 1851; second edition, 1853; third edition, 1867.

The *Lapidarium Septentrionale: a Description of the Monuments of Roman Rule in the North of England*, 1875; edited by the present writer.

In the *Collectanea Antiqua*, Vols. II. and III., Mr. Charles Roach Smith gives a graphic account of the journeys he made to different parts of the Barrier, some of them in the company of the author.

To the munificence of His Grace the Duke of Northumberland, antiquaries are indebted for two works of the greatest importance—*A Survey of the Watling Street from the Tees to the Scotch Border*, made in the years 1850 and 1851, and *A Survey of the Roman Wall*, made in the years 1852—1854. The late Mr. Henry McLauchlan, to whom the responsible task was committed, has performed it with great skill and the most scrupulous fidelity. Whoever possesses the *Survey of the Wall*, and its accompanying *Memoir*, may not only enter advantageously upon his pilgrimage, but when it is over, can easily retrace, upon the accurately engraved plans, every step of his journey.

II.—Historical Data.

Pytheas of Marseilles made an exploratory voyage to Britain, about B.C. 330.

Julius Cæsar landed in Britain B.C. 55. The legions which he brought on this occasion were the seventh and the tenth.

He withdrew the same year. The next summer he made a second descent, bringing five legions with him. One of these legions, the seventh, is specified by Cæsar ; the others are not. This army was likewise withdrawn before the approach of winter.

The Emperor Claudius visited the island in person A.D. 43, having previously sent over a considerable army, consisting of the second, the ninth, the fourteenth, and the twentieth legions, together with a proper proportion of auxiliary troops. Most of these legions had an important part to perform in the history of Roman Britain. The second continued in the island until it was finally abandoned by the Romans, having Caerleon, the Isca Silurum of the Romans for its head quarters. The ninth was surprised and nearly cut to pieces by Boadicea ; and afterwards, when in Scotland, under the command of Agricola, it met with a similar misfortune. A slab found in York in 1854, commemorating the erection of a building in the reign of Trajan, by the ninth legion, furnishes us with probably the last trace of it. Horsley conjectures that the remains of this legion were incorporated with the sixth legion, which Hadrian brought over with him, and which eventually settled in York, the Eburacum of the Romans. The fourteenth legion was recalled by Nero ; it was sent back again to Britain by Vitellius, and finally withdrawn in the reign of Vespasian. The twentieth must have remained until nearly the close of the period of Roman occupation. It had the city of Chester, the Deva of the Romans, for its head quarters.

It was in the year A.D. 50 that Caractacus and his family fell into the hands of Ostorius Scapula, Claudius' Proprætor in Britain ; they were heavily ironed and sent to Rome.

In the reign of Nero, A.D. 61, when Suetonius Paulinus, the Roman general, was upon an expedition in Anglesea, the Britons, commanded by Boadicea, arose and destroyed the Roman settlements at Colchester, St. Albans, and London.

By command of the Emperor Vespasian, Julius Agricola repaired to Britain as commander-in-chief. On his arrival, late in the summer, A.D. 78, he subdued the Ordovices (occupying the north west portion of Wales), and reduced the Isle of Anglesea, The next year he brought into subjection the inhabitants of the Lower Isthmus of Britain. Before advancing northwards he planted some forts in the district already subdued so as to secure his retreat, if necessary, and to prevent his being attacked in the rear. The year 80 saw him ravaging the country as far north as the Firth of Tay. The year 81 he spent in securing his Caledonian conquests, especially by the establishment of forts in the district of the Upper Isthmus. Having done this, he overran the country northwards; and in A.D. 84 he gave battle to 30,000 Caledonians under Galgacus. Shortly afterwards, from motives of jealousy, he was recalled by Domitian, who, on the death of Titus, had assumed the purple.

During the reigns of Nerva and Trajan we hear little of Britain. Hadrian became Emperor in the year 117; and towards the close of A.D. 119, in consequence of the turbulent state of the island, visited it in person. It was on this occasion that the sixth legion, which had previously been stationed in Germany, came to our shores.

To this period the building of the Roman Wall of the North of England must be referred. The Emperor did not remain in the country long enough to see the completion of his works, but he left behind him Aulus Platorius Nepos, his Legate and Proprætor, under whom they were carried forward.

Antoninus Pius succeeded Hadrian A.D. 138. During his reign the Barrier extending between the Firth of Forth and the Firth of Clyde was reared; the management of the work was committed to Lollius Urbicus, Imperial Legate and Proprætor.

Whilst Marcus Aurelius Antoninus, styled the "Philosopher," held the reins of government, Britain was in a turbulent state; Calpurnius Agricola, of whom some memorials remain in the inscribed stones of the Wall, with difficulty repressed the excited passions of the people. In the reign of Commodus, the son of Marcus Aurelius, the warlike tribes broke out into open insurrection. Dion Cassius gives us the following account of the affair:—"Commodus was also engaged in several wars with the barbarians . . The Britannic war, however, was the greatest of these. For some of the nations within that island having passed over the wall which divided them from the Roman stations, and besides killing a certain commander, with his soldiers, having committed much other devastation, Commodus became alarmed, and sent Marcellus Ulpius against them. (*Monumenta Historica Britannica*, p. lix.) The Wall, its stations and guard chambers, bear to this hour extensive marks of devastations which were probably committed at this period. The name of Ulpius appears upon the fragment of a stone at Chesters, the ancient CILURNUM.

Other legates—Perennis, Pertinax, Albinus, and Junius Severus, came in succession to Britain, during the reign of Commodus; but their efforts were not successful in establishing permanent peace, or even in preventing occasional seditions and insurrectionary movements in the army itself.

Commodus was strangled A.D. 192. When Lucius Septimius Severus found himself firmly established on the throne, he turned his attention to the state of Britain. His legates

being unable either to purchase peace or compel the submission of the natives, he came over in person in the year
208, bringing with him his sons, Caracalla and Geta. He
spent some time in making preparations. He gathered his
troops from all quarters; improved the roads, restored the
ruined stations, and repaired the Wall. At length, in A.D.
209, all being ready, he advanced against the Caledonians.
He spent three years in the enterprise, and lost fifty thousand
men. Worn out with disease and vexation, he returned to
York to die. His ashes were taken with much ceremony to
Rome. His two sons, Caracalla and Geta, succeeded him
A.D. 211; but in the year following the younger fell a victim
to his brother's ambition.

In A.D. 217, Caracalla was himself assassinated, when
Opilius Macrinus was declared Emperor, to be assassinated
in his turn, next year.

In A.D. 218, Marcus Aurelius Antoninus, commonly called
Elagabalus (of whom some lapidarian memorials have been
found upon the Wall), was proclaimed Emperor.

In the year A.D. 222, Elagabalus was slain, and Severus
Alexander became Emperor. Severus Alexander's assassin-
ation took place in the year A.D. 235.

Maximinus, who succeeded him, met with the usual fate
of emperors, A.D. 238. Gordian (III.) became Emperor in
238, and was slain A.D. 244. Marcus Julius Philippus was
next chosen Emperor; and he associated with himself in the
management of the Empire his son Philip. On their assassin-
ation, A.D. 249, Quintus Trajanus Decius was proclaimed
Emperor, and slain two years afterwards.

Trebonianus Gallus became Emperor A.D. 251; and in
the year following, associated his son Volusianus with him in
the Empire.

Publius Licinius Valerianus and his son Gallienus became joint Emperors A.D. 254.

In the year 260, Gallienus became sole Emperor. During his reign a large number of usurpers arose, who are commonly denominated the "Thirty Tyrants;" of these Victorinus, Postumus, the two Tetrici, and Marius, are supposed to have been acknowledged in Britain, as their coins are found in greater abundance here than on the continent. Claudius, surnamed Gothicus, became Emperor A.D. 268; L. Domitus Aurelianus A.D. 270; M. Claudius Tacitus A.D. 275; M. Annius Florianus A.D. 276, (he reigned only 88 days); Aurelius Probus A.D. 276; M. Aurelius Carus A.D. 282, (who associated his sons, Carinus and Numerianus with him as Cæsars); and Aurelius Diocletianus A.D. 284. Diocletian associated with himself in the Empire M. Aur. Valer. Maximianus.

In A.D. 287, Carausius, who had charge of a fleet to repress piracy in the English Channel, revolted, and assumed the sovereignty of Britain, which he retained until A.D. 293, when he was treacherously slain by Allectus, who then assumed the government of the Island. In A.D. 296, Constantius Chlorus repaired to Britain, slew Allectus, and reduced the country to its allegiance. Constantius and Galerius, who had for some years acted as subordinate Emperors or Cæsars, obtained the sovereign authority A.D. 305. In the following year Constantius died at York; and his son Constantinus, afterwards surnamed the Great, obtained the purple. In the same year (306), Maxentius, son of Maximianus, was proclaimed Emperor at Rome.

In the year A.D. 330, Constantine transferred the seat of empire to Byzantium, which henceforth took the name of Constantinople. Constantine died A.D. 337; and his three sons, Constantinus, Constantius, and Constans were proclaimed Emperors. Magnentius, whose father was a Briton, claimed, A.D. 350, the imperial purple; but he died by his own hands the following year. Julian, surnamed the Apostate, became Emperor A.D. 361; and was succeeded by Florus Jovianus, A.D. 363. Flavius Valentinianus assumed the purple A.D. 364; and took his brother Valens as colleague; he afterwards further associated with himself his sons, Gratianus and Valentinianus the younger. At this period Britain was in a deplorable state; Picts, Saxons, and Scots, made it the object of incessant attacks. Gratian having become, A.D. 379, by the death of his colleagues, sole Emperor, he chose as his partner in the Empire, Theodosius, afterwards styled the Great. In the year 383, Theodosius shared the Empire with his son Arcadius. At this time Clemens Maximus, who had been sent to Britain to repel the incursions of the Picts and Scots, was proclaimed Emperor by the soldiers; in order to support his claim, he passed over with his forces to the continent, draining the island of its youth.

Theodosius dying, A.D. 395, was succeeded by his two sons, Arcadius and Honorius, Honorius being made Emperor of the West, and Arcadius of the East.

In the year 396, the Britons sent ambassadors to Rome, asking for assistance. A legion is said to have been sent to them, by command of Stilicho, and their enemies were for a time repressed. We are not told what legion was sent, and no inscriptions have been found or other evidence discovered to betoken its presence.

A.D. 407. This was a season of intestine tumult in Britain. The soldiers successively invested Marcus, Gratian, and Constantine with the purple. Constantine transferred his army to Gaul, and made a successful stand against Honorius; again draining the island of its military strength.

A.D. 410. Honorius, harassed by the Goths and other enemies, wrote to the Britons informing them he was no longer able to help them, and that they must look to themselves for safety.

A.D. 418. *The Saxon Chronicle* says, "This year the Romans collected all the treasures that were in Britain; and some they hid in the earth, so that no one has since been able to find them; and some they carried with them into Gaul."

A.D. 446. "Britain abandoned by the Romans."—*Horsley*.

The series of Roman coins found in the North of England practically ends with Gratian, who was slain A.D. 383; there have, however, occasionally been found coins of Theodosius, who died A.D. 395, of Arcadus, who died A.D. 408, and of Honorius, who died A.D. 423.

III.—MILITARY DATA.
The Notitia.

A document has come down to our times from the Roman age, which is of great use in elucidating the arrangements of the Wall. It is entitled *Notitia Dignitatum et Administrationum omnium tam civilium quam militarium in partibus orientis et occidentis*, and contains an account of the disposal of the chief dignitaries of the Empire, civil and military, throughout the world. The following is the portion of it which relates to the Wall; the section is headed *Item per lineam Valli*—also along the line of the Wall.

The Tribune of the fourth cohort of the Lingones at SEGEDUNUM.
The Tribune of the cohort of the Cornovii at PONS ÆLII.
The Prefect of the first ala, (or wing,) of the Astures at CONDERCUM.
The Tribune of the first cohort of the Frixagi (Frisii) at VINDOBALA.

The Prefect of the Savinian ala at HUNNUM,

The Prefect of the second ala of Astures at CILURNUM.

The Tribune of the first cohort of the Batavians at PROCOLITIA.

The Tribune of the first cohort of the Tungri at BORCOVICUS.

The Tribune of the fourth cohort of the Gauls at VINDOLANA.

The Tribune of the first cohort of the Astures at ÆSICA.

The Tribune of the second cohort of the Dalmatians at MAGNA.

The Tribune of the first cohort of Dacians, styled "Ælia," at AMBOGLANNA.

The Prefect of the ala, called " Petriana," at PETRIANA.

The Prefect of a detachment of Moors, styled "Aureliani," at ABALLABA.

The Tribune of the second cohort of the Lergi at CONGAVATA.

The Tribune of the first cohort of the Spaniards at AXELODUNUM.

The Tribune of the second cohort of the Thracians at GABROSENTUM.

The Tribune of the first marine cohort, styled "Ælia," at TUNNOCELUM.

The Tribune of the first cohort of the Morini at GLANNIBANTA.

The Tribune of the third cohort of the Nervii at ALIONIS.

The Cuneus of men in armour at BREMETENRACUM.

The Prefect of the first ala, styled Herculean, at OLENACUM.

The Tribune of the sixth cohort of the Nervii at VIROSIDUM.

The precise period when the *Notitia* was compiled is not known. It was probably written about the beginning of the fifth century, and certainly before the abandonment of Britain by the Romans. By it the names of the stations are ascertained. Thus, for example, when in a camp, now called Housesteads, many altars are found bearing the name of the first cohort of the Tungri, a body of troops which the *Notitia* places at BORCOVICUS, the inference is natural that Housesteads is the BORCOVICUS of the Romans ; and this probability becomes a moral certainty when the stations on either side of it yield tablets inscribed with the names of the first cohort of the Batavians, and the fourth cohort of the Gauls, the troops which the *Notitia* places in the stations immediately to the east and west of Borcovicus.

Antonine's Itinerary.

The *Itinerary* of Antonine is another work of much importance in settling the names and locality of the Roman stations in Britain as well as in other countries. It gives the routes pursued by the soldiers in their marches, the stations at which they halted, and the distance between them in Roman miles. It is usually ascribed to the reign of Caracalla.

The Army and its Officers.

The legion was the main division of a Roman army. At first none of the lower class were admitted into the army; afterwards, the legion was composed of any one having the rank of a Roman citizen. In early times, the legion consisted of about 4,000 foot soldiers; in the time of Hadrian its complement was 6,000.

Each legion had a troop of 300 or 400 horse soldiers attached to it. Originally the cavalry consisted entirely of *equites*, knights; in later times foreign troops were used for this purpose, and hence they were regarded as auxiliaries simply, and as not belonging to the legion. As the cavalry generally formed the wing of an army, a troop of horse was termed an *ala*, or wing. Attached to each legion, was a number of foreign troops (besides the cavalry) called auxiliaries. In later times the Roman army chiefly consisted of these.

Each legion was divided into ten cohorts, each cohort into three maniples, and each maniple into two centuries. Each century consisted, when complete, as its name implies, of 100 men.

The principal officers in the legion were tribunes, of which there were six to each legion. Each century was commanded by a centurion. Each centurion had under him two officers, acting as lieutenants, called *optiones*, and two *signiferi* or standard-bearers. The term *vexillarius* was also applied to the bearer of the standard *(vexillum)*. In inscriptions found on the Wall, the term *vexillatio* is occasionally met with; it is supposed to refer to a body of soldiers drafted from different cohorts or even legions for some special purpose and fighting under the same *vexillum* (or standard); it is applied to both horse and foot soldiers.

Each *ala* or troop of horse (about 300 in number), was divided into ten squadrons called *turmæ*, and each *turma* into three *decuriæ* (consisting usually of ten men). The *decuria* was commanded by a decurion. A prefect (equivalent in rank to the tribune of the legion) commanded the whole *ala*. The term *numerus* occurs in the *Notitia*, and in inscriptions. It seems to be a general term, similar to our word band or troop. It is most frequently applied to cavalry, though not exclusively.

Mention is made in inscriptions of officers of a superior class to any of those already named. The Proconsuls and Proprætors were the governors of the province. The office of Consul was in its origin essentially of a military nature, and that of Prætor of a judicial or civil character. When a province was in a state of revolt, the command of it was conferred upon a Proconsul, but when the development of its internal resources was the object of most importance, a Proprætor was appointed; this distinction, however, was not always observed. The Legate was a military officer, not attached to any particular corps, but exercising a general superintendence of a country, under the provincial governor. His rank corresponded to that of a lieutenant-general in a modern army. The following terms are also met with:—

Emeriti, soldiers who had served their full time; *evocati*, veterans again called out as volunteers—the Emperor's body guard; *ex-evocati*, veterans a second time discharged; *beneficiarii*, soldiers who have received some honour or special exemption from the drudgeries of service; *duplares*, soldiers receiving double pay as a reward.

IV.—Height above the Level of the Sea of the Principal Points of the Wall.

These are taken from the 6-inch ordnance maps of Northumberland and Cumberland.

	Feet.		Feet.
Benwell (Camp)	416	Hotbank Crags	1074
Chapel Hill	374	Cats' Stairs	900
Rutchester	448	Winshields	1230
Harlow Hill	495	Great Chesters	600
Down Hill...	666	Walltown Crags	860
Halton Chesters	600	Carvoran	700
Wall 1½ m. west of Halton	870	Birdoswald	515
St. Oswalds	745	Bankshead	510
Limestone Corner ...	822	Hare Hill	426
Carrawburgh	785	Castle-steads	177
Carraw House	795	Walton	248
Sewingshields Crags ...	1068	Newtown of Irthington ...	248
Housesteads	800	Stanwix	110

CHAPTER II.

A GENERAL VIEW OF THE WORKS.

The Roman Wall, or as it used to be called, the Picts' Wall, is a great fortification intended to act not only as a fence against a northern enemy, but to be used as the basis of military operations against a foe on either side of it.

It cannot have been reared as a fence, marking the northern limit of the Roman Empire ; for (1) every station and every mile-castle along its course seems to have been provided with a wide portal, opening towards the north ; and (2) there are some stations situated far to the north of the Wall, on the line both of the Watling Street and of the Maiden Way, which can be proved to have been garrisoned by Roman troops until near the close of the period of Roman occupation in Britain.

This great fortification consists of three parts :—

1. A Stone Wall, with a ditch on its northern side.   2. An Earth Wall, or Vallum, south of the stone wall.   3. Stations, Castles, Watch-towers, and Roads, for the accommodation of the soldiery who manned the Wall, and for the transmission of military stores.   These lie, for the most part, between the stone wall and the earthen lines.

The whole of the works proceed from one side of the island to the other in a nearly direct line, and in comparatively close companionship.   The stone wall and earthern rampart are generally within sixty or eighty yards of each other.   The distance between them, however, varies according to the nature of the country.   In one instance they approach within thirty yards of each other, while in another, they are half a mile apart.   It is in the high grounds of the central region that they are most widely separated.   Midway between the seas, the country attains a considerable elevation ; here the stone wall seeks the highest ridges, but the Vallum, forsaking for a while its usual companion, runs along the adjacent valley.   Both works are, however, so arranged as to afford each other the greatest amount of support which the nature of the country allows.   The Wall usually seizes those positions which give it the greatest advantage on its northern margin; the Vallum, on the other hand, has been drawn with the view of occupying ground that is strongest towards the south.

The stone wall extends from Wallsend on the Tyne to Bowness on the Solway, a distance of about seventy-three English miles and a half. (MacLauchlan's *Memoir*, p. 5.) The earth wall falls short of this distance by about three miles at each end; not extending beyond Newcastle on the east side, and Dykesfield * on the west.

Most writers who have treated of the Roman remains in Britain, have considered that the various parts of the fortification are the work of different periods.

Horsley conceived that the stations and the north agger of the Vallum were the work of Agricola; that the southern mounds and fosse of the Vallum were the work of Hadrian; and that the stone wall was reared by Severus. Other writers maintain that the stone wall was erected by Theodosius and Honorius, about the close of the fourth and the beginning of the fifth century.

In all probability, the whole series of fortifications were the work of one period, and were reared at the command of Hadrian. Deferring the discussion of this question until the works have been examined in detail, it will meanwhile be convenient to speak of the whole series as being but different parts of one great engineering scheme.

The most striking feature in the plan, both of the Murus and the Vallum, is the determinate manner in which they

---

* Some writers represent the Vallum as extending as far west as Drumburgh. According to Mr. MacLauchlan's Plan it proceeds no further than Dykesfield. Horsley says, "Whether Hadrian's work has been continued any further than this marsh, or to the water-side beyond Drumburgh, is doubtful," p. 156.

pursue their straightforward course. The Vallum makes fewer deviations from a right line than the stone wall; * but as the Wall traverses higher ground, this remarkable tendency is more easily detected in it than in the other. Shooting over the country, in its onward course, it only swerves from a straight line to take in its route the boldest elevations. So far from declining a hill, it usually selects one. For nineteen miles out of Newcastle the road to Carlisle runs upon the foundation of the Wall, and during the summer months its dusty surface contrasts well with the surrounding verdure. Often will the traveller, after attaining some of the steep acclivities of his path, observe the road stretching for miles in an undeviating course to the east and to the west of him, resembling, as Hutton expresses it, a white ribbon on a green ground. But if the Wall seldom deviates from a right line, except to occupy the highest points, it never fails to seize them, as they occur, no matter how often it is compelled, with this view, to change its direction. This mode of proceeding involves another peculiarity. The Wall is compelled to accommodate itself to the depressions of the mountainous region over which it passes. Without flinching, it sinks into the "gap," or pass, which ever and anon occurs, and, having crossed the narrow valley, ascends unfalteringly the acclivity on the other side. The antiquary, in following the Wall into these ravines, is often compelled to step with the utmost caution, and in clambering up the opposite ascent, is as frequently constrained to pause for breath.

* This peculiarity of the Vallum has been strikingly brought out in Mr. MacLauchlan's Survey. West of Harlow Hill it runs for nearly five miles in a straight line. West of Limestone Corner it runs in the direction of Sewingshields Crags three miles and a half without bending. Between Banks-hill and Sandysike, a distance of three miles and a half, it pursues a direct course.—*Memoir*, pp. 18, 34, 61.

I.—THE WALL.

In no part of its course is the Wall entirely perfect, and therefore it is difficult to ascertain what its original height has been. Bede, whose cherished home was the monastery of Jarrow, anciently part of the parish of Wallsend, is the earliest author who gives its dimensions. He says, "It is eight feet in breadth, and twelve in height, in a straight line from east to west, as is still visible to beholders." He probably speaks of it as he saw it in his own neighbourhood.

Subsequent writers assign to it a greater elevation. Sir Christopher Ridley, writing about the year 1572, gives it the following dimensions:—"The bredth iij yardis, the hyght remaneth in sum placis yet vij yardis." Samson Erdeswick, an English antiquary of some celebrity, visited the Wall, in the year 1574. His account is:—"As towching Hadrian's* Wall, begyning abowt a town called Bonus standing vppon the river Sulway now called Eden, and there yet standing of the heyth of 16 fote, for almost a quarter of a myle together, and so along the river syde estwards." Camden, who visited the Wall in 1599, says :—"Within two furlongs of Carvoran, on a pretty high hill, the Wall is still standing, fifteen feet in height, and nine in breadth." These statements leave upon the mind an impression that the estimate of Bede is too low. In all probability, the Wall would be surmounted by a battlement of not less than four feet in height, and as this part of the structure would be the first to fall into decay, Bede's calculation was probably irrespective of it. This, however, only gives us a total elevation of sixteen feet. Unless we reject the evidence of Ridley and Erdeswick, we must admit,

* Thus early was the stone wall ascribed to Hadrian.

even after making due allowance for error and exaggeration, that the Wall, when in its integrity was, in some parts of its course, about eighteen feet high. This elevation would be in keeping with its breadth.

The thickness of the Wall varies considerably; in some places it is seven feet, in others nine feet and a half (in the foundation course). Probably the prevailing width is eight feet, the measurement given by Bede.

The frequency with which the thickness of the Wall varies favours the idea that numerous gangs of labourers were simultaneously employed upon the work, and that each superintending centurion was allowed to use some discretion as to its width. The northern face of the Wall is continuous, but the southern has numerous outsets and insets, measuring from four to twelve inches at the points where the sections of the different companies joined.

Throughout the whole of its length, the Wall was accompanied on its northern margin by a broad and deep fosse, which, by increasing the comparative height of the Wall, added greatly to its strength. This portion of the Barrier may yet be traced, with trifling interruptions, from sea to sea. Even in places where the Wall has quite disappeared, its more lowly companion, the fosse, remains.

When the ditch traverses a flat or exposed country, a portion of the materials taken out of it has frequently been thrown upon its northern margin, so as to present to the enemy an additional rampart. In those positions, on the other hand, where its assistance could be of no avail, as along the edge of a cliff, the fosse is intermitted.

No small amount of labour has been expended in the excavation of the ditch; it has been drawn indifferently through alluvial soil, and rocks of sandstone, limestone, and basalt. The great labour which this involved is well seen at the top of Limestone Bank, where enormous blocks of whinstone lie just as they have been lifted out of the fosse. How they were lifted is a matter of wonder to many. The fosse never leaves the Wall to avoid a mechanical difficulty.

The size of the ditch in several places is still considerable. To the east of Heddon-on-the-Wall, it measures thirty-four feet across the top, and is nearly nine feet deep; as it descends the hill from Carvoran to Thirlwall, it measures forty feet across the top, fourteen across the bottom, and is ten feet deep. To the west of Limestone Corner is a portion which, reckoning from the top of the supplemental mound on its northern margin, has a depth of twenty feet. The dimensions of the fosse were probably not uniform throughout the line; but these examples prepare us to receive, as tolerably correct, Hutton's estimate of its average size. "The ditch to the north was as near as convenient, thirty-six feet wide and fifteen feet deep."

II.—THE VALLUM.

The Vallum or earth wall, is uniformly to the south of the stone wall. It consists of three ramparts and a fosse.

One of these ramparts (*a*) is placed close upon the southern edge of the ditch, the two others of larger dimensions stand, one (*b*) to the north, and the other (*c*) to the south of it, at the distance of about twenty-four feet. The annexed section of the works near the 18th mile-stone west of Newcastle exhibits their present condition.   It is drawn to the scale of seventy-five feet to the inch.   The wall itself, though shown in the cut, is, in that part unhappily, entirely removed.

The aggers or ramparts, in some parts of the line, stand, even at present, six or seven feet above the level of the neighbouring ground.   They are composed of earth, mingled, not unfrequently, with masses of stone.   Occasionally, the stone preponderates to such an extent as to yield to the hand of the modern spoiler ready materials for the formation of rough stone walls.   In several places they are being quarried with this view.

The fosse of the Vallum is of a character similar to the fosse of the stone wall; but, judging from present appearances, its dimensions have been rather less.   It, too, has been frequently cut through beds of stone.

Although the distance between the stone Wall and the Vallum is, as already observed, perpetually varying, the lines of the Vallum maintain amongst themselves nearly the same relative position throughout their entire course.

No apparent paths of egress have been made through these southern lines of fortification.   The only mode of communication with the country to the south originally contemplated seems to have been by the gateways of the stations.

The aggers of the Vallum were probably fenced with stakes—*chevaux de frise.*

If we adopt the theory that the Wall and the Vallum exhibit unity of design, a question of some importance arises —With what view was the Vallum constructed?   The true answer to this inquiry seems to have been hit upon even before Horsley's time.   That able antiquary, referring to the relative position of the Wall and the Vallum, says:—"Such considerations as these have induced some to believe that what now goes by the name of Hadrian's work was originally designed for a fence against any sudden insurrection of the provincial Britons, and particularly of the Brigantes" (p. 125). A careful examination of the country over which the Wall runs, and the fact which Horsley thus states:—"That the southern prospect of Hadrian's work, and the defence on that side, is generally better than on the north; whereas the northern prospect and defence have been principally or only taken care of in the Wall of Severus," almost necessarily lead to the conclusion that whilst the Wall undertook the harder duty of warding off the professedly hostile tribes of Caledonia, the Vallum was intended as a protection against sudden surprise from the south. Agricola is represented by Tacitus as saying:—"With me it has long been a settled opinion, that the back of a general or his army is never safe." The natives of the country on the south side of the Wall, though conquered, were not to be depended upon; in the event of their kinsmen in the north gaining an advantage, they would be ready to avail themselves of it. The Romans knew this, and with characteristic prudence made themselves secure on both sides.

The existence of the Murus on one side of the military way and the Vallum on the other would be of great service in securing "the safety of the soldiers in their marches, and of the transit of provisions and military stores."

Mr. Hodgson, who makes this remark, further adds:— "Besides the protection of the military way from station to station, the interval between the Walls might have its use as a secure enclosure for the horses and cattle of the garrisons to depasture in."

III.—STATIONS, MILE-CASTLES, AND TURRETS.

The third part of the fortification consisted of the structures that were formed for the accommodation of the soldiery.

These consisted of Stations, Mile-castles, and Turrets.

At distances along the line, which average nearly four miles, stationary camps *(stationes* or *castra stativa)* were erected. These received their distinctive appellation in contradistinction to those contemporary camps which were thrown up when an army halted for a night or some brief period.

The stations on the line of the Wall were military cities, suited to be the residence of the chief who commanded the district, and providing secure lodgment for the powerful body of soldiery he had under him.

Some of the stations of the Wall are believed to have been Agricola's forts, but adopted by the engineer of the Wall as suitable to his purpose, though independent of the great Wall. In the case of the other stations, they would probably be built before the Wall was stretched from the one to the other, as the securing of a safe retreat for the soldiers employed upon the work would necessarily be the first care of the builder.

The stations are quadrangular in their form, though rounded at the corners, and contain an area of from three to five acres. The station of Birdoswald, which is the largest, contains five acres and a half. Drumburgh contains only three-quarters of an acre; but this is an extreme case. A stone wall, from five to eight feet thick, incloses them, and has probably in every instance been strengthened by a fosse; occasionally an earthen rampart is added. They usually stand upon ground which slopes to the south, and is naturally defended upon one side at least.

The Wall, when it does not fall in with the northern wall of a station, usually comes up to the northern cheek of its eastern and western gateways. The Vallum, in like manner, usually approaches close to the southern wall of the station, or comes up to the defence of the southern side of the eastern and western portals. At least three of the stations, it must, however, be observed, are quite detached from both lines of fortification, being situated to the south of them. They probably belonged to Agricola's series of forts.

All the stations have, on their erection, been provided after the usual method of Roman castrametation, with at least four gateways; in several instances these gateways have been partially walled up at some period prior to the final abandonment of the fortification.

In some of the best preserved stations the main streets leading from the four gateways, and crossing each other at right angles, may be discerned. The minor streets which communicated with these were very narrow, but parallel to the main ones. The remains of suburbs, for the accommodation, probably, of the camp followers, have been found outside the walls of most of the great camps. The officer commanding the garrison has, in several instances, had a villa outside the station to which he could resort in times of quietness, and where he would have a greater degree of comfort than within the contracted lines of the camp.

In selecting a spot for a station, care has been taken that a copious supply of water should be at hand. The springs, rivulets, wells, and aqueducts, whence they procured the needful fluid, are still, in many places, to be traced.

The stations, as we might expect on an enemy's frontier, have been constructed with a view to security, not luxury or display. In this respect they show a striking contrast with the Roman buildings in the south of England. No traces of a tesselated pavement have been found in the mural region; the nearest approach to it being some lozenge-shaped flooring tiles at Birdoswald.

For the most part, the stations now present a scene of utter desolation. The wayfarer may pass through some of them without knowing it. The sheep, depasturing the grass-grown ruins, look listlessly upon the passer-by, and the curlew, wheeling above his head, screams as at the presence of an intruder. Whether or not sites naturally fertile were chosen for the stations does not appear ; but certain it is that they are now, for the most part, coated with a sward more green and more luxuriant than that which covers the contiguous grounds. Centuries of occupation have given them a degree of fertility which, probably, they will never lose. One can scarcely turn up the soil without meeting, not only with fragments of Roman pottery and other imperishable articles, but with the bones of oxen, the tusks of boars, the horns of deer, and other animal remains.

It is not a little remarkable that the names of the stations, which must have been household words in the days of Roman occupation, have for the most part been obliterated from the local vocabulary. The truth is, that military reasons dictated the choice of the stations,—commercial facilities gave rise to modern cities.

The number of stations given in the *Notitia* list, as being situated *per lineam Valli*, is twenty-three. Horsley conceived that eighteen of these were immediately connected with the Wall, and that the rest were supporting stations to the north and the south of it. This opinion is probably near the truth, but as the stations following *Amboglanna* towards the west have not been ascertained with certainty, it may be most prudent not to attempt to give their Roman names until the discovery of some inscriptions in them shall enable us to do so correctly.

In addition to the stations, Castella or Mile-castles were provided for the use of the troops which garrisoned the Wall. They derive their modern name from the circumstance of their being usually placed at the distance of a Roman mile, or about seven furlongs from each other. They were quadrangular buildings, differing somewhat in size, but usually measuring about sixty feet from east to west, and fifty from north to south. They have evidently been built at the same time as the Wall; their walls being of the same kind of masonry as the Wall, and of the same thickness. They are placed immediately within the Wall, that structure forming their north wall. Though generally placed at the distance of a Roman mile from each other, the nature of the ground, independently of distance, has frequently determined the site of their location. Whenever the Wall has had occasion to traverse a river or a mountain-pass, a mile-castle has usually been placed on the one side or the other to guard the defile. Judging from the most perfect specimens which remain, these mile-castles have been provided with wide portals of massive masonry in the centre of their northern and southern walls. Their southern angles have been rounded off on the outside. It is not easy to conjecture what were the internal arrangements of these buildings; probably they afforded little accommodation beyond what their four strong walls and well-barred gates gave. It is not unlikely that temporary erections were placed within them, with roofs leaning against the walls of the main building. The foundations of such structures have been found in several of them.

Between the mile-castles three, or according to Horsley, four subsidiary buildings, generally denominated Turrets or Watch Towers, were placed. They were little more than stone sentry-boxes. Horsley, in his day, complained that "scarce three of them could be made out in succession." When the first edition of this book was published not one was to be seen along the whole course of the Wall.* They fell a prey more easily than other parts of the great structure to the rapacity of the spoiler. Recent excavations have displayed examples at East Brunton, Black-Carts Farm, and Walltown Crags. They are recessed into the great Wall, and contain an area of about twelve feet by ten feet; their walls are three feet thick.

IV.—THE MILITARY WAY.

But all these arrangements were not enough ; without Roads, one important element in the strength of the Great Barrier would be wanting. Nothing economises military force more effectually than the possession of means for quickly concentrating all available resources upon any point which the enemy may select for attack. Neither stone walls nor ditches, nor earthen ramparts, would alone have proved material impediments to the incursions of the Caledonians :—

> An iron race, ...
> Foes to the gentler genius of the plain.

It is reported that Agesilaus, when asked where were the walls of Sparta, pointed to his soldiers, and said " There."

* Hutton says, "I have all along inquired for turrets, but might as well have inquired among the stars."

The Romans placed their chief reliance on the valour and discipline of their armies, though they did not despise the assistance of mural lines. In a foreign country, to which it was difficult to transmit relays of troops, it became a matter of great importance to economise the lives of the soldiery. Hence arose the Wall.

The Military Way is usually about eighteen feet wide. It is composed of rubble stone, chiefly trap. Its surface is rounded, the centre being elevated a foot or eighteen inches above the adjoining ground. The mode of its formation seems to have been this :—A couple of stones were placed edgewise in the centre; others were placed on each side of these, slightly leaning upon them, and when the proper width was attained, stout kerb-stones defined each margin and perfected the work. By this means the pressure was distributed over the whole surface. When carried along the slope of a hill, the hanging side of the road was made up by unusually large kerb-stones. In most places where the way still remains, it is completely grass-grown, but may, notwithstanding, be easily distinguished from the neighbouring ground by the nature of its herbage; the dryness of its substratum allowing the growth of a finer description of plant. For the same reason a sheep-track generally runs along it. For the accommodation of the soldiery, the road went from castle to castle, and so from station to station. In doing this it did not always keep close to the Wall, but took the easiest path between the required points. In traversing the precipitous grounds between Sewingshields and Thirlwall, the ingenuity of the engineer has been severely tried; but most successfully has he performed his task. Whilst, as previously observed, the Wall shoots over the highest and steepest summits, the road pursues its tortuous course from one platform of the rock to another, so as to bring the traveller from mile-castle to mile-castle by the easiest possible gradients.

Besides the road now described, which, throughout its entire length, keeps within the two great lines of fortification, and goes from mile-castle to mile-castle; another, situated to the south of both Murus and Vallum, has afforded a direct line of communication between the eastern and western stations. From Chesters to Carvoran the Wall forms a curved line in order to gain the highest hills of the district. For the accommodation of those whose business did not require them to call at any intermediate point, this other road went, like the string of a bow, direct and upon comparatively level ground from one of these stations to the other. This road, named the Stanegate, is shown upon the map, it passes near the modern village of Newburgh, and skirts the north gate of the station at Chesterholm, near to which place a Roman mile-stone stands. In all probability this road was continued westwards. In Mr. MacLauchlan's Survey it is seen stretching from Carvoran to the vicinity of Birdoswald, and again, from the vicinity of Irthington to the neighbourhood of Stanwix.

The existence of this direct line of road to the south of both Murus and Vallum bears strongly upon the question whether or not the north agger of the Vallum was a military way. With one line of transit close to the Wall and another going in a direct line from one extremity (or nearly so) of the Barrier to the other, there was no need for a third in close vicinage with the first.

In estimating the resources of this great fortification, we must also bear in mind that two great lines of communication —the Watling Street and the Maiden Way—intersected the country from north to south, and that many subsidiary roads bore down upon them. The sixth legion, whose head-quarters was York, would have no difficulty at any season of the year in coming to the aid of the auxiliaries to whom the defence of the Wall was more immediately intrusted, at whatever point their assistance might be required.

If tradition is to be credited, the Romans were not satisfied with roads as a means of rapidly communicating information; speaking-trumpets or pipes, we are told, ran along the whole length of the Wall. It may perhaps be sufficient to say that no one is known to have seen these speaking-tubes; though earthen and lead pipes, for the conveyance of water, are not unfrequently met with in the stations. Besides, such means of transmitting information would not be needed. Horsley, speaking of the turrets, says:—"By placing sentinels in each of these, who must have been within call of one another, the communication quite along the Wall might be kept up, without having recourse to the fiction of a sounding trumpet, or pipes laid underground from one end of the Wall to the other."

V.—Quarries and Mode of Building.

The Masonry of the Wall next demands attention. The stones employed in building the Wall and stations were very carefully selected. When good stones were to be had near at hand, they were taken; but those of inferior quality were never used to avoid the labour of bringing better from a distance. In some parts of the line, in Cumberland especially, the stone must have been brought from quarries seven or eight miles off. A quartzose grit was generally selected, not only on account of its hardness, but because its rough surface gave the mortar firmer adhesion to it.

The quarries from which the stone has been procured can, in many instances, be precisely ascertained. On Fallow-field Fell, not far from Chollerford, are a series of ancient quarries, on the face of one of which are to be seen the words—

[P]ETRA FLAVI[I] CARANTINI,

The rock of Flavius Carantinus.

On opening out, in the year 1837, some old quarries on the high brown hill of Barcombe, near Thorngrafton, a small copper vessel was found, containing a large number of coins, all of the Upper Empire. North of Busy Gap the wedge-holes yet remain in some slabs of rock that rise to the surface. A Roman quarry existed on Haltwhistle Fell, on which was formerly the inscription, LEG.VI.V. In Cumberland there are several Roman inscriptions on the face of the ancient quarries. About two miles west of Birdoswald, and little more than a quarter of a mile south of the road, is Coome Crag, on which are several Roman inscriptions, made apparently by the quarrymen. The most remarkable of this class of antiquities is the "Written Rock of the Gelt," near Brampton, which is here shown. The general purport of the inscription is:—

"A vexillation of the second legion, under an *optio* called Agricola, were, in the consulship of Flavius Aper and Albinus Maximus [A.D. 207 employed here to hew stone]."

East of the Glebe Farm at Irthington, are extensive remains of ancient quarries.

The exterior masonry of the Wall consists, on both sides, of carefully squared freestone blocks; the interior, of rubble of any description firmly imbedded in mortar. The character of the facing-stones is peculiar, yet tolerably uniform. They measure on the face eight or nine inches by ten or eleven; their length, which is perhaps their characteristic feature, some-times amounts to twenty inches or more. The part of the stone exposed to the weather is cut across "the bait," so as to

D

avoid its scaling off by the lines of stratification ; the stone
tapers towards the end which is set into the Wall, and has a
form nearly resembling that of a wedge. Owing to the extent
to which the stones are set into the Wall, the necessity of
bonding tiles—so characteristic of Roman masonry in the
south of England—is altogether superseded. Stones of the
shape and size which have now been described were just those
which could be most easily wrought in the quarry, most conveniently carried on the backs of the impressed Britons to the

Wall, and most easily fitted into their bed.*   The uniformity
in their appearance is such as to enable us, after a little
practice, at once to recognise them in the churches, castles,
farm-buildings, and fences of the district through which the
Wall runs.

The stones of the ramparts of some of the stations (CILUR-
NUM for example) are smaller than those of the Wall. The
internal buildings of the stations have also been composed of
comparatively small stones.

* The figures shewn in the text are copied from Trajan's column at Rome.
They show the mode in which the stones were carried for the erection of the
buildings which were erected during the course of the Dacian campaigns.
Hadrian accompanied Trajan during the first of these expeditions. When
the quarry was at a distance from the line of the Wall, and a sufficiently
level road could be obtained, wheeled vehicles would doubtless be used.

The front of the stones, both of the Wall and stations, is roughly "scabbled" with the pick. In some parts of the line, this tooling takes a definite form; when this is the case, the marking called the "diamond broaching" is most common. Sometimes the stone is scored with waved lines, called "feather broaching," or with small squares, or with nearly upright lines.

The tenacity of the mortar which was used forms an important element in the strength of the whole fabric. It has evidently been of a nature similar to the grout and concrete of the present day. The lime on being taken from the kiln was ground (not slaked with water), and was then mixed with sand and gravel. When about to be used, but not before, water was freely added to the mass. Mortar thus prepared speedily hardens.

Occasionally, but by no means frequently, small pieces of charcoal are mixed with the mortar. These have evidently been derived from the wood used in burning the lime. Excepting in the buildings of the stations, pounded tile, so characteristic of the Roman mortar in the south of England, is not a common ingredient in the mortar of the Wall. Limestone is abundant in most parts of the district through which the Wall passes. The Romans probably burnt it in "sow kilns." The limestone and fuel being arranged in alternate layers, the whole was carefully covered with turf and ignited. This simple method was in more recent times much resorted to when lime was wanted for farm purposes, before the introduction of railways.

Supposing the stones to be now quarried and squared, the lime burnt and mixed with sand and gravel, the next point to be attended to is the method of using them. The foundation was prepared by the removal of the natural soil to the width of about nine feet. In the hill district, a very scanty portion of earth covers the rocks; in the richer regions an excavation of from fifteen to eighteen inches has been made before the subsoil was reached. On the outer and inner margins of the ground thus bared, two rows of flags, of from two to four inches in thickness, and from eighteen to twenty in breadth, were generally laid; no mortar was placed under them, but not unfrequently a quantity of well-puddled clay. On these was laid the first course of facing-stones, which were usually the largest stones used in the structure. In the higher courses the facing-stones are uniformly of freestone, but in the ground course a "whinstone" is occasionally introduced. The flagstones of the foundation usually project from one to five inches beyond the first course of facing-stones, and these again usually stand out an inch or two beyond the second course, after which the wall is taken straight up.

One or two courses of facing-stones having been placed in their beds and carefully pointed, a mass of mortar in a very fluid state was poured into the interior of the wall, and stones of any kind or shape that were of a convenient size were "puddled" in amongst it. Whinstones, as being most abundant in the district, are generally used for the filling. Course after course was added, and one mass of concrete imposed upon another, until the wall reached the required height. When the whole was finished it formed a solid, compact mass, without any holes or crevices in the interior, and in a short time became as firm as unhewn rock.

In some parts of the line the mortar has been "hand-laid." The rubble of the interior having been first disposed in its place, the mortar has been laid upon it with a trowel. In this case the mortar never penetrates the interstices of the mass, and does not make such solid masonry as the method generally pursued. When, however, this plan is adopted, the rubble stones are often laid upon their edges in a slanting position, somewhat in the fashion of herring-bone masonry.

On gently waving ground the courses of the Wall follow the undulations of the surface, but on steep inclines the stones are laid parallel to the horizon.

It is sometimes asked, "How long would the Wall be in building?" From calculations that have been made, founded upon the experience gained by the construction of the vast works connected with modern railways, and supposing ten thousand men were employed upon it, it is considered that, in the existing circumstances of the country at the time, the *Vallum* and the *Murus* could not be reared, even supposing the labour to have been uninterrupted, in a shorter period than two years. The cost of it, in our present currency, would be upwards of a million of pounds.

About fifteen thousand men would be required to garrison the stations of the Wall.

CHAPTER III.

LOCAL DESCRIPTION.

I.—WALLSEND TO NEWCASTLE.

THE village of Wallsend, once so famous for its coal, takes its name from the Roman Wall. Here was the eastern extremity of the great structure. At this point the river became sufficiently wide to prove of itself a strong barrier. Here was planted the station of SEGEDUNUM, the first of those given in the *Notitia* as being *per lineam Valli*. The site of the station is good. Without being so much elevated as to give it a painful exposure to the blast of the north and the east, it commands an extensive view in every direction. The ground in front of it has a full exposure to the mid-day sun. The station stands upon an angle of the river, formed by two of the longest "reaches" which the stream makes in the whole of its course. The "Long Reach" extends downwards as far as the high end of South Shields, and the "Bill Reach" stretches nearly two miles up the water. In both directions, therefore, any operations conducted on the river could be easily discerned by the Roman garrison.

Although it was not thought requisite to extend the Wall farther along the northern bank of the Tyne than Wallsend,* special precautions were taken to guard the mouth of the estuary. Proofs of Roman occupation have been found on the promontory where the ruins of Tynemouth Priory now stand, and at the western extremity of North Shields, where a camp known as Blake Chesters once stood; whilst on the southern side of the river, camps have been planted on the Lawe at South Shields, and at Jarrow.

In a neighbourhood where mining operations have, in modern times, been conducted on a large scale, any very marked indications of Roman occupation cannot be expected.

---

* Horsley, in whose days the banks of the river were comparatively undisturbed by modern buildings, is very decided upon this point. He says, (p. 104), "The Wall at the east end manifestly terminates in a station near to Cousins's house, the ruins of which station are yet very visible"; and again (p. 130), "It is very certain that Severus's Wall never came to Tynemouth."

Besides this, extensive building operations have of late been carried on here and are still in progress. It is satisfactory, however, to find (1884) some slight traces, but to discover these the stranger had better seek the assistance of some one who knew the place in happier days. The grass-grown mound of the eastern rampart may be still noticed, defended by its ditch. The southern rampart may also be partially detected. The rounded angle formed by the junction of these walls is tolerably distinct. The defile which formed the strength of the station on its west side has been filled up; the commencement of its dip may, however, be seen. The house, long occupied by Mr. Reay, and more recently by Mr. Wilson, is just within the eastern rampart of the station ; and that which was so long known as Mr. Buddle's house, and more recently occupied by Mr. Leslie, but which is now being pulled down, is just within the line of what was its western rampart. The shaft of the famous Wallsend colliery is a few yards to the west of the western rampart.

In order to prevent an enemy passing between the station and the river, a wall came down from the south-east angle of the station into the river. Some traces of this wall might be noticed before the width of the river was contracted and its new-made banks covered by buildings.* Mr. Buddle, the famous coal engineer, told the writer that when bathing in the river, as a boy, he had often noticed the foundations of this wall extending far into the stream. Mr. Leslie had seen it go as far into the water as the lowest tides enabled him to observe. The station is supposed to have contained an area of three acres and a half.

* The whole aspect of the river and its banks, in this neighbourhood, has been entirely changed since the writer commenced his mural investigations.

Numerous proofs of Roman occupation have, at various times, been found in the station. Roman pottery and coins have frequently been found. Bones of all kinds have been dug up in considerable quantities. In excavating a cellar under the dining-room of Wallsend House, a well was found. The inscribed stones which have been found at this station are not of much importance. One was found not long ago bearing the words LEG. II. AVG.—"The second legion, styled the August." The northern portion of the station is quite obliterated. There can be no doubt that its north rampart lay to the north of the present road. Recent excavations show that it has been correctly laid down in the map of the Ordnance Survey.

Feeble as the traces now are of the ancient station of SEGEDUNUM it is to be feared that these will soon be entirely obliterated. The whole of the ground occupied by the camp and its vicinity is being laid out as building ground, and modern streets and houses will probably soon utterly efface the last trace of the ramparts which for upwards of three centuries were defended by Roman valour.

The Wall in its course westwards has probably proceeded from the north jamb of the western gateway, allowing the northern part of the station to project beyond it. A new row of houses, appropriately called "The Roman Wall," represents its course.

Carville Hall,* now in a ruinous condition, is the Cousins's House of Horsley. The fosse on the north of Carville, which is filled with water and serves as a duck-pond, is a remnant of the north fosse of the Wall, and as such will be hailed with delight by the despondent antiquary. Let him look westward

* Carville Hall is now let out in tenements.

and he will detect its course. The stone dike which forms the fence of the next field contains many Roman stones. We come almost immediately to Stote's Houses, the Bee Houses of Horsley; the old houses here are almost entirely composed of Roman stones. On the north of them the fosse of the Wall is filled with water, and forms two ponds. Here some traces of the foundation of the Wall may be seen. About sixty yards to the south of these houses are traces (becoming increasingly faint) of two tumuli, one on each side of the little valley descending to the Tyne; the easterly one is the most distinct. These may cover the ashes of some ancient British chiefs who fought and died before the Romans reached these northern parts. The cart track is now on the Wall; the fosse is less distinct—a wire fence runs along it. Sixty years ago the Wall in this vicinity was standing between three and four feet high, covered with brushwood. About half way between Stote's Houses and Old Walker is a small stream; at the point where the Wall crosses it several stones (possibly walling stones) lie in its bed. West of the brook the core of the Wall is seen in the footpath. On the top of the rise, about eighty yards from the brook, is the site of the first mile-castle. The ground is under tillage, but its slightly elevated surface may possibly enable the traveller to hit upon its site. The fosse of the Wall becomes encouraging as we proceed.

The Farm-house of Old Walker is now reached. Many Roman stones appear in its walls; the fosse is used as a duck-pond. After this for some distance there is little to engage the attention of the observer; he may, however, detect some traces of the north fosse. Presently he will notice that the site of this ditch is enclosed. The road now runs on the north of the ditch some distance. The site of the fosse all the way to Byker Hill is enclosed between hedges, and used as potato gardens. It was left waste long after the neighbouring ground was brought into tillage. The road that is seen stretching in a straight line up the hill to Byker indicates the direction of the Wall. It is the first, but by no means the most remarkable, instance that we shall meet with of the unflinching and straightforward tendencies of this remarkable structure.

In the second field from Byker Hill, Mr. McLauchlan, aided by his measuring chain, lays down the position of the second mile-castle. It is seven furlongs from the last. A while ago the attentive observer might possibly detect it by its gently swelling surface, but it is now covered by a brick-kiln. On Byker Hill is a large quarry, from which the Romans doubtless procured stone for the Wall, which entirely obliterates the remains. We now lose all traces of the object of our inquiry, and we shall not again meet with them until we reach the western limits of Newcastle. An entirely new town has within recent years been planted upon Byker Hill, which baffles all antiquarian search. The wall in this vicinity must, however, in the year 1725, have been standing in stately grandeur, as appears from the "Prospect of it from Byker Hill," which Stukeley gives in his *Iter Boreale*. He made this drawing because "the country being entirely undermined it might, sometime or other, sink, and so disorder the track of this stately work." It must have remained in an encouraging state of preservation until 1800, for in the *Monthly Magazine* of that year we read, "At this period a portion of the foundation of the Roman Wall was taken up at Byker Hill, for the purpose of repairing the highways." This process has been carried on in other parts of the Wall up to the present period (1884), Board-schools notwithstanding.

The Wall ran through Byker in a line with the street called "Shields Road," and began its descent down the steep bank which leads to the Ouseburn, a few yards to the south of the new Byker bridge. Having crossed the stream it climbed, in a straight line, the opposite bank. No traces of it now remain. A mile-castle stood at the point where the Wall began its descent to the Ouseburn, from which two large stones (one of them inscribed) were taken, and are now preserved in the Antiquarian Museum, Newcastle. Having reached the western bank of the valley, the Wall made straight for the Red Barns, now the Dominican Monastery. Hence it is supposed to have passed over the rising ground called the Wall Knoll to the Sallyport Gate. It then went on to Pilgrim Street, a little to the north of Silver Street, which perhaps then formed its military way, and so over Lork Burn (now Dean Street) to the west door of St. Nicholas' Church, where remains of it were found in 1763. Leland tells us, on the authority of Dr. Davel, then Master of St. Mary's Hospital, Newcastle, that "the church of St. Nicholas stands upon the Picts' Wall." In its passage from the town westwards it went by St. John's Church, and in front of the palisades of the Assembly Rooms, up Westgate Hill. The range of houses called Cumberland Row very nearly represents the line of the Wall, and the present road is probably identical with the ancient military way.

II.—NEWCASTLE-UPON-TYNE.

Newcastle was the second station on the line. It bore the name of PONS ÆLII; deriving this designation from the bridge which Hadrian, who was of the Ælian family, built over the Tyne. The present Swing Bridge occupies the same position as did the bridge of Hadrian. Hadrian's bridge seems to have served (with various renovations) the traffic of the district till about A.D., 1248, when a new bridge was built. The mediæval bridge was destroyed by a flood in A.D., 1771. It was found that in its construction the piers of the ancient Roman bridge had, to a considerable extent, been made use of. When the bridge of 1775 was removed to make way for the present structure, the wooden piles and framework of the foundation of one at least of the Roman piers were met with and removed. On both occasions Roman coins were found.

The position of the station has not been ascertained with certainty. On the north side of Collingwood Street, close to the Groat Market, strong remains of the Roman Wall were exhumed in 1810. Near the western extremity of the same street, but on its south side, another piece of Roman Wall was met with in 1853. These fragments were no doubt portions of the north wall of the station. In laying down some water-pipes in Collingwood Street, in 1852, two walls of Roman masonry were exposed, which were, as near as the eye could judge, at right angles with this north wall; these must have been parts of the station. We shall probably not greatly err if we suppose PONS ÆLII to have lain between St. Nicholas' Church on the one side and the Literary and Philosophical Society on the other; and, having the north side of Collingwood Street for the site of its north rampart, to have extended as far south as Bailiffgate, where the ground begins to dip rapidly down towards the river. When the Town Hall buildings were reared no traces of Roman building were found. This might have been expected, for the site is to the north of our supposed station. In other directions, no

doubt, suburban buildings clustered round the camp. When the present Assize Courts (beside the Old Castle) were built, numerous Roman remains were found, and a Roman well still exists under the centre of the building.

One of the most interesting of the remains of the Romans found in Newcastle is the altar shown on the opposite page. It was dredged up from the bottom of the river in three several pieces, and at different times, when the works of the Swing Bridge were in progress. It is dedicated to Neptune by the Sixth Legion, surnamed the victorious, pious, and faithful. This legion, or some important detachment of it, having safely traversed the stormy waters of the North Sea reared this altar in token of their gratitude to the god of the seas. The altar is at present in the Museum of the Society of Antiquaries of Newcastle.

According to the *Notitia*, a cohort of the Cornovii, under the command of a tribune, garrisoned PONS ÆLII. Who the Cornovii were we have no means of knowing; neither does any inscription exist, either to confirm or to correct the statement of the *Notitia*.

There are some buildings in Newcastle which will interest the Roman antiquary. The mother church of the town (now a Cathedral) is dedicated to St. Nicholas. Masses of Roman ruins on the site of this church probably led in Saxon times to the building of some homely temple, which long ago disappeared. Tradition speaks of a Norman church, founded in the reign of William Rufus. It, too, is gone, having been destroyed, it is believed, in 1216. The present church, which is chiefly in the "decorated" style, was finished in 1350. The steeple is a subsequent addition.

The Old Castle is one of the most interesting Norman fortifications remaining in England. Robert Curthose built a castle here, which must soon have perished, as we find William Rufus engaged in the work of reconstruction. The present

Keep was erected in the reign of Henry II. It was commenced in 1172, and finished in 1177. Though not so large as many of the Norman Keeps of England, it exhibits in a very clear manner the spirit and design of that class of building. In 1813 the battlements and flag-tower were placed

upon it by the Corporation. The woodcut represents its appearance as seen from the west, before these additions were made. It shows the gateway, now removed, which led into the inner bailey. The Black Gate, the principal entrance into the Castle precincts, was built by Henry III. in the year 1248. The upper portions of it, which had long been in a ruinous condition, have been recently restored by the Society of Antiquaries of Newcastle. Here are deposited a collection of Roman altars and other antiquities, chiefly derived from the Wall, more extensive than is elsewhere to be met with in England.

III.—FROM NEWCASTLE TO THE NORTH TYNE.

We now pursue the Wall on its course westward. In addition to the Murus or stone wall, we will now have the companionship of the Vallum or earth wall. As already observed, the Vallum is not met with at either extremity of the line. With respect to the eastern end, Horsley's testimony is very emphatic. "There is not, in all the space between Cousins's House and Newcastle, the least vestige or appearance of Hadrian's Vallum, or any thing belonging to it." The Vallum is supposed to have proceeded from the southern rampart of the station of PONS ÆLII, and to have run up Westgate Hill parallel with the Wall. In the days of the writer's youth it was to be seen at the back of the houses on the left hand of the road, about half way up the hill.

At the top of Westgate Hill, at a place called the Quarry House, Horsley found traces of a mile-castle. Neither Quarry House nor traces of a mile-castle now exist.

The mounds and fosse of the Vallum are met with on the left of the road, opposite to the Union Workhouse. As we pursue our way to the Firth of Solway, these works will seldom be out of sight. On the right hand side of the traveller the fosse of the stone Wall soon comes into view. The additional rampart formed on its northern edge by the throwing out of the excavated materials, will here, and in many other places, be noticed.

Benwell Hill.

The third station on the line, Benwell Hill, the CONDERCUM of the Romans, is about two miles from Newcastle. Its form is nearly obliterated. It lies partly to the north of the road, and partly to the south. The northern portion is now occupied by the high service reservoir of the Newcastle Water Company. South of the road some interesting traces of it remain. The eastern rampart and the south-east angle of the station show boldly in the grounds of G. W. Rendel, Esq.; its southern and western ramparts may be traced, though more obscurely, in the neighbouring grounds of J. P. Mulcaster, Esq. On the sunny slope leading down to the river are manifest traces of foundations. The Vallum has come up to the southern rampart of the station; the Wall has probably joined it at the point where the road now crosses it. The suburban buildings of this station have been extensive. One of these, on the east side, was excavated a few years ago by Mr. Rendel. A small temple, terminating at its southern extremity in a circular apse, is seen. The engraving shows it. Two altars found in the temple now stand in the place which they originally occupied. One of these is most tastefully adorned; it is dedicated to a god, unknown to classical mythology, Antenociticus, and to the deities of the emperors, by Ælius Vibius, a centurion of the

twentieth legion, surnamed the Valerian and Victorious. The other altar is of a ruder kind, but it has a longer inscription, which may be thus translated :—"To the god Anociticus by the decrees of our best and greatest Emperors, given under Ulpius Marcellus, a man of consular rank; Tineius Longus, of the præfecture of knights, adorned with the broad clasp, and a quæstor dedicated [this altar]." Probably the Anociticus which we have here is only a contracted form of the Antenociticus which we have on the other altar. Ulpius Marcellus was a jurist who flourished in the reigns of Antoninus Pius and Marcus Aurelius. The emperors intended are no doubt Aurelius and his colleague Lucius Verus. The altar will thus belong to a period between A.D. 161 and 169. In Mr. Mulcaster's grounds may be seen some fragments of millstones and other Roman remains, and in particular the capital of a column, having a species of moulding which was afterwards adopted by Norman architects. This station was garrisoned by a troop of horse—the first wing of the Asturians, a people of Spain.

The Romans are supposed to have wrought the coal in the vicinity of Benwell. When the lower water-reservoir was formed here, several years ago, some ancient coal workings were exposed, but nothing was found to indicate decisively the period to which they belonged. They were probably Roman.

The Wall on the south side of the road here is chiefly composed of Roman stones. The larger stones are no doubt derived from the Wall, the smaller description from the buildings in the station.

Leaving CONDERCUM, we again pursue our journey westward. We now pass the second milestone from Newcastle. The road runs for several miles upon the foundation of the

E

Wall. Formerly the facing stones were in many places seen
protruding through the "metal;" but since the diversion of
the greater part of the traffic from the road to the railway,
the remnants of this great relic of antiquity have, in several
instances, been removed to supply material for mending the
turnpike. The north fosse, as we pursue our journey, becomes
more distinct on the right hand. Descending Benwell Hill,
the village of East Denton is reached. Here, on the left hand

side, we meet, for the first time, with a remnant of the Wall
rising above the ground. The cut shews it. It is 9½ feet wide.
The trunk of the apple tree which long grew upon it fell
several winters ago. Denton Hall, on the right, an antique
building, redolent of the memories of Mrs. Montague and Dr.
Samuel Johnson, and the scene of sundry ghost stories,* is
soon reached. Here a few sculptured stones from the Wall
are preserved. Opposite to Denton Hall the core of the Wall
is in good preservation, and at the bottom of the field on the

* See *Richardson's Table Book*, Legendary, Vol. III., p. 310.

south all the features of the Vallum are well developed. The next village is West Denton. Just before reaching the lodge of West Denton House, a mound will be observed on the left of the road. This consists of the ruins of a mile-castle.

The geologist will be interested in knowing that, a little to the south of this spot, very near where the ditch of the Vallum crosses the brook, the course of the Ninety-fathom Dyke is still to be seen. This "fault will be detected by the perpendicularity of the strata." (*MacLauchlan*, p. 15). At West Denton the Murus and Vallum are about 200 yards apart; after this they slowly converge until they reach Walbottle Dean, where they are but sixty yards distant from each other. After that they keep nearly parallel and in close contiguity until reaching Rutchester. Ascending the hill from West Denton, the fosse of the Wall is boldly developed. The Vallum is feeble. Passing the fourth mile-stone, we arrive at Chapel House. The view here is extensive. On the south of the road Horsley observed "some foundations of stone ramparts." They are now completely eradicated. A little beyond this—half way down the hill—we should meet with the site of another *castellum ;* it is now scarcely discernible. On the slope of this hill and the rise of the next, several traces of the Wall are to be seen in the road. Passing Walbottle (*botle* is the Saxon for an abode), we come to the fifth mile-stone; the Vallum here is good, and it is well seen ascending the hill before us. At Walbottle Dean House, another *castellum* has stood. The remains of its southern gateway are to be seen within the grounds. There is a beautiful prospect from this place. As we proceed onwards, two or three courses of stones may be seen in the bank on the traveller's right hand. These appear to have formed the

foundation courses of the Wall. The road here has bee
recently lowered and slightly altered in its course. No trac
of the bridge by which the Wall crossed the dean remai
Proceeding onwards, a lane crosses the road. The turning 1
the left hand takes us to Newburn. At Newburn the rive
for the first time, becomes fordable. In ancient times it wa
consequently a place of importance. Its knolls bear marl
of early fortifications, and several stones in the present churc
are undoubtedly Roman. There is reason to believe that th
Romans laid a framework of stone across the bed of the rive
to improve the ford.

In 1346 David, King of Scotland, crossed the ford on h
way to Neville's Cross. In 1640 the Scotch forces unde
General Lesley defeated the troops of Charles I. at Newburr

We have now arrived at the colliery village of Throckley
Beyond it we find a Wesleyan chapel and the Schools of th
Throckley Coal Company. Just before reaching the sixt
mile-stone we come to the filter beds of the Newcastle an
Gateshead Water Company, by which the water intended fo
domestic use in these towns is purified. After passing th
sixth mile-stone, Throckley Bank Top is reached. Both th
fosse of the Wall and the Vallum may be traced. Anothe
mile-castle is reached; besides the gentle elevation, th
difference in the colour of its soil or the tint of its vegetatioi
will often be noticed. The traveller will observe that ver
often the gate into a field is placed on the spot where
mile-castle stood. The reason is obvious; the ruins of th
building formed a hard surface, which was useless for agri
cultural purposes, but most excellent for sustaining traffic
The facing stones of the Wall may be seen in the road, givin;
to the structure a width of 8 feet 6 inches. A little furthe

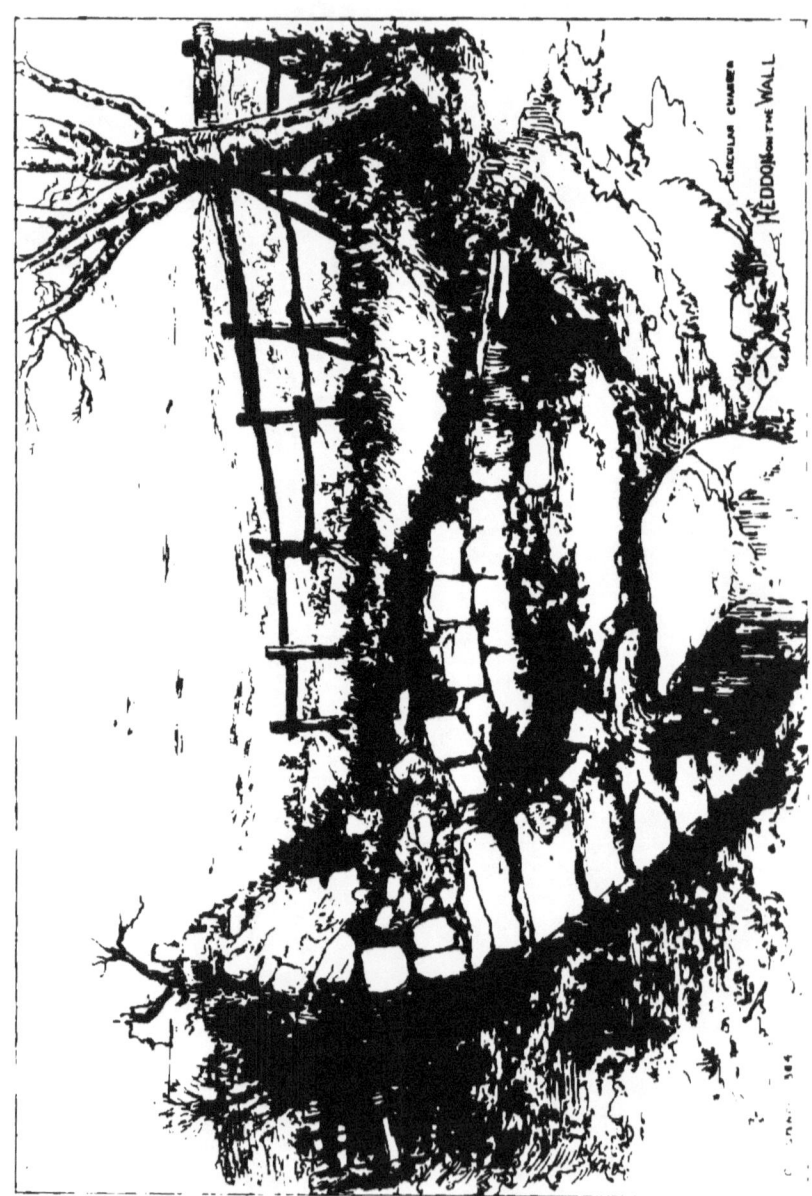

CIRCULAR CHAMBER

HEDDON ON THE WALL

on, a range of houses attracts the eye on the right of the road. It is the Frenchmen's Row, originally built for the workmen employed in Heddon Colliery, but afterwards used as the residence of a number of refugees, who fled to England on the occasion of the first French Revolution. The dial was constructed by them.

At Heddon Banks the facing stones of both sides of the Wall used to be seen in the road, but the northern range of them has been recently torn up.

On the top of the eminence which we reach before coming to Heddon-on-the-Wall, the north fosse will be seen to be deeper than we have yet noticed it. The works of the Vallum, about fifty yards to the south, are also finely developed. In both cases the ditch is cut through the free-stone rock. In the sides of the south ditch the tool-marks of the excavators are visible. Before entering the village, let the traveller clamber over the tree-crowned wall which skirts the road on his left. He will here see an interesting though small fragment of the Wall. Its north face is destroyed, but five courses of its southern face remain. Somewhat nearer the farm-house the remains of a circular chamber appear in the substance of the Wall, which is shown in the opposite engraving, having a diameter of seven feet, with a small aperture, leading out of it, in a slanting direction. This kind of structure is quite peculiar; has it been intended for a turret? At Heddon-on-the-Wall, the Wall is only about thirty-five yards from the ditch of the Vallum. The fosse of the Vallum is seen cutting boldly through the village; in the low ground it is used as a pond. A *castellum* must have stood hereabouts; it has probably been destroyed by the erection of the village. The seventh mile-stone is passed

just as we leave the place. The road that turns off to the left
leads to Horsley and Corbridge. The road that we have been
travelling upon, and which we are to keep for several miles
further, goes nearly straight forward. It is General Wade's
Military Road. When the Pretender's forces appeared before
Carlisle in 1745, the royal troops were lying at Newcastle,
where the enemy had been expected. At that time, no road
that would bear the transit of artillery existed between
Newcastle and Carlisle, so that General Wade was obliged
to leave Carlisle to the mercy of the enemy, and proceed in
search of him by a southerly route. He met him at Preston;
with what effect is well-known. After this the road between
Newcastle and Carlisle, now known throughout the district
as "The Military Road," was made. For miles together the
Wall was pulled down to form it.

This statement prepares us for a brief extract from the
journal of that eminent man, John Wesley. He writes:—
"Wednesday, 21 May, 1755. I preached at Nafferton, near
Horsley, about thirteen miles from Newcastle. We rode
chiefly on the new western road, which lies on the old Roman
Wall. Some part of this is still to be seen, as are the remains
of most of the towers, which were built a mile distant from
each other, quite from sea to sea. But where are the men of
renown who built them, and who once made all the land
tremble? Crumbled into dust! Gone hence, to be no more
seen, till the earth shall give up her dead!"

Not much that calls for observation occurs before reaching
the next station—Rutchester. About midway between
Heddon-on-the-Wall and Rutchester is the site of a mile-
castle; it is very indistinct.

Rutchester.

Rutchester, the ancient VINDOBALA, is the fourth station on the line of the Wall. It was garrisoned by the first cohort of Frixagi, or, as it should probably be written, Frisii. The Frisians were a tribe occupying a portion of what is now the kingdom of the Netherlands. Unless the traveller be on his guard, he may pass through the middle of VINDOBALA without knowing it. A lane crosses the road just as you come up to it.

The great Wall seems to have joined the station at its gateways, leaving a considerable portion of the camp projecting to the north, and a still larger to the south of it. The station, the general form of which may be discerned, has had an area of about three acres and a half. The turnpike road probably represents its *via principalis*. To the north of the road the station is under the plough, but the general elevation of its surface, and the slight though yearly diminishing traces of its ditch, serve sufficiently well to mark its position. South of the road, the western and southern ramparts remain in a fair state of preservation. The farm-buildings are all to the south of the camp.

The Vallum here, as is usually the case in the immediate vicinity of stations, is indistinct ; but it seems to have joined the fort in a line with its southern rampart. The suburbs have been to the south of the station. The present farm-house is formed on the nucleus of a mediæval stronghold ; some of its ancient features being retained. To the west of the farm-house, on the brow of the hill, an ancient trough-like excavation has been made in the solid rock. Its use is not known. It was once popularly called the "Giant's Grave." Another account of its use is recorded in Sir David Smith's MSS., now preserved in Alnwick Castle : "The old peasants

here have a tradition that the Romans made a beverage somewhat like beer of the bells of heather (heath), and that this trough was used in the process of making such drink." *
The cistern is twelve feet long, four feet six inches broad, and two feet deep, and has a hole close to the bottom at one end. When discovered, in 1766, it had a partition of masonry across it, and contained many decayed bones, and an iron implement described as being like a three-footed candlestick. About the middle of last century a figure of Hercules was found here and is now preserved in the Castle of Newcastle.

In 1844 four altars were discovered a few yards to the west of the "Giant's Grave." One of them is shown in the woodcut. The sculpture on its base (a bull, which was sacred to Mithras), as well as other circumstances, leaves no doubt that the god intended is not the one true and living God, but Mithras, the Eastern Apollo. The altar is neatly designed; a wreath encircles the word DEO, and two palm branches wave over it. The inscription may thus be read in English—"Lucius Sentius Castus [a centurion], of the sixth legion, piously dedicated this altar to the god [Mithras]." It is now at Otterburn. Most of the stones of the farm-buildings and

* The opinion long prevailed in Northumberland, that the *Picts* had the art of preparing an intoxicating liquor from heather-bells, and that the secret died with them.

adjacent fences are Roman. A few fragments of inscriptions are built up in the walls; one, in a coach-house, bears the letters, AVR. RIN. XIT. NIS. It is no doubt part of a monumental tablet; when complete it would probably be —*Diis Manibus* A∪R*elius Victo*RIN*us vi*XIT *an*NIS. At the door in front of the house are some fragments of altars and other stones among which is a centurial stone that reads—[CO]H III Ɔ PEDIOVI—the century of Pediovus of the third cohort.

We now continue our journey. About one-third of a mile forward, on a knoll beside the field gate, the site of another mile-castle occurs. Presently we pass, on the left of the road, a house formerly used as a public house, and known as "The Iron Sign." Some of the buildings are entirely composed of Roman stones. In a wall abutting upon the road, are some centurial and sculptured stones. They are read with difficulty, but in a favourable light one of them seems to be COH. VIII.; another, Ɔ HOS. LVPI. A side light is the best for reading weathered inscriptions. Passing the ninth mile-stone, we stand upon the top of an eminence, called Round Hill, or sometimes Eppie's Hill. We have here a good view of Harlow Hill and the adjacent country. The north fosse is very distinct, forming a deep groove on the right of the road all the way to Harlow Hill. The Wall and the Vallum are at this point within thirty yards of each other. They soon separate; for whilst the Wall inclines to the north in order to secure, in conformity with its usual practice, the high ground, the Vallum continues to move onward in a nearly straight line. In doing so it runs along the flanks of Harlow Hill. Had the Vallum been an independent barrier, it would probably have kept to the high ground. From a point opposite the next mile-castle to Carr Hill, a distance of five miles, the Vallum goes in a perfectly straight line.

A little more than half a mile beyond Round Hill, we pass the site of a mile-castle; the Vallum is here 400 yards from the wall.   We soon arrive at Harlow Hill.   The Wall has passed through the fold yards on the south side of the turnpike road.   A mile-castle has stood here, but no traces of it now exist.   On the high ground north of the village are the remains of a tumulus and entrenchments.   The Romans would not leave so important a position undefended.   From the quarries under this summit the builders of the Wall seem to have obtained both freestone and lime.   Some barrows to the north of this place, and graves filled with human bones, confirm the traditionary account of bloody battles having been fought here in "the troublesome times."

Descending the hill, we come to the Whittle Dean reservoirs of the Newcastle and Gateshead Water Company.

The village of Welton is about half a mile to the south of the road.   Its most prominent feature is the ancient fortlet called Welton Hall.   It is built entirely of Roman stones. Over the door are the initials and date—"W W. 1614." Strange stories are still told of the enormous strength of old Will of Welton.

Ascending the hill, just after passing the reservoirs, the site of another mile-castle is seen on the left hand.   At this point the Vallum, after crossing one of the reservoirs, again comes into close companionship with the Wall.   At the usual distance (seven furlongs and a half) westward of the castle, the site of another may be discerned.   It is about a furlong west of the Robin Hood Inn, where a road turns down to a farm-house.   Wall Houses is next reached.   Between this point and the fourteenth mile-stone all the lines of the Barrier are developed in a degree that is quite inspiring.   The north fosse is, for some distance, planted with trees, which will, for a considerable time, save it from the plough. Another house, the remnant of a village, called High Wall Houses, is next approached. After passing what was a turnpike-gate, a road on the left leads to Corbridge, distant about four miles, and Hexham about seven miles. About a mile to the south of us is Shildon Hill, which forms a conspicuous feature in the landscape. It has an oval-shaped entrenchment on its summit, belonging, probably, to the ancient British era. At Matfen-Piers Lodge there is another mile-castle. The Wall, as seen in the road, is a little less than eight feet thick. The road on the right leads to Matfen. At Matfen Hall, the seat of Sir Edward Blackett, Bart., are several important inscribed and sculptured stones and other antiquities derived from the Wall, especially from the station of Hunnum. We now pass the fourteenth milestone.

At Halton Shields was another *castellum*, though all decided traces of it are now obliterated. "Like the man at Halton Shields," was a saying that was common a while ago. This celebrated personage set off on a journey, and, after travelling laboriously all night, found himself at his own back door next morning.

On the top of the next summit, Carr Hill, the facing stones of the Wall are seen in the road, and the angle which it here makes, bending away to the south, may be observed. It measures nine feet six inches in width. The Wall and Vallum are fifty-five yards apart. They go on in tolerable parallelism for some distance, when the Vallum suddenly bends to the south, evidently to avoid a small barrow-like elevation called Down Hill. Having done this, it returns as quickly to something like its former direction. The Wall pursues a straightforward course, and cuts across the hill where its north fosse is well marked.

These appearances strongly corroborate the opinion that the various lines of the fortification are but parts of one great scheme. If the Vallum had been constructed as an independent defence against a northern foe, and nearly a century before the Wall, an elevation which so entirely commands the Vallum would surely not have been left open to the enemy, especially as it would be just as easy to take the Vallum along the north flank of the hill as the south.

Down Hill has a number of depressions upon it, caused no doubt by the Romans quarrying lime here. There is a modern lime quarry on the western edge of the hill.

Passing Halton Red House, we reach the station of HUNNUM.

Halton Chesters.

The Wall came up to the lateral gateways of this camp; consequently, the turnpike-road, its present representative, goes through the midst of it. Unless the traveller be on the alert, he will pass through the station without knowing it, as did Sandy Gordon the Scottish Antiquary, and William Hutton the first time he visited it. The Vallum came up to the southern rampart. Horsley gave this camp the name of Halton Chesters, from the village of Halton, which lies about half a mile to the south of it. This station does not occupy the elevated position which most of the stations do. It has the usual rectangular form, but it possesses this peculiarity, that an angular portion has, as it were, been cut out of its north-west corner. The nature of the ground has probably dictated this arrangement. The station has contained an area of four acres and a quarter. The distance between the last station (Rutchester) and this is greater than usual, being seven miles and two furlongs in a direct line. The station of HUNNUM was garrisoned by a troop of horse, called in the *Notitia*, "Ala Saviniana" or "Sabiniana." This troop probably took its name from Sabina, the wife of Hadrian. There is reason to believe that the Empress accompanied Hadrian to Britain, and that the imperial court was established here for the winter of 119-120 (*Merivale*, Vol. VII., p. 438.) The only inscription confirming the *Notitia* in its statement of the occupation of Hunnum, is one which was first noticed by Camden, and is now preserved at Cambridge. It is part of a monumental slab, dedicated to the shades of Noricus, who died at the age of 30, by Messorius Magnus, a brother of the deceased, and a *duplaris* of the *Ala Sabiniana*.

The portion of the station north of the road was brought into cultivation in the year 1827. It is called the "Brunt-ha'penny Field," from the number of corroded copper coins which have been picked up in it. Numerous buildings, most carefully constructed, were found in it. One of them was an elaborate structure, containing at least eleven apartments. These were heated by the transmission of hot air under their floors and up their sides. The idea has been extensively adopted that all the buildings provided with hypocausts were public baths. The Romans were great bathers, but we must not overlook the difference between the climate of Italy and Britain. Warmth would be the first requisite here. Nearly all the remains found in Northumberland prove that the necessities of war were chiefly attended to, not the requirements of luxury. The remains of "The Baths" at Hunnum were most carefully examined and described by the Rev. John Hodgson and Mr. Dobson (*Hist. Nor.*, Pt. II. Vol. III. p. 317);

but though we are told which was the *apodyterium*, which the *tepidarium*, the *caldarium*, and the *frigidarium*, nothing is said about those essential requisites in a public bathing establishment—the pipes for the introduction of the water, the boilers for heating, and the basins for holding it. These did not exist. A portion of one of the smallest of the chambers here was indeed walled off and carefully lined with cement, so as to form a reservoir, ten feet long by seven feet three inches broad, but this was the only real indication of a bath. Similar

cisterns have been found at CILURNUM, BORCOVICUS, and elsewhere; these were probably the only arrangements made for bathing, even in the dwellings of the tribunes and the prefects, and these were probably supplied by hand, with hot or cold water, at the command of the master of the house. The whole of this building was removed as soon as it was discovered. The part of the station which is to the south of the road has a gentle slope and a fair exposure to the sun. It is known by the name of the Chesters; in Horsley's day it had the additional designation of Silverhill, no doubt from the discovery, on some occasion, of a number of denarii in it.

An elaborately carved slab, shown on the opposite page, commemorating some work done by the second legion, styled the
August, was found here in 1769, and is preserved at Alnwick
Castle. As the ground has not been recently ploughed, it
exhibits, with considerable distinctness, the lines of the outer
entrenchments, as well as the contour of the ruined buildings
and streets of the interior. The road to Halton runs through
the middle of the station, probably on the very site of the old

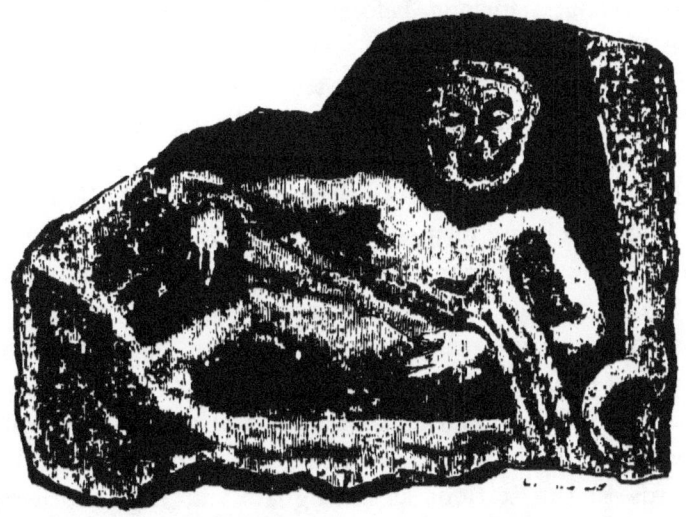

Roman *via* leading from the Prætorian to the Decuman
gate. The suburbs have covered a fine tract of pasture
ground to the south.

Halton Castle and Church are chiefly composed of Roman
stones. In the church-yard is a Roman altar placed upside
down, but its inscription is obliterated. Before the door of
the house is a small altar showing the *patera* on one side and
a *præfericulum* on the other, and in the garden wall is a
much weathered stone, on which is carved the figure of a man

reclining on a couch—probably part of a funereal stone. It
is shown in the woodcut on the previous page. In the wall
of one of the back buildings is the much-defaced figure of a
man, which is also probably a part of a funereal stone.

On leaving the station, it will be noticed how much the
defile on its west side strengthens the military position of the
camp. About a furlong before reaching Portgate the faint
traces of a mile-castle may be seen.

Passing the sixteenth mile-stone, we come to another
castellum, and, continuing to ascend the hill, we soon reach
the point where the ancient Watling Street, running from
south to north, crosses the Wall at right angles.* This road.
which was probably formed by Agricola, in his first advance
into Scotland, is in many places, as here, still used as a high-
way; in others it is grass-grown and deserted, but even in
these instances it retains, often for miles together, all the
features of its original construction. The Watling Street, on
its way from the South, passes the stations of Binchester.
Lanchester, Ebchester, Corchester, and, crossing the Wall,
proceeds to the stations at Risingham and High Rochester.
It reaches the Scottish border at Chew Green, where there is
a group of camps of remarkable construction.

There can be little doubt that the station of HUNNUM was
intended to guard the passage of the Wall by the Street.

The Wall and Vallum are parallel in this place, and are
about eighty yards apart. The earthworks now become
exceedingly interesting, and continue to be so for the next
two or three miles. The north fosse is in many places very
bold; the materials that have been turned out of it are

* In Horsley's day there seems to have been a species of fortification here.
He says, "At Watling Street gate there has been a square *castellum*, half
within the Wall and half without."

lying on the outer margin, rough and untrimmed, as if the labourers had left the work but to obtain some refreshment, and were about to return to it. Ascending the hill, on the top of which is a fir plantation, the foundations of the Wall may be well seen. Before reaching the plantation, a mile-castle will be observed. At this point it will be well for the antiquary to forsake the turnpike road and examine the Vallum. He will not find it in a more perfect state in any other part of the line. Old Mr. Hutton was charmed with it. "I climbed over a stone wall," he says, "to examine the wonder; measured the whole in every direction; surveyed it with surprise, with delight; was fascinated, and unable to proceed; forgot I was upon a wild common, a stranger, and the evening approaching; lost in astonishment, I was not able to move."

On passing the crown of the hill, and beginning the descent, the Wall may be measured (in the road) ten feet five inches in width.

After passing a clump of trees on the right hand, and before reaching the eighteenth mile-stone, the site of another mile-castle may be distinctly noticed. On Errington Hill Head, about half a mile to the north of this point, are some ancient encampments; they command a magnificent view of the Erring Burn and of the valley of North Tyne. The Hallington reservoir of the Newcastle Water Company and Swinburne Castle are to be seen to the north. About a furlong before reaching the nineteenth mile-stone, the feeble traces of a mile-castle may perhaps be recognised. Directly opposite to this, on the north of the Wall, and about a furlong from it, "is a small quadrangular enclosure, on the top of the crag, which is presumed to be the remains of a small Roman camp, made to protect the workmen while they were quarrying and building the Wall." (*MacLauchlan*, p. 24.) This camp has been a good deal disturbed.

In several other instances, which we shall notice as they occur, Mr. MacLauchlan found a similar arrangement to exist —a small earthen camp opposite a mile-castle. There can be no doubt that the reason he assigns for them is the true one. This camp is to the north of the Wall; in nearly every other instance the camp is to the south of the Wall. Advancing a little further along the road, we observe north of the Wall a round hill, which, to all appearance, is a tumulus. Into the front of one of the houses at St. Oswald's Hill Head, a

 centurial stone is built, bearing the inscription, CHO. VIII. >CAECILI CLIIME.—The century or company of Cecilius Clemens of the eighth cohort. Immediately south of this place, distant about a quarter of a mile, is Fallowfield Fell, where the Roman quarryman, Carantinus, has left his name upon the rock, as already stated (p. 31). The "written rock" is not easily found, in consequence of its being but slightly elevated above the general 'level.* The view from the Fell is very extensive and fine.

Onwards, we come to St. Oswald's Church. Opposite to it is a field called Mould's Close, where, according to local

---

* If the reader chooses to see it let him attend to the following directions:—On the rise, to the south of St. Oswald's Hill Head, is a fir plantation. The "written rock" is to the south of this plantation, and a little to the east of it. A cairn of stones erected by some good Samaritan at present (1884) stands upon it; long may it be spared!

tradition, the hottest of the fight between King Oswald and Cadwalla raged. Bede tells us:—"This last king (Oswald), after the death of his brother Eanfrid, advanced with an army, small indeed in number, but strengthened with the faith of Christ; and the impious commander of the Britons was slain, though he had most numerous forces, which he boasted nothing could withstand, at a place, in the English tongue called Denisesburn, that is, Denis's-brook. This place is shown to this day, and held in much veneration, where Oswald being about to engage, erected the sign of the holy cross, and on his knees prayed to God that he would assist His worshippers in their great distress. . . . Advancing towards the enemy with the first dawn of the day, they obtained the victory, as their faith deserved. . . . The place in the English tongue is called Hefenfeld, or the Heavenly Field. . . . The same place is near the Wall with which the Romans formerly enclosed the island from sea to sea, to restrain the fury of the barbarous nations, as has been said before. Hither, also, the brothers of the church of Hagulstad, which is not far from thence, repair yearly on the day before that on which King Oswald was afterwards slain, to watch there for the health of his soul, and having sung many psalms, to offer for him in the morning the sacrifice of the holy oblation. And since that good custom has spread, they have lately built and consecrated a church there, which has attached additional sanctity and honour to that place." *Bede's Ecclesiastical History*, Book III., ch. vii.

The Rev. Dr. Greenwell has adduced strong evidence to show that Denisesburn was in the vicinity of Dilston. The existence of the church of St. Oswald, however, fixes the spot where the cross was raised, and where probably, also, the

battle was begun, but the fight may have extended towards
Dilston, and the slaughter of Cadwalla taken place there.

Some faint traces of the next mile-castle may be seen at
the field-gate on the right of the road, opposite Plane-trees
Farm House. The house is in the ditch of the Vallum. A
little further on, also on the right of the road, is the Black
Pasture Quarry, which yields stone of the same nature as that
used in the Wall in this vicinity. The stone is a close-grained
sandstone, and may be obtained in blocks of any size. The
storms of centuries have little or no effect upon it.

Before reaching the twentieth mile-stone, we come to
Plane-trees Field, where, on the left of the road, a conspicuous
piece of the Wall remains. It has, in some places, three or four
courses of facing-stones entire; the grout of the interior, which
rises still higher, gives root to some fine old thorns. The Wall
was in still better condition just before Hutton passed that way,
He says:—" Had I been some months sooner I should have been
favoured with a noble treat; but now that treat was miserably
soured. At the twentieth mile-stone I should have seen a piece
of Severus' [Hadrian's] Wall, seven feet and a half high, and
two hundred and twenty yards long; a sight not to be found
in the whole line. But the proprietor is now taking it down
to erect a farm-house with the materials. Ninety-five yards
are already destroyed, and the stones fit for building removed.
Then we come to thirteen yards which are still standing, and
overgrown on the top with brambles." According to local
tradition, it was owing to Mr. Hutton's entreaties and tears
that the fine piece of Wall which we meet with in the Brunton grounds was spared. In the grounds of Brunton*—the

* The genuine antiquary does not need to be reminded that before
entering the private grounds of a gentleman leave must be asked and
obtained.

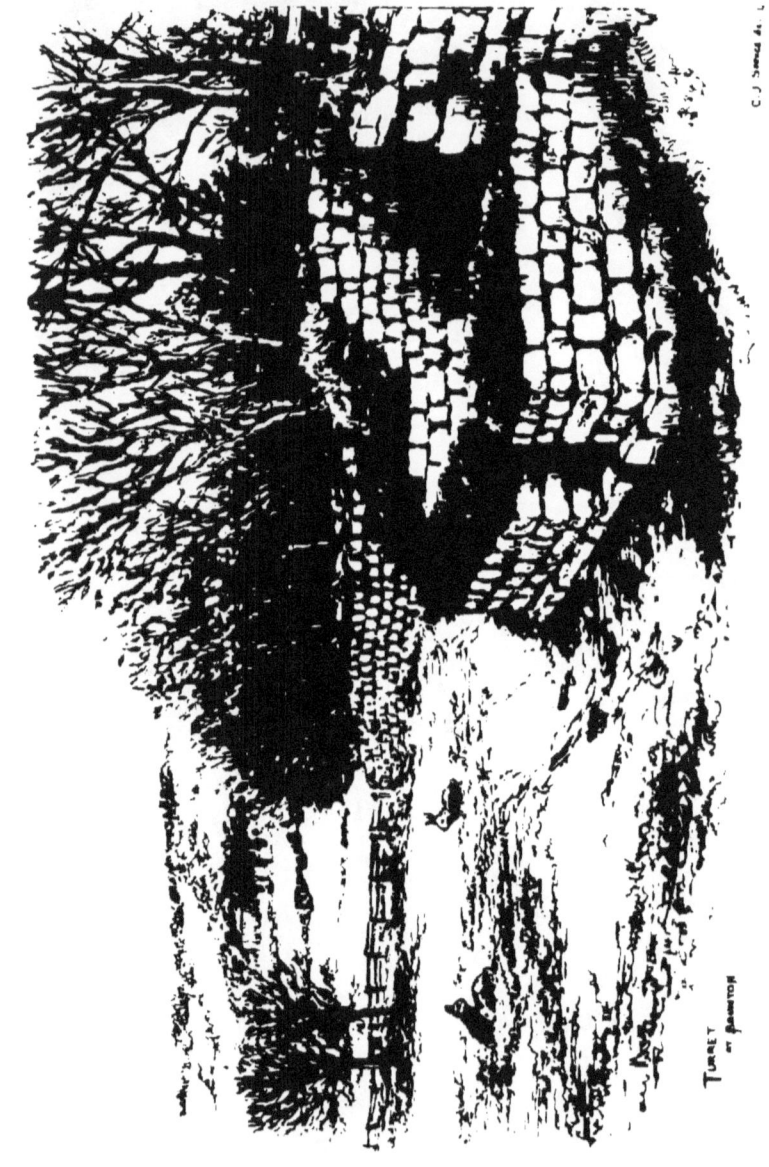

TURRET at ...

residence of Major Waddilove—a little below this, a piece of
the Wall is to be seen, in a state of very great perfection. It
is seven feet high, and presents nine courses of facing-stones
entire. The mortar of the five lower courses is good. The
north fosse, along which we walk in coming to this relic, is
very boldly developed; and being, during the spring and
summer months, thickly covered with ferns and wild flowers,
is an object of great interest.

We now get over the Wall to examine its south face.* A
couple of years ago it was covered up in its own ruins. It has
recently been excavated by Mr. Clayton, the proprietor of the
estate, and not only is a fine stretch of the Wall displayed,
but a turret, the first that we have met with in our journey
hitherto, has been brought to light. The turret is a small
quadrangular building, inclosing a space of twelve feet nine
inches by eleven feet six inches. It has a doorway nearly
four feet wide. The turret is recessed into the Great Wall
about four feet. The Wall, which forms the north wall of
the turret, is standing eleven courses high, giving an elevation
of eight feet and a half. The side walls of the turret are two
feet nine inches thick. Its south wall is nearly four feet high.
Altogether this is the finest specimen of the turret that we
shall meet with in our peregrinations. It is well shown in the
etching on the opposite page.

The road, which for nearly the whole distance from
Newcastle has run upon the line of the Wall, now deviates
considerably to the north of it. This was done by the
Government Surveyor, in order to take advantage of a bridge
which crossed the river at Chollerford. This was no doubt

* By a little detour we reach a gate which takes into the field south of
the Wall, and so avoid getting over the structure.

the bridge for the repairs of which thirteen days' relaxation of enjoined penance were granted to contributors by Bishop Skirlaw, in the time of Richard II. Unfortunately it was carried away by the great flood of 1771, shortly after which time the present bridge was built. The Romans went straight down the hill notwithstanding its steepness, and crossed the river where it was comparatively narrow.

On the east bank of the river towards the north is a conspicuous building, called Cocklaw Tower. It is roofless, but forms a fine and characteristic specimen of the border peel. On the walls of one of its apartments are traces of fresco-painting. On the opposite side of the river, is Haughton Castle, the seat of George Crawshay, Esq. The situation of this castle is most lovely, and the building itself, consisting as it does of an ecclesiastical fabric, adapted to the purposes of border warfare, furnishes the antiquary with a study of considerable intricacy, but great interest.

The inn at Chollerford, as is well known to many anglers and some antiquaries, has long had the reputation of being a comfortable one.

Leaving Brunton, the Wall continues its onward course to the North Tyne in a straight line. A little before reaching the railway a gently elevated mound indicates the site of a mile-castle. Next we meet with the most remarkable feature on the whole line of the Wall—the remains of the bridge over the North Tyne. This is nearly half a mile down the river from the railway station. As foot passengers are necessarily debarred from walking on the line, a traveller approaching it from this quarter should take the stile at the east end of Chollerford Bridge, and find his way through fields and along the river's brink to the object of his search.

The lines both of Wall and Vallum may be distinguished as they approach the river. The Wall, as it enters the little plantation on the river's brink, has been laid bare.   It is six feet four inches thick, and in one place stands eight feet eight inches high.   It terminates temporarily in a square building or *castellum*, formed of stones of the same character as those used in the Wall.   Several layers of wood ashes were found when this building was excavated.   In front of it we have the land abutment of the bridge.   It consists of a solid mass of masonry, of a form well calculated to resist the thrust of the descending stream, and the regurgitation of the waters when passed.   The abutment presents to the river a face of twenty-two feet, and from it the platform of the bridge would spring. From each side of this projecting face the walls retire in an oblique direction.   The southern portion of the abutment has originally been formed upon the same plan as the northern, but an addition has afterwards been made to it, probably to give increased space for defensive works. In the northern part of the abutment, five courses of facing-stones remain, giving a height above the foundation course of six feet.   Some of the stones are very large ; one is four feet ten inches long, and eighteen inches thick.   The stone is from the Black Pasture Quarry, already referred to (p. 68).   All the facing-stones have been placed in their position by the *luis*, and they have been bound together by rods of iron embedded in lead.   The grooves for the rods remain, and, in some places, when first excavated, portions of the lead were seen.   The peculiar feathered tooling of the facing-stones will be noticed.   It is the opinion of some antiquaries that, whilst the great mass of the bridge is the work of Hadrian, these facing-stones are the work of Severus.   It is probable that, by his time, the bridge would require repairs, and these he would effect, both here and in other parts of the mural fortress, before entering upon his Caledonian expedition. At Housesteads and many other places stones that have evidently been used in repairs have this peculiar kind of broaching.

One other circumstance requires attention. Embedded in the centre of the abutment is a piece of masonry which is independent of all the rest, and has the form of a water pier. The river in this part of its course has a tendency to recede from its eastern bank and encroach upon its western. The present abutment is some distance from the river, while that upon the other side is entirely submerged. There can be little doubt that this tendency has always existed, and that the pier which we now see in the middle of the land-abutment of Hadrian's Bridge was formerly one of the water piers of a bridge of earlier date, probably one erected by Agricola. The stones of this pier are bound together, individually, by wedge-shaped cramps, not grouped by long rods, as the facing-stones of the abutment and the piers in the river are.

The platform of this bridge was undoubtedly of timber. Several of the stones which lie on the ground have grooves in them for admitting the spars. No arch stones have been found among the ruins.

From coins, from the sculptures on Trajan's column, and other authentic sources of information, we learn that the approaches to a bridge on an enemy's frontier were always defended by appropriate fortifications. Here, particularly on the south side, as already observed, there was ample space for these defensive bulwarks. When the whole structure was complete it must have had a very formidable appearance.

A covered way, evidently posterior to any of the other

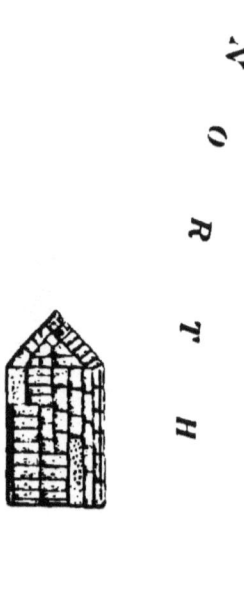

NORTH TYNE

ROMAN BRIDGE
OVER THE
NORTH TYNE.

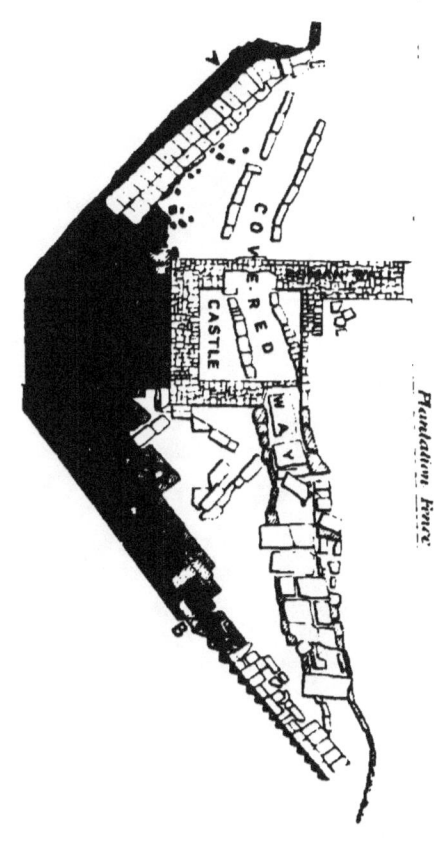

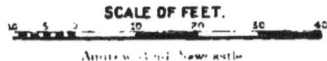

SCALE OF FEET.

works, will be observed crossing the abutment and cutting through the square castle in which the Wall terminates. It goes beyond the extent of the excavations in both directions. It is formed in a great measure of stones that have been used in the bridge. As it is founded upon a bed of silt at least a yard thick, its construction cannot have taken place until the works of the bridge had been overwhelmed by some terrible devastation. No probable conjecture has yet been formed of its use. The idea of a water-course naturally rises in the mind; but the joints of the passage are by no means close, and, though covered on the top, the bottom of it consists simply of the sandy alluvium of the river. Most of the slabs which form the covering have been snapped across, apparently by the weight of the deposit upon them, though some of them are two feet thick; they were found precisely as they now lie.

Several stones among the debris will attract attention. Amongst them is one about four feet in length, resembling an axletree. It has orifices as if for receiving handspikes. Its use is not known. There is also a circular shaft, about nine feet long and two feet in diameter, which has several peculiarities. It has, apparently, been used as an upright post at one extremity of the bridge for the purpose of attaching the balustrade to it. It bears marks of having had an iron rod inserted into it.

Unhappily no inscribed stone has been found to detail the history of the bridge. One large stone was found; but the greater portion of it having been exposed to the roll of the river for centuries, its inscription is entirely obliterated, except the last three lines, which happened to be covered by the gravel of the stream; but they only give us the name of the prefect who had charge of the works, Ælius Longinus—not the name of the emperor by whose command they were executed.   They are

. . . . CURANTE AELIO LONGINO PRAEF EQQ.	. . . . Under the care of Ælius Longinus, a prefect of cavalry.

As we have not previously met with a prefect of this name, we are in ignorance of the date of the inscription.

Shortly before the first edition of this work was published, the whole of this piece of masonry was buried under the accumulated deposits of the river; and, as if more effectually to conceal the architectural treasure beneath, a thriving plantation occupied the surface.   The late Mr. William Coulson, of Corbridge, who had acquired considerable experience as an explorator of Roman remains at BREMENIUM, suspected the truth.   It was at his suggestion, and partly under his superintendence, that the excavations were undertaken by Mr. Clayton, the proprietor of the stations of CILURNUM, PROCOLITIA, BORCOVICUS, and VINDOLANA, and of extensive tracts of Wall between and beyond them—a gentle man to whom, more than any other, the antiquary is indebted for the preservation and skilful display of the best remnants of Imperial Power in Britain.

The plan of the bridge which is here inserted will give the reader a correct idea of it.   In a paper by Mr. Clayton, in the *Archæologia Æliana*, N.S., Vol. VI., p. 80, he will find a fuller account than the limits of this little volume allow, of this important structure.

We now turn to the other works of the bridge.   There have been three water piers.   It has been ascertained, by

. partial excavation, that one of them lies immediately under the eastern bank of the river. Two others are, when the water is low and placid, to be seen in the bed of the stream. Blocks of masonry, which have resisted the roll of this impetuous river for more than seventeen centuries, are a sight worth seeing, even at the expense of being immersed in cold water to the full extent of the lower extremities. That end of the piers which is directed towards the stream is pointed. The *luis* holes remain in the stones. The grooves formed for the iron rods and cramps can also be discerned. The western abutment has been of the same form and construction as the other, but it is in a great measure submerged by the encroachments of the river. In favourable circumstances it can be seen from the bank. There are indications which render it probable that the western abutment, as well as the eastern, was furnished with a tower of defence. In leaving this subject, a short extract from Mr. Clayton's interesting paper may be introduced. "Those who have seen the magnificent remains of the Pont du Gard (justly the pride of Gallia Narbonensis), lighted by the glorious sun of Languedoc, may think lightly of these meagre relics of the bridge of CILURNUM, under the darker skies of Northumberland; but it may be safely affirmed, that the bridge over the Gardon does not span a lovelier stream than the North Tyne, and that so much as remains of the masonry of the bridge of CILURNUM, leads to the conclusion that this bridge, as originally constructed, was not inferior in solidity of material, and excellency of workmanship, to the mighty structure reared by Roman hands in Gaul."

IV.—OBJECTS OF ROMAN INTEREST WITHIN THE LINES OF THE GREAT BARRIER.

Before proceeding to the examination of the station of CILURNUM, to which the Roman bridge over the North Tyne introduces us, it is fitting that we should notice two places lying to the south of the Wall which have been occupied by the Romans—Corchester and Hexham.

Corchester.

To the west of the little town of Corbridge, and distant about six hundred yards from its church, are traces of an extensive Roman settlement. The situation is one which would recommend itself to a Roman engineer. It rises gently above the general surface, and is defended on its southern margin by the river Tyne and its somewhat precipitous bank, and on its western by the more humble stream, the Cor-burn.

It was, probably, a Roman town rather than a purely military settlement. Its shape and size favour this idea. Mr. MacLauchlan, after diligently tracing out the course of its ramparts, came to the conclusion that its form was an irregular ellipse, and that it contained an area of about twenty-two acres. All the camps we have hitherto had occasion to notice assume the form of parallelograms, and have a much smaller area than this. Owing to the peculiar fertility of the soil, the site has long been subject to the plough, and all the erections of the Roman era have been overthrown or obscured.

Numerous important inscriptions have been found here. Amongst them are two altars bearing Greek inscriptions. It is curious to think that the Greek language must at one time have been more or less spoken by the inhabitants of the place. An engraving of one of these altars is here introduced. This altar is now at Netherby. The Astarte of this altar is the Ashtoreth of the Scriptures, the "abomination of the Zidonians." The other Greek altar found here was dedicated

ΑΣΤ[ΑΡ]ΤΗΣ
ΒΩΜΟΝ Μ
ΕΣΟΡΑΣ
ΠΟΥΛΧΕΡ Μ'
ΑΝΕΘΗΚΕΝ

——

Of Astarte
the altar me
you see.
Pulcher me
dedicated.

to the **Tyrian Hercules** by Diodora, the archpriestess. During the period of the Roman occupation of Britain the superstitions and the impure worship of the East were largely followed in this land.

The church of Corbridge, especially the tower, is largely

composed of Roman stones.   Built into the front of a house
on the east of the town is a fractured inscription to the
Emperor Marcus Aurelius Antoninus.   Which of the emperors
of that name is intended is uncertain; from the excellence
of the lettering the earliest of them is probably the person.
Some small sculptured stones are to be met with in some of
the houses.   Numerous important coins have here been found,
amongst them an *aureus* of Domitian, now in the cabinet of
the Duke of Northumberland.   Several inscribed stones from
Corchester are preserved in the Museum of the Society of
Antiquaries of Newcastle.

Hexham.

The appearance of Hexham from the railway is very pic-
turesque.   This is no doubt the site of a Roman station, but
its Roman designation has not been satisfactorily ascertained.
Stukeley says, "This town was undoubtedly Roman; we
judged the *castrum* was where the castellated building now
stands, east of the market place, which is the brow of the hill,
and has a good prospect."   About the year 674 Bishop Wilfred
built a church here.   The only portion of Wilfred's building
that remains is the crypt; the church itself seems to have been
laid in ruins by the Danes in 867, in which state it long continued.   The present church is an exceedingly beautiful
specimen of the early English style.   It was probably erected
at the close of the twelfth or beginning of the thirteenth
century.   The nave is said to have been destroyed during an
incursion of the Scots in 1296, and has never been rebuilt.
This church had the privilege of sanctuary.   The Saxon frid-
stool, or seat of safety, is preserved in the church.   In the
aisle of the south transept are two Roman altars, which

were discovered in pulling down some buildings close to the church, in 1871. One of them is uninscribed. The other contains the following inscription :—

APOLLINI
MAPONO
· · TERENTIVS
· · · F OVF
FIRMVS · SAEN
PRAEF · CASTR
LEG · VI · V · P · F
D D

"Dedicated to Apollo Maponus by · · Terentius Firmus, the son of · · · , of the tribe of Oufentina, a native of Siena, and prefect of the camps of the Sixth Legion, the victorious, pious, and faithful."

The term Maponus is supposed to have reference to the name of some place in England where Apollo was specially worshipped.

In the south transept of the church is preserved a finely-carved tombstone, which was discovered in 1881 by Mr. Robt. Robson, the parish clerk, beneath the floor of the porch adjoining the south transept. The woodcut on the opposite page shows it. It represents the deceased soldier, with the standard in his right hand, riding rough-shod over a prostrate enemy. The inscription is—

DIS MANIBVS FLAVINVS
EQ · ALAE PETR · SIGNIFER
TVR · CANDIDI AN · XXV
STIP · VII H · S

"To the gods the Shades. Flavinus, a soldier of the cavalry regiment of Petriana, standard-bearer of the troop of Candidus, being twenty-five years of age and having served seven years in the army, is here laid."

The crypt has special attractions for the Roman antiquary. It was accidently discovered in the early part of the last

century. After being almost forgotten, attention was again
called to it by the late Mr. Fairless, in the second volume of
the *Journal of the Archæological Institute*. A similar crypt
exists at Ripon, where Wilfred also built a church. It is
entirely built of Roman stones. The use of its various parts

is quite a mystery. Mr. Fairless says:—"There have been
three approaches to this solemn and drear retreat, one of
them at present reaching nearly into the body of the church;
another, to the south, leading to the cloisters; the third rising

into the nave." The woodcut represents one of its chambers. For a long time the only entrance to it was by a ladder, from the church-yard; now it is entered more conveniently by a passage from the transept, which has more recently been discovered. Besides some exceedingly graceful mouldings and devices, which were afterwards adopted by the Saxon and Norman builders, two Roman inscriptions have been built up into the crypt. The more important of these is the one shown in the woodcut. The inscription reads—

IMP · CAES · L · SEP · · ·
PERTINAX ET IMP · C · ·
AVR · ANTONINV · · ·
VS · · · · · · ·
· · · · · COHORTE · · ·
VEXILLATION · · · · ·
FECERVNT SVB · · · ·

The Emperor Cæsar Lucius Septimius [Severus] Pertinax, and the Emperor Cæsar [Marcus] Aurelius Antoninus [and Publius Septimius Geta Cæsar] by the cohort · · · · and the vexillation · · · erected under the superintendence of · · ·

The inscription is imperfect. The name of Geta after his murder by his elder brother was, as in this instance, struck out of all the inscriptions in the empire.

As previously remarked, Severus, before commencing his Caledonian campaign, seems to have repaired Hadrian's Wall, and put in order all the stations on the Watling Street. He may have made Hexham his headquarters while attending to these operations.

The other inscription forms the head-way of one of the arches of the crypt. It is probably part of another altar to Apollo Maponus.

One of the stones at the top of the staircase at the north-west corner of the tower of the Priory Church is a Roman altar, on which are represented an ox's head, with a garland and some sacrificial instruments. The number of inscribed and sculptured stones found in Hexham gives strong confirmation to the opinion that it was a post held by the Romans. Some have supposed that the Roman stones used in the construction of the church have been brought from Corchester. This surely cannot have been the case, as there is abundance of stone in the immediate vicinity of Hexham.

In the year 1832 the sexton, when digging a grave deeper than usual, on the west side of the north transept of the church, struck upon a vessel of Saxon workmanship, containing, it is calculated, about eight thousand Saxon coins. These proved to be *stycas*, a small coin peculiar to Northumberland. The vessel, in a fragmentary condition, and about 300 of the coins, were transmitted to the British Museum. The coins are about a quarter of an inch in diameter, composed of a mixture of metals nearly resembling the Corinthian brass of the ancients. They are most beautifully executed, the letters being sharper and better formed than those of the Norman and Plantagenet series. The coins belong to a period extending from A.D. 790 to A.D. 844.*

V.—FROM THE NORTH TYNE TO THE TIPALT.

We resume our mural investigations at the point where we discontinued them—the North Tyne in the vicinity of Chollerford. A pleasant walk of a little more than half a mile along the turnpike road brings us from Chollerford to Chesters, the seat of John Clayton, Esq., F.S.A. Leave to enter the grounds will not be denied to a brother antiquary who courteously requests it.

Chesters.

Chesters is the CILURNUM of the *Notitia*. It is known in the neighbourhood as "the Chesters," to distinguish it from other camps of less importance. As this station is more accessible than most of the others upon the line of the Wall, and is more frequently visited, it may be well to give a fuller description of it than can in other instances be indulged in. A few general observations will prepare us for taking a personal survey of it.

Excepting AMBOGLANNA, the modern Birdoswald, CILUR-NUM is the largest station on the line of the Wall. It contains an area of five acres and a quarter. It has, as usual, the form of a parallelogram ; and as its surface is slightly raised above the general level of the ground, in consequence of the masonry

* A full account of this remarkable find, with numerous illustrations, from the pen of the late John Adamson, Esq., F.S.A., long the senior secretary of the Newcastle Society of Antiquaries, is to be found in the "Archæologia," Vol. XXV and XXVI., and in the "Archæologia Æliana," Vol. III., quarto series.

which it contains, and the quantity of *debris* which covers it, its outlines may be easily discerned. The practice of the Romans in rounding the angles of their stations is here well seen. The ramparts are five feet thick, and in several places the fosse, which gave them additional strength, may be noticed outside them.

Most of the stations on the Wall, as we have already seen, have four gateways, one in the centre of each rampart. A street about eighteen feet wide proceeds from the north gateway to the south of each, and another from the eastern gateway to the western; these streets cross each other in the middle of the station at right angles. As it was necessary to expose as small a surface as possible to the attack of an enemy, and hence to compress the station within the most confined limits, the other streets of the camps are exceedingly narrow—scarcely a yard wide.*

The stations of CILURNUM and AMBOGLANNA form an exception to the other stations, in this respect, that they have six gateways instead of four. This, doubtless, was owing to their being larger than the others. In each of these cases there is a second gateway in the eastern and western ramparts. The second gateway is, however, only about half the size of the others, having only one portal instead of two. The existence of this second gateway implies the formation of an additional street, running between the eastern and western ramparts.

In many instances the Great Wall comes up to the northern rampart of the stations, and is in the same straight line with it; but in other cases, of which CILURNUM is an example, the

---

* Horsley speaking of Birdoswald, says, "I found the breadth of the passage between the rows of houses or barracks to be no more than thirty-two inches."

CILURNUM.

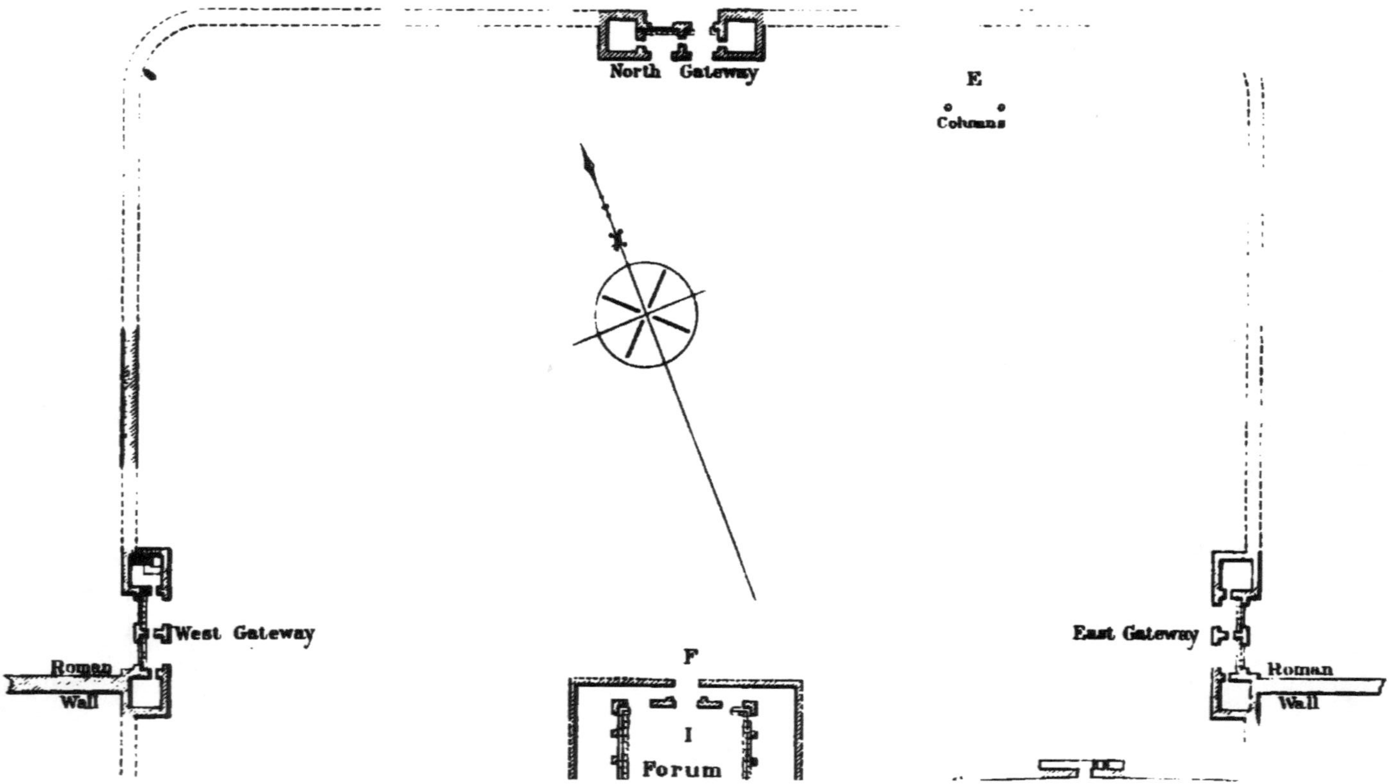

East Gateway

Roman Wall

E.
Columns

North Gateway

F
I
Forum

West Gateway

Roman Wall

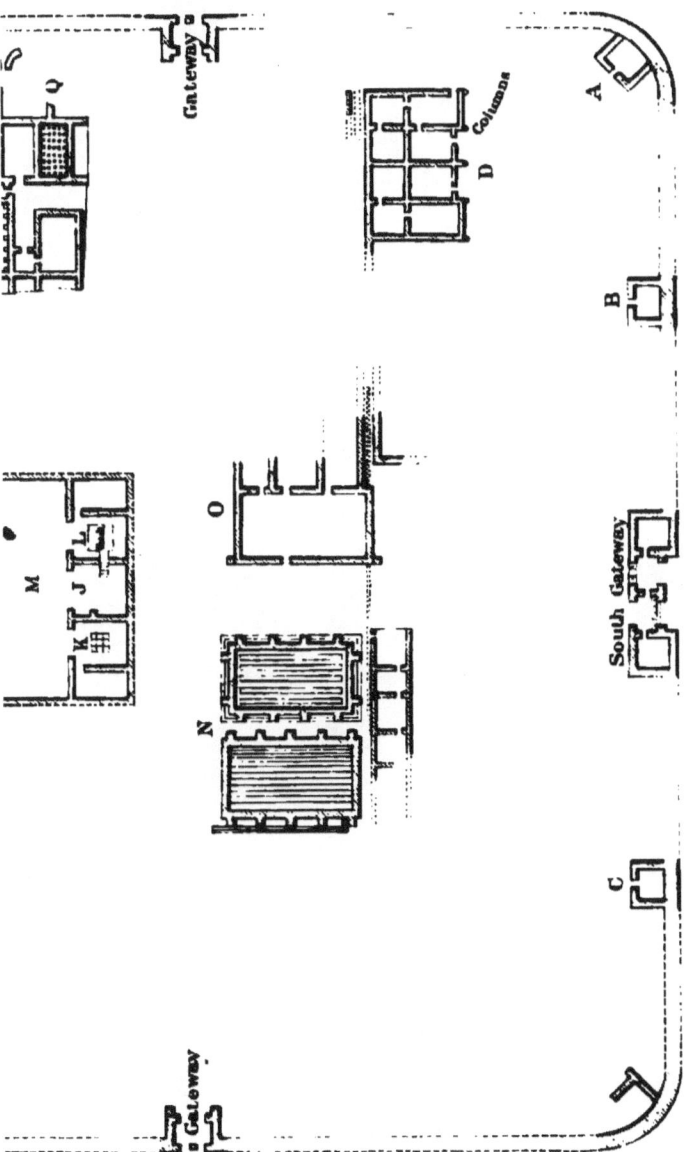

Gateway E

Q

Gateway C

D Colonnade

A

B

M

J K L

O

N

South Gateway

C

Scale of Plan

Feet 10 5 0 10 20 30 40 50 60 70 80 90 100 110 120 130 140 150 Feet

ll strikes the eastern and western ramparts at some dis-
ce from their northern extremity, thus leaving a part of the
:ion, say one-third, to project northwards beyond the Wall.
We have said that at CILURNUM and AMBOGLANNA there
two gateways in the eastern and western ramparts of the
ips. The most northerly of these gateways is of the size
l form usually adopted in the stations. The gateway that
constantly meet with may be thus described. It has two
tals, about eleven feet wide each. A wall, with a narrow
sage through it, divides the one portal from the other.
:h portal has been spanned by an arch, both on its outer
inner margin. Each portal has been closed by two-
red gates, which have rotated upon pivots shod with iron.
ε pivot holes in many instances still exist. When closed,
gates have struck against a rim of stonework which crosses
threshold, or against a stone set up in its centre.
Having made these general remarks, we may now begin
personal exploration of the camp. The accompanying
n, reduced by the kind permission of Mr. Clayton from one
his possession, will enable us the more readily to under-
ld its arrangements.
In passing from the mansion of Chesters to the camp, we
ιd a foot-path which lies in the north fosse of the Wall.
; ."-ll, represented by a slightly elevated grass-grown
ιnd, is on our right hand. If the earth were removed,
or three courses of stones would probably be displayed.
On reaching the station the line of its western rampart
be observed. A little to the north of us a portion of the
ll has been laid bare. On looking still further to the north,
notice how the western rampart blends with the northern
ιpart in a rounded corner. If now we turn to the south

and look along the rampart until it reaches a fine cluster of sycamore trees, we will detect the south-western corner of the station bending round like the rest in a circular fashion.

The principal western gateway of the station is immediately in front of us; we notice its double portal and its two guard chambers. The great Wall is seen coming up to the southern jamb of the gateway. It is here seven feet wide, and it is standing to the height of six courses of stones. The fact that the Wall comes up to the southern margin of the gate rather than the northern will excite surprise. We shall revert to this subject when we examine the corresponding gate in the eastern rampart. That this gateway has, at an early period, been diverted from its original use is evident from the fact that a small tank has been formed in its northern guard chamber, into which, gutter-stones that are still in their place have, no doubt, introduced water from the outside.

Proceeding southwards along the rampart for the distance of about forty-eight yards, we come to the site of a second gateway in it. It is a gateway with a single portal; but as it is precisely similar to one on the opposite side of the camp, which is left exposed, it was not thought necessary to do more than ascertain its existence and its form; it is now covered up. At the south-west angle of the station to which we next proceed, traces of internal walls will be observed, proving the existence of a building, probably a tower, similar to some others which we shall presently see. Going along the south rampart we come to one of these (c in the Plan)— a square building with a doorway on its inner side. On this side are a number of gutter-stones for receiving the rainfall from the roof, which were found, when the excavation was made, precisely in the position in which they now are. As we proceed along the south rampart we will notice a gentle depression on its southern margin, caused by the fosse which surrounded the station.

The southern gateway, at which we next arrive, has some peculiarities which we will do well to notice. Its double portal and its two guard chambers will be observed. The wall separating the two portals is in a more complete condition perhaps than in any other instance. The iron which has begirt the pivot of one of the gates of the western portal is to be seen in the pivot hole. The iron was found in the other pivot-hole when the gate was first excavated, but, becoming loose, it was removed.

The excavations which, from time to time, have been made in the stations and mile-castles of the Wall, have afforded abundant proof that in more than one instance the northern foe has succeeded in driving the garrison from their defences, and in occupying their posts. As they could not long expect to hold them, they have availed themselves of the opportunity of committing all the damage they could; they have burnt everything that was combustible, and have damaged the masonry to the utmost of their power. When the Roman troops, having obtained reinforcements, succeeded in repulsing the foe and regaining possession of their strongholds, they have not been able thoroughly to retrieve the damage which had been done. As time was pressing, they have not removed the whole of the fallen rubbish, but, making all as smooth as possible, they have laid new floors and raised the walls that were partially demolished, or built new ones upon the higher foundation. We have proofs of all this in the gate before us. When the eastern guard chamber was excavated three layers of ashes were found. And let the visitor now look at the eastern portal of the gate before us. Its floor is raised considerably above the level of that of the western portal by a mass of loose stones; and that it must have occupied this higher elevation when the Romans abandoned the fort, is evident from the existence still, at the upper level, of the pivot-holes of the gate and of the central stone against which the doors struck when shut.

Another fact must be mentioned. Towards the close of the period of Roman occupation, when supplies of men and money were withheld, the garrisons became weak and demoralised. They no longer depended upon their valour and their generalship, but availed themselves of mechanical contrivances to protect themselves from the foe. Amongst other things, they diminished the size of many of their gateways, and walled-up others altogether. In the case before us, the western portal had been walled-up entirely, and only the eastern made use of. This walling has been removed, and the portal now presents the aspect it had when first built.

Let the visitor now enter the eastern guard chamber and he will, on the upper course of its eastern wall, notice a stone on which is carved in faint characters LEG. VI. VI. *Legio sexta victrix* (The Sixth Legion surnamed the Victorious). The letters have been formed by a series of puncturings.

In this guard chamber was found the larger portion of a bronze tablet of more than national importance—a diploma or *Tabula honestæ missionis*, conferring the right of Roman citizenship and the right of marriage upon certain soldiers who were then employed in Britain. Mr. Clayton has generously presented this tablet to the British Museum, where three other tablets of a similar nature (found in England) have been deposited. A full description of this interesting document, together with an engraving of it, will be found in the Appendix at the end of this volume.

Some gutter-stones are to be seen on the outer margin of this gate, which have received the drippings from the roof of the gateway.

It is impossible to examine the camp thoroughly without having to retrace our steps occasionally; but we will endeavour to avoid this as much as possible.

Let us now, for a little, forsake the southern rampart and examine the buildings to the north of us. In the plan of the station some buildings, having the form of parallelograms, are laid down at (N) and (O). Those at (N) were conceived from their construction to have been granaries; but as the masonry of them was defective it was thought best to remove them. The chamber to the east of these at (O) presented no features of interest, and being fragile, was removed also.

The enclosure in the centre of the station is that important series of buildings which, in a Roman city, was denominated the Forum. That CILURNUM should be provided with a structure of this kind shows that it must have been not a mere garrison, but a military city commanding an extensive district, rich in commercial resources, and having a considerable population.

As that part of the station which is occupied by the Forum is more depressed than the neighbouring parts, it seemed as if no buildings of importance would be found below the sod, and it was long before it received the attentions of the excavator. Mr. Clayton, however, wishing to know what connection the crypt (L), which we shall presently examine, had with the contiguous buildings, ordered excavations to be made in this part. The spade of the excavator had laid bare but a small part of the neighbouring walls when Mr. Clayton discovered in their arrangement a resemblance to that which he had seen in the Forum at Pompeii. He therefore ordered the whole enclosure to be laid bare, with the results which we see before us.

The Forum was easy of access. The street from the north gate of the station comes right down to its north gate, and the two streets from the lateral gateways of the station passed along its northern and southern ends. Streets passed from the one to the other of these two ways on the eastern and western sides of the Forum at (H) and (G). The Forum has three gates, one in the centre of its northern, its western, and its eastern walls. We will now enter the enclosure by its western gateway at (H). This gateway has had a roof over it, as is proved by the gutter-stones which still remain, and which carried off the rainfall. The steps remain as they were found by the excavator.

The northern half of the Forum consists of a square enclosure (I), which is surrounded by a covered colonnade. The base of the columns which have supported the roof on the inner side remain, and the gutter-stones which received the water which fell from it occupy their original position. In the interior space, goods which were not liable to injury from exposure to the weather would be offered for sale. It has been flagged, but it has not been fully excavated. Goods that have been brought to the market in wheeled vehicles have been introduced by the eastern gate (G), it still having in it the grooves formed by the action of the wheels.

At the southern end of the Forum are three halls (J, K, L), each having a wide portal—eighteen feet in extent. The wedge-shaped stones which lie about the place show that these entrances have been spanned by an arch. The central chamber (J) is believed to have been the *ærarium* of the station, the place where the treasure chest of the regiment was kept, and where all pecuniary business connected with it was transacted; the chambers on each side of it (K, L) are believed to be the *curiæ* in which courts-martial were held and the justice of the district dispensed. Connected with each *curia* is a smaller chamber in which prisoners or persons connected with the court might remain in readiness.

When towards the close of the Roman occupation of Britain the garrison declined in physical and moral strength certain changes in these buildings have been effected. The vault which now occupies a part of the *ærarium* (J) and of

the eastern *curia* (L) was built for the more effectual preservation of the treasure chest, and the entrance into the courts
was walled up leaving only a narrow doorway.

The vault was discovered in the early part of the present
century.   A tradition existed in the country that the station
had been occupied by a cavalry regiment and that the stables,
which were capable of accommodating 500 horses, were
underground.   The rustics when they came upon this vault
naturally enough thought that the latter part of the legend
was about to be verified and that they would soon enter the
stables; it was not to be so, however.   An oaken door, bound
and studded with iron, closed the entrance into this chamber,
but it fell to pieces shortly after being exposed.   On the floor
were found a number of base denarii, chiefly of the reign of
Severus.   The roof of the apartment is peculiar.   It consists of
three separate arches, the intervals between them being filled
up by the process called "stepping over."   The woodcut on the
previous page represents the structure as seen from the inside.

Between the important public buildings which we have
now described and the market-place is an open walk (M) which
would, during the hours of business, be occupied by traders
and litigants attending the markets or the courts.

If the visitor chooses he may now examine the north
gateway of the station, which is constructed on the same plan
as the others, but is in a less perfect condition.   A drain to
carry off the waste water of this part of the station finds vent
here.   A road has proceeded from this gateway in the direction of the Watling Street, to which attention will presently
be called.

We now come to the south-eastern portion of the station.
On the Plan at (D), a series of longitudinal chambers are marked,

and five cylindrical columns which are about four feet high. The walls of these chambers were of very loose masonry, their foundations were at different depths, and they were manifestly of late construction. Being fragile, they have been removed. The pillars stand as they were found; the tops of them have evidently been broken off. It is difficult to say what the object of them has been. On the south side of them was found a road with a hard bottom, formed of river-side gravel. This road probably ran all round the station.

Near the north-east angle of the station (F) there has been a similar arrangement of pillars, only two of which are now standing. A road ran along the north of them. Here also were a number of buildings of loose construction and probably of late date.

Attached to the southern rampart of the station are two chambers (B, A), similar to the one we have already seen at (C); they stand about twelve courses of stones high and have an area of about thirteen feet by ten. They are entered by a door on their inner side. Almost at the bottom of the chamber marked (B), were found the skeletons of two infants.

It will be well to notice the masonry on the outside of the south-east angle of the station. It is exceedingly good, and there are eight courses of it.

Proceeding northwards along the eastern rampart, we come to the smaller of the two gateways on this side. It has only a single portal, which is twelve feet wide. By means of this small eastern gateway the most of the traffic to the bridge and onwards must have been carried. It may be mentioned, however, that the remains of a Roman bridge, of similar structure to the one we have already examined, have been found about midway between the bridge already described

and the modern bridge at Chollerford. The north gateway
of the station would be the one by which the traffic proceeding
over this bridge would have egress from the station. Traces
of a road leading in that direction have been found. This
gateway and the bridge we have now referred to would, when
the country was in a state of quietude, relieve the traffic proceeding from the small eastern gateway, especially that
portion of it which was intended for the Watling Street.

Proceeding onwards about forty-five yards, we come to
the great gateway of the eastern rampart. The etching here
introduced gives a view of it from the interior of its southern
margin. It is in a state of excellent preservation. The
guard chambers are unusually complete, their walls being, in
one place, twelve courses of stones high. The gates, when
closed, have struck against a rim of stonework which crosses
the threshold. Each portal, both at back and front, has as
usual been crowned by an arch. The springer of the arch
on the southern pier at the back of this gateway remains,
and the large slabs of stone which formed the foundations of
the arches in front of the gateway are in their proper position.
A drain is seen in the flooring of the gateway.

The great Wall (as was the case at the western gateway)
comes up to the southern jamb of this gateway, instead of
the northern, as we might have expected; giving apparently
a great advantage to a northern foe. This circumstance may
perhaps be accounted for in the following manner:—The
station, as we have already said, was probably one of Agricola's,
and had been constructed to guard the passage of the river,
and command the valley of the North Tyne. When Hadrian
resolved upon the construction of the Wall, his engineer saw
the necessity of including this station in its range. For some

THE EASTERN GATEWAY
CILURNUM

reason, however, which we cannot discover, he thought fit to bring up the Wall to the southern instead of the northern margin of these great gateways, thus rendering them useless in ~~~ of war to the garrison. They were accordingly walled up in front and rear, the interior space being filled with rubble. This mass of building would form an excellent platform on which to plant catapults and ballistæ, which probably was done.*

Entering once more within the walls of the station, we have a series of buildings (P Q R) which will well repay examination. They have probably been the prætorium or general's quarters, and were excavated by Mr. John Clayton in 1843. The annexed woodcut gives a good sketch of part of them. An

* By way of showing the extent to which engines of war were used by the Romans it may be stated that when Vespasian attacked the city of Jotapata, in Palestine, be brought a hundred and sixty engines to play upon it, and that whilst some of them projected large stones, others threw lances, fire, or a multitude of darts.—*Josephus, Wars of the Jews,* III., vii., 9.

account of the excavation from the pen of Mr. Clayton will be found in the *Archæologia Æliana*, O.S., Vol. III., p. 142. Although the frosts and rains of forty winters have had some effect upon them, the ruins are still stately. We may enter the enclosure by the wicket at (s). The narrowness of the streets, on which we have already commented, will be noticed. It will be observed that the floors of the chambers are supported upon pillars of brick or stone. The object of this was to allow heated air to circulate under the floors, and thus communicate warmth to the apartments. The hot air was likewise carried up the walls by means of flue tiles. As the floors were thick, an equable heat would be communicated at a small expenditure of fuel. The site of the furnace (Q) is near the south-east portion of the buildings. The tiles composing it, as well as the stone pillars in its vicinity, having been strongly acted on by fire, have for the most part crumbled into a shapeless mass. In one of the chambers on the northern side of the group are two receptacles that look like baths, or tanks for holding water. When first exposed they were found to be lined with red cement, which has peeled off through the action of the weather. It will be noticed that some of the *pilæ* supporting the floors are portions of columns that have ornamented some previous building. The excellency of the masonry of some parts of these structures will strike the observer. The woodcut on the opposite page represents a buttress (R) at the north-east angle of the group. These ruined walls are the favourite habitat of some wild plants of great beauty and some rarity, especially the *corydalis lutea*, the *erinus Hispanicus*, and the *geranium lucidum*. It is interesting to see life, fragrance, and grace springing from the grave of empire.

In the course of his peregrinations the traveller will have noticed in the vicinity of the more recent explorations some of the minor objects that have been thrown up by the spade of the excavator. Fragments of vessels of Samian ware are frequent, so are portions of wine amphoræ, mortars, and glass vessels. The shells of oysters, mussels, cockles, and limpets

will be noticed; the Romans were fond of this species of food, and though CILURNUM is thirty miles from the sea, the garrison found means to procure it. The bones of animals— the red deer, the roe-buck, the ox, the wild boar, and the sheep—are frequent. The conclusion seems inevitable that the occupants of the camp, when at their meals, threw the

H

bones of their food, after they had picked them, amongst the rushes that covered their floors, and allowed them to remain there. The bones do not occur at the lowest level of the excavations. It would thus appear that this disreputable practice was not in use when the regiment was in its prime.

We now make our way to the river's edge. The course of the road leading from the station to the bridge will be discerned. It would seem as if buildings had been reared on both sides of it, the foundations of which are now covered by the turf. A portion of the great Wall has been laid bare in this vicinity. In the margin of the river, when the stream is clear, the foundations of the western abutment of the bridge are seen.

On the south side of the road in this neighbourhood, and near the edge of the river, a large and lofty range of buildings will quickly arrest the gaze of the visitor. Their existence was not dreamt of a few months ago. In attempting to make a drain from the camp to the river, some walls were unexpectedly hit upon. The spade of the excavator, laboriously applied, has since revealed the mass of building, which we will now by the aid of the accompanying Plan attempt to describe.

We will begin our examination at the north-east angle of the group. Here we meet with a courtyard (A in the Plan) about forty-five feet long and thirty feet wide. It is paved with rough flags, and is enclosed on all sides with walls, though only a small portion of its eastern wall remains. The wall at its western extremity is rendered remarkable by being pierced on its inner side by seven niches or recessed arches. Each niche is three feet high, two feet wide, one foot six inches deep, and is raised eight inches above the level of the floor. No reasonable conjecture has been formed as to the

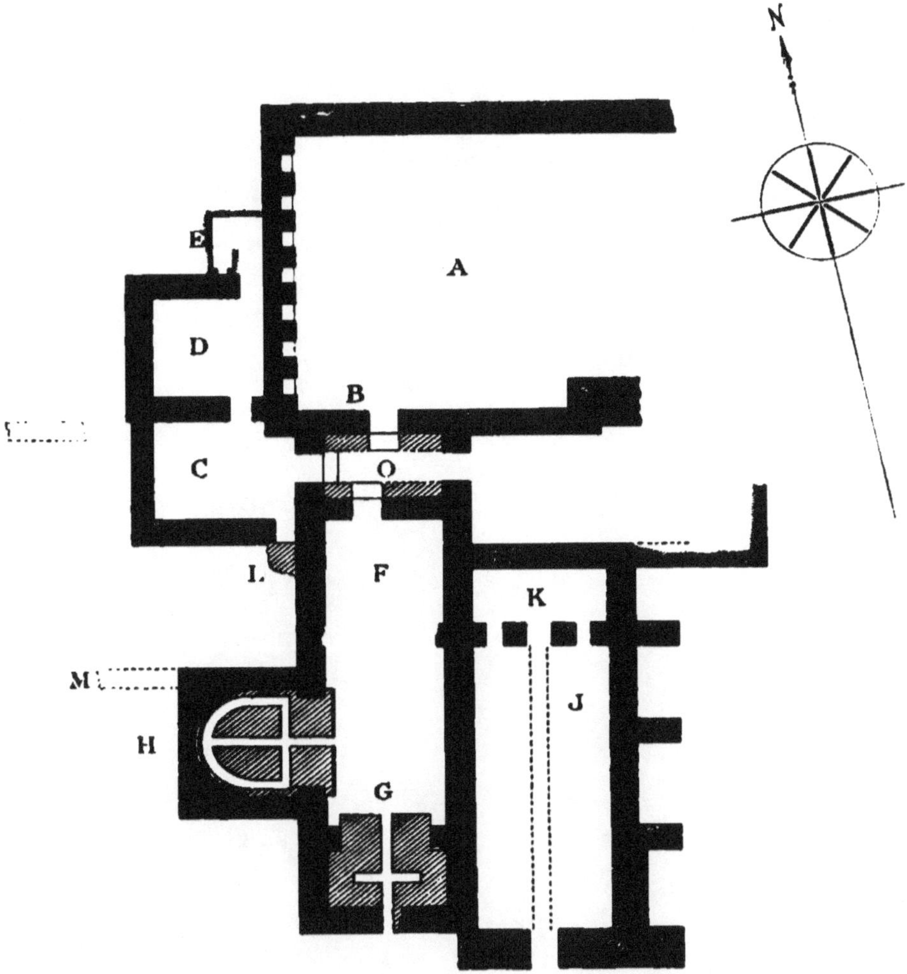

N

E

A

D

B

C

O

I.

F

K

M

J

H

G

EXCAVATIONS near the RIVER at
CILURNUM.

Scale of Feet.

0   10   20   30   40   50 Feet

And ꟸ Reid. Newcastle

CILURNUM

use of these niches. Some have supposed that they were intended to hold statues or images; but they are too near the ground for such a purpose. The accompanying etching gives a good representation of this wall and the court.

Passing out of this courtyard by a doorway (B) in its south wall, we come into a passage (O), the flags of which, and the steps that lead into the neighbouring chamber, are much worn by the tread of feet. This passage has a low wall on each side of its main walls, intended, perhaps, for seats. At its western extremity is a square chamber (C), whose walls stand sixteen courses of stones, or seven feet six inches high. It is provided with a hypocaust, and in its south wall is an air course, formed of flue tiles, for taking the hot air upwards. The jambs of the door leading out of this chamber are masses of well-chiselled stone, six feet high; the pivot-holes of the door, and the holes for fastening it, will be noticed. Passing into the next room (D), we notice the excellence of the masonry of its walls, and observe that it has been provided with a hypocaust. This room leads into another which, judging from the rudeness of its masonry, is of later date than the others that we have passed through. In the floor of it are what appear to be the remains of the furnace which has supplied the hypocausts and flues with hot air.

Returning to the passage which we have just left (O), we find a doorway in its south wall leading into a chamber (F), which at present is thirty-four feet long by thirteen and a half broad; but it seems at one time to have been divided into two. Its floor is of concrete, and in one place where it is partially removed, a flue is seen, the upper part of which is coated with soot. In excavating this chamber numerous small blocks of concrete, of the form shown in the woodcut here given, were found. It is difficult to divine the use of them. In the lowest course of masonry in the east wall of this chamber are two small stones slightly carved; one of them bears a phallic representation, on the other is a bird, having over it the word NEILO (?). At the southern extremity of this chamber is a

SIDE VIEW. square bay (G) filled with a mass of masonry, about three feet high, and intersected by a longitudinal and a transverse flue carefully constructed.

There is another chamber which is entered by a passage through the south wall of the large hall (F). It is marked (H) in the Plan. This chamber terminates in a circular bay, in which is a splayed opening or window, resembling in form the windows of a mediæval castle. The width of the window is four feet; the upper part of it is wanting. With the exception of one of a similar kind in the Forum of the camp at South Shields, no other example of a window has been found in any Roman structure in the North of England. The writer found on the ground outside this window some fragments of Roman window glass. The Romans in making their window glass seem to have poured the melted vitreous matter upon a stone slab. The under side of the plate is thus dull, bearing marks of the granulation of the stone, the upper is smooth and bright. The edge of the plate is rounded and smooth. A longitudinal and transverse flue, and one following the form of the circular bay, have supplied this chamber with hot air; its floor being supported in the same manner as the chamber (G) —by solid blocks of masonry. The external masonry of this chamber is square; it presents twenty-three courses of stones, and is nine and a half feet high.

To the east of the long room (F) is another apartment,

twenty-nine feet long by fourteen broad. It has had a concrete floor, underneath which there are appearances of a
channel, which may be a flue. At the north end of this
chamber (J) is a small room (K), the floor of which is at a
lower level than that of the one with which it communicates.
When first opened, this smaller room was filled with sand up
to the level of the floor of the other, which also had a covering of sand over it. There are three apertures in the wall
separating these two chambers. The east wall of the long
chamber (J) is strengthened on its outside by four buttresses.
Its south wall has no buttresses; but it is four feet six inches
thick, and is built in stages. There is an aperture in this
wall, probably for carrying a flue through.

On clearing away the soil from the eastern and southern
faces of these chambers, thirty-three human skeletons were
found, all of them in a remarkably perfect condition. The
skeletons of two horses and that of a dog were also met with.

On inspecting the western face of this cluster of buildings,
a vacant space will be noticed between the chamber with the
circular bay (H) and the chamber (C). At the north-east angle
of this opening will be noticed a rough piece of masonry (L),
hollow within. This has probably been a channel to carry the
hot air coming from the furnace at (E), and passing through
the chambers (D and C) to the hall at (F), and elsewhere.

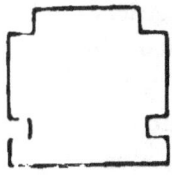

Scattered about the vacant space
to which we have now referred, were
found a number of carefully dressed
stones, slightly wedge-shaped, and furnished with a groove. The woodcuts
represent them. They are supposed

SIDE VIEW.

END VIEW.

to have formed an arch which may have stood in this vicinity,
but with what object does not appear.

Several large channel stones, very skilfully wrought, have
been found in various parts of the ruins. They are very
superior to the ordinary gutter-stones so often seen in Roman
stations. One of them was found in the aperture at the south
end of the chamber (J). What their original position may
have been we have no means of knowing.

Close to this aperture, and partly resting upon the gutter-
stone, was found an altar inscribed :—

DAE	To the goddess Fortune
FORT · CO	the preserver, Venenus a
NSERVATR	
ICI VENENV	German (dedicates it) will-
S · GER · L · M	ingly to a deserved object.

On the face of it, between the first two lines and the
remainder of the inscription, is a carved figure of the deity.
There was nothing to induce the supposition that the altar
was found in its original position, or that this chamber was
devoted to sacred purposes.

On the western side of this range of buildings is a wall (M)
of good masonry, leading to the supposition that this block
may have had some connection with others nearer the station.
The other wall at (N) is, to all appearance, mediæval.

During the progress of the excavations fewer coins,
weapons, vases, ornaments, and articles of domestic use have
been found than usual. The dearth of these things leads to the
idea that these halls have not been used as ordinary barracks,
but have been put to some special service. What that use
has been, conjecture has as yet failed to find out. Can they
have been intended to defend the passage of the river?

A slight inspection of the buildings will show that they
have not all been built at the same time. Changes have been

effected in them at different periods; the masonry of some of them is good, of others inferior. Marks of fire appear in several places. No doubt that element has been employed, along with other means, in effecting their final destruction. It is, however, somewhat strange to find such considerable buildings as these, which have withstood, in this busy England, the lapse of perhaps thirteen or fourteen centuries.

It was hoped that some inscription would have been found in the course of the excavations which would have told us the purpose of the building and the name of its constructor. In this we are disappointed. Beside the altar to Fortune, which we have already noticed, portions of four inscriptions have been found, but they are very fragmentary. Two of them manifestly belong to the time of Elagabalus and Severus Alexander. The first of them is here shown :—

. . . RIBVS COM

. RO SALVTE DE

. . . VR SEVERI

The inscription may be conjecturally restored and expanded thus:—*Mat*RIBVS COM*munibus p*RO SALVTE DE*curiæ Avrelii* SEVERI *Alexandris.* "To the Mothers, common to all horsemen for the safety of the decuria or troop of Aurelius Severus Alexander." The value of the inscription consists in the last line, which, though the lower half of the letters is wanting, seems to give us with certainty the name of Aurelius Severus Alexander. He was Cæsar when Elagabalus was Augustus, and he was the immediate successor of that emperor.

The next stone is here shown :—

PER · CL . . . .
LEG · PR . . . .
SEP · NIL . . . .

which may be thus expanded :—PER CL*audium Apellinium* LEG*atum*, PR*oprætorem instante* SEP*timio* NIL*o præfecto equitum.* It no doubt refers to a building which was erected by direction of Claudius Apellinius, under the superintendence of Septimius Nilus. In an inscription found at this station (which will be given in a subsequent page), belonging to the time of Elagabalus and Severus Alexander, we meet with the name of Septimius Nilus ; and in an inscription found at BREMENIUM, which also belongs to this period, we meet with the name of Claudius Apellinius (*Lap. Sep.*, No. 572, C.I.L. VII., No. 1,045). Another stone belonging to this period was also found in the station here, erected by the second ala of Astures for the safety of the emperors, so that it seems certain that extensive building operations went on at CILURNUM about the years A.D. 220, 221.

The remaining two stones which were found in the new excavations are here figured. One of them seems to be part of an altar to Jupiter, erected for the safety of Galerius Verus or Verecundus. The other, beyond reminding us of the well-known formula DD. NN., *domini nostri*, yields no information. They are both here figured :—

In addition to the suburban buildings which we have now described, the remains of similar structures have been found in unusual numbers to the south and west of the camp.

The burying ground of the station was to the south of it, at a point where the river bends rapidly to the east, and where the sunk fence defining the park of Chesters joins the river's bank. This fact has been inferred from the number of monumental slabs that have been found here. It is a place of peaceful repose and great natural beauty.

CILURNUM was garrisoned, as numerous inscriptions prove, by the second ala of Astures—a people from the modern Asturia, in Spain. The Rev. John Hodgson says :—"The Astures in exchanging the sunny valleys of Spain for the banks of tawny Tyne, might find the climate in their new situation worse; but a lovlier spot than CILURNUM all the Asturias could not give them."

Several very important inscriptions, sculptures, and other relics of the Roman era found in this and neighbouring stations are preserved in the mansion and grounds of Chesters. To a few of these the attention of the student is now directed.

In the portico fronting the house are some important altars. In the doorway are two large altars dedicated to Mars Thingsus, and two female deities, hailing from Alesia, which have recently been found at Chapel Hill, to the south of the station of BORCOVICUS. Along with them was found a portion of a large semi-circular slab (here preserved), on which we have probably a representation of the god and the two nymphs. Here, too, is an altar to Cocidius, a native British god, found not far from the station of VINDOLANA, and another to the same god (in association with the Roman deity Silvanus) which was found at BORCOVICUS. To the right of the doorway are two cylindrical stones; these are milestones from the vicinity of the Caw Gap, one of them bears the name of Hadrian (much erased), the other of Severus Alexander. One very fine altar, figured on the opposite page, will attract the visitor's attention. It bears the following inscription :—

I O M
CETERISQVE
DIIS IMMORT
ET GEN PRAETOR
Q PETRONIVS
Q F FAB VRBICVS
PRAEF COH IIII
GALLORVM
. . . . . .
EX ITALIA
DOMO BRIXIA
VOTVM SOLVIT
PRO SE
AC SVIS

"To Jupiter, the best and greatest, and the other immortal gods, and the genius of the camp, Quintus Petronius Urbicus, the son of Quintus, of the Fabian tribe, the prefect of the fourth cohort of the Gauls, . . . from Italy, a native of Brixia (the modern Brescia), [erected this altar] in discharge of a vow for himself and his family."

This altar was found at VINDOLANA, Chesterholm, where the *Notitia* places the prefect of the fourth cohort of the Gauls. The altar thus confirms the statement of the *Notitia*. One line of the inscription has been erased. This had pro-

bably contained an epithet of the legion (perhaps *Anton-iniana*) derived from the name of some emperor (Elagabalus)? who had assumed the name Antoninus, but who having fallen into disgrace the epithet was renounced. The sides of the altar are ornamented with figures of the stork. This bird is remarkable for its attachment to its young. Urbicus seems to have been fond of his family, as he associates them with himself in the benefits which he expects to result from his devotion to the gods. Hence probably the introduction of the stork.

In the shed to the right of the portico are a number of sculptured stones and inscriptions brought from the station of PROCOLITIA, Carrawburgh. Two of the largest are grave-stones, one of them being to a standard bearer, who is repre-sented at full length with his standard in his hand. Here, too, are a number of small uninscribed altars which were got out of the well at PROCOLITIA, and which will be referred to afterwards.

Of the antiquities on the left of the doorway, our space will only allow us to notice two. One of these is the small inscribed stone which is here engraved. The inscription, when complete, has probably stood thus:—

IMP · T[ITO AEL]
IO · HAD · [ANTONI]
NO · AVG · [PIO PP.]
COS · LEG · [II AVG ·]

"The second legion, styled the august, dedicates this building to the Emperor Titus Ælius Hadrianus Antoninus Augustus, pious, the father of his country, and consul. . . . ."

Antoninus Pius was consul for the first time A.D. 138. This is the earliest inscription found at CILURNUM. It was procured in excavating the large gateway in the eastern rampart.

The other object respecting which the visitor may require some information, is a large fir cone ornament of red sandstone. It is from the Roman station at Papcastle. This emblem, the cone of the Italian pine, was used by the Etruscans and Romans to signify the resuscitating powers of nature. It was placed among their tombs, and carved upon their gravestones, perhaps to indicate their hope of a life beyond the grave. There is a smaller figure of the same kind in this portico; it was brought from VINDOLANA, Chesterholm.

If we now turn our steps to the Antiquity House, a tasteful rustic structure in the garden, we shall find in it many other objects of antiquarian interest. An important slab, shown in the engraving, and found in this station, fronts the entrance. The inscription, a considerable part of which is effaced, is as follows :—

IMP · CAES M AVREL . . . .

AVG . . . .

. . . . P . M . TRIB . P . IIII COS III P . P . DIVI

DIVI SEVER . NEP . ET M . . . .

CAESAR IMPER . . . .

ALAE II ASTVR . . . VETVSTATE . *conlaps. restitu-*

ERVNT . PER . MARIVM . VALERIAN . . . . . .

INSTANTE . SEPTIMIO . NILO . PRAE . . . . . .

DEDICATVM III KAL NOVEM GRATO ET SELE . . .

"To the Emperor Cæsar Marcus Aurelius Antoninus Augutus
. . . . high priest, possessed of the tribunician power for
the fourth time, consul for the third time, father of his country,
of the deified [Antoninus Magnus son], of the deified Severus
grandson, and Marcus [Aurelius Alexander . . .] Cæsar,
heir to the empire. The [soldiers] of the second cavalry
regiment of Asturians restored [this temple], [which had
fallen down] through age, by command of Marius Valerianus
[imperial legate and proprætor] under the superintendence
of Septimius Nilus, the prefect. It was dedicated on the third
of the Kalends of November (Oct. 30th), Gratus and Seleucus being consuls." Gratus and Seleucus were consuls A.D.
221. Elagabalus, who took to himself the name of Marcus
Aurelius Antoninus, was then upon the throne, and Severus
Alexander was his adopted son and heir. On his being
murdered a few months afterwards, his name was as usual
struck out of all the documents of the empire. Hence the
erasures in the tablet. Severus Alexander was himself
murdered a few years afterwards. This inscription confirms
the statement of the *Notitia*, that the second ala of Asturians
was in garrison here. As the *Notitia* was not compiled until

the beginning of the fifth century, we have thus direct proof that the same regiment was quartered here for at least two

hundred years. It was probably brought here long before the time of Elagabalus; most likely in the time of Hadrian.

Two figures opposite the visitor will strike his eye. The more important of these is the headless figure of Cybele, the mother of the gods, standing upon what was probably intended for a bull. It was found in the southwest corner of the station, and when first exhumed was used in building a stone fence which protected some young trees at the south-west corner of the station. The sculpture, as will be seen from the engraving, is of a masterly character. The dress of the goddess is precisely that which was in vogue in the salons of Paris and London a year or two ago. The figure on the left of Cybele is that of Victory. It too has been much mutilated, probably by the Caledonians immediately after the departure of the Romans. It was found inside the eastern gateway of the station of BORCOVICUS by Mr.

Clayton's excavators in 1852. She holds a palm branch in her left hand, in her right would be a coronal wreath wherewith to deck the victor's brow.

Not far from Victory is a stone lintel found in CILURNUM on which are carved (see woodcut) in bold relief two sea monsters. A sea goat and a Pegasus formed the usual badge of the second legion; this carving is probably a variety of the accustomed symbol. A boar was the badge of the twentieth legion. One or two examples of this will be seen in the stones here exhibited. The group of stones shown in the woodcut on the following page is of some interest. The composite capital, found in the station of CILURNUM, enables us to form an idea of the ornate character of some of the buildings that were con-

tained within its walls. The other stones of the group are

specimens of a numerous class found upon the Wall, of which there are many in this repository, and which are called "centurial stones." They are supposed to have been built into the Wall with the view of indicating that the portion in which they occur was built by the troops under the command of a particular centurion. The inscription is usually preceded

by a reversed ɔ, or an angular stroke thus >, which is sup-posed to be equivalent to the word *centuria*. Thus one of the stones before us reads (in English) the Century of Valerius Maximus, and the other the Century of Rufus Sabinus— these troops having built, as is supposed, the portions of the Wall in which they were found.

I

The figure of a soldier lies on the ground. It was found in the station of Borcovicus. It is badly damaged, but enough remains to show the ability of the soldier-artist from whose chisel it proceeded. The spear is in the warrior's right hand, his shield is in his left; his helmet is more ornamented than usual.

In this apartment are two fragments of an inscription, which was probably attached to every mile-castle. The inscription, when entire, has stood thus:—

J STOREY DE.

IMP CAES TRAIAN
HADRIANI AVG
LEG II AVG
A PLATORIO NEPOTE LEG PR PR

"[In honour of] the Emperor Cæsar Trajanus Hadrianus Augustus. The second legion [styled] the august [erected this, by command of] Aulus Platorius Nepos, legate and proprætor."

One of the fragments referred to was got from the mile-castle to the west of Housesteads, the other from that at Cawfields. Reference will afterwards be made to these stones when we discuss the question, "Who built the Wall?"

Three small altars have on them the peculiar inscription, DIBVS VETERIBVS—to the ancient gods. One is shown in the

woodcut. These precious stone fragments afford negative evidence of a change of faith in the occupants of the mural region. While many yielded to the truth, as heralded by the servants of Christ, others stuck up for the old gods (as they supposed them to be)—Jupiter, Mars, Apollo, and others.

Before leaving the stones in the Antiquity House, we

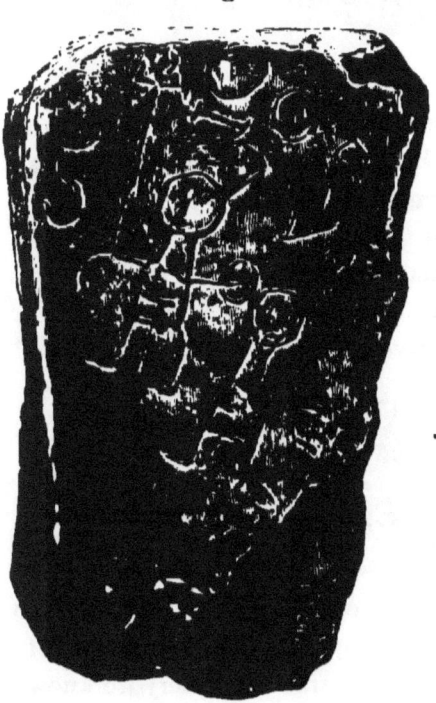

may notice the juvenile efforts of some aspiring artist. On one stone is carved a soldier, bearing in his left hand a small circular shield, and in his right a spear; with other figures. The next (over leaf) represents a sporting scene. A man is thrusting at a stag whose head is turned towards him; in the background is a wild boar. Human nature is the same in every age. Boys will be boys, whether their native tongue be that of Homer, or Virgil, or Milton.

In the mansion at Chesters are preserved a great variety of antiquities, derived from the stations and portions of the Wall, which are the property of Mr. Clayton.   As only those persons who are specially introduced can expect to have access

to them, a slight notice of them here will suffice.   Here may be seen a graceful figure of the Genius of the North Tyne, which was found between the two gates in the east rampart of the station here.   The woodcut represents it.

Many vases of Samian ware and earthen vessels of native manufacture, together with intaglios, gems, and rings of the precious metals derived from various parts of the Wall, are preserved in their various cases.

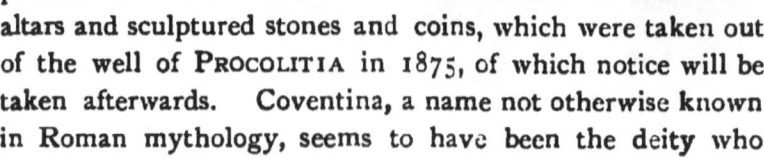

Here too are preserved the altars and sculptured stones and coins, which were taken out of the well of PROCOLITIA in 1875, of which notice will be taken afterwards.   Coventina, a name not otherwise known in Roman mythology, seems to have been the deity who

presided over this renowned fountain. The woodcut repre-
rents a slab dedicated to her honour. She floats upon the

leaf of a water lily,
holding a water-plant
in her right hand and
a flowing goblet in her
left. The inscription
is :—

DEAE

COVVENTINAE

T · D · COSCONIA

NVS · PR · COH

I · BAT · L · M

"To the goddess Cov-
entina Titus Domitius
Cosconianus, prefect
of the first cohort of
Batavians [dedicates
this] willingly to a
most deserving object."
Besides this, a carving
(p. 125) representing
three water nymphs (the attendants of the deity), ten altars
inscribed to her honour, and two elaborately constructed vases
are here preserved. These were probably kept in a little
chapel built over the mouth of the well, and were thrown
into it, together with the treasure chest of the station, and carefully covered over with stones, in an hour of extreme peril.

Leaving the mansion at Chesters, and proceeding towards
the plantation which lies to the west of the house, we meet with

a piece of the Wall, frequently covered with honeysuckle and
other plants, and presenting four courses of facing-stones in
position.   The fosse behind it is used as a duck-pond.   Beyond
this, the foundation of the Wall forms the slightly elevated
crown of a path leading through the plantation.   The fosse
is seen to the north of it.

Emerging from the grounds of Chesters, we are once more
upon the turnpike road, and climb the hill which leads to
Walwick.   The lines of the Vallum are seen in the field on

the left.   A fine ash-tree is growing on the north agger.
The foundations of the Wall are often seen in the road.
The woodcut here introduced was prepared under unusually
favourable circumstances; no new "metal" had for long been
placed on the road, and recent thunder-showers had removed
all dust.   The large house on the top of the hill was formerly
an inn.   In front of the cottage, a little further on, a mile-
castle formerly stood; no traces of it now remain.   Walwick

Hall is next passed. The view from Walwick is exceedingly fine, commanding, as it does, the vales of Tyne, Warden Hill, the hill behind Wall (both of which have been fortified by the Ancient Britons), and Hexham, with its Priory Church, beautiful even in the distance. After passing Walwick, the turnpike road leaves the Wall, and runs by the side of the Vallum; the fosse of the Wall is on our right and is in excellent condition.

Ascending the next hill, called Tower Taye, we come to a small tower, built a century and a half ago out of the stones of the Wall. Reaching the summit of the hill, all the lines of the Barrier come grandly into view. Proceeding onwards, we find, on our right, the remains of a mile-castle very distinctly marked. On the hill to the left of us are some ancient quarries which have doubtless been used by the Romans. To the south of the quarries is an earthen en-

trenchment, the gateways of which are furnished with traverses.
It was no doubt occupied by the Romans when the Wall was
in course of construction. The road now runs upon the north
agger of the Vallum, which has been spread out to form it.
A very fine piece of Wall, six feet high, is seen on our right,
running along the Black-carts farm.

In the course of clearing the southern face of the Wall, a
turret was laid bare in 1873 by Mr. Clayton, the proprietor
of the farm. Its area is eleven feet ten inches by eleven feet
four inches, inside measurement. Like the turret at Brunton,
it is let into the Wall; but the Wall for a short distance on
each side of it is made thicker than usual. The front wall
of the turret is nearly gone, only its base course remaining,
but the Wall at its back is fourteen courses high. In the
south front is a doorway three feet wide. The woodcut on the
previous page represents this interesting building.

Proceeding onwards, we come to a break in the Wall
through which a road runs to the North: this is called the
Hen Gap. The Wall beyond this has been recently cleared.
It will well repay examination. The etching opposite represents it. The facing stones are rather larger than usual.

The fosse of the Vallum is here exceedingly good. Before
reaching the summit of the Limestone Bank, the traveller
may with advantage enter the plantation on the left hand of
the road. He will here see the ditch of the Vallum in a
condition approaching perfection; and if the season of the
year be favourable, he will be delighted with the profusion
of wild flowers which diversify the rugged surface of the
plantation.

On the summit of this hill, Limestone Bank, several
things demand our attention. The view to the north is fine

THE WALL OF LIMESTONE BANK

embracing the valley of the North Tyne, with Chipchase Castle* on its north bank, and the Simonside and Cheviot Hills in the distance. A *castellum*, with which the stone dykes of the fields unfortunately interfere, is on the summit. Here we, for the first time, meet with a piece of the military way which accompanied the Wall throughout its entire length. It is seen coming up to the south gateway of the *castellum ;* and then, bending away from it, proceeds on its course westwards. The road has unfortunately been largely robbed by General Wade, or some of his subordinates, in order to supply material for forming the military road.

The fosse both of Wall and Vallum may next be examined; a grander sight Britain can hardly afford us. In each case it has been cut through the basalt which forms the summit of the hill, and the excavated masses lie upon the brink. How the Romans managed to dislodge such large blocks of this tough material without the aid of gunpowder is a marvel. Dr. Lingard, in his MS. *Tourification of the Wall*, says:—"It is a most astonishing sight." The fosse of the Wall is specially curious. On its northern margin lies a stone, now split into three pieces by the frosts of winter, which when laid upon its present bed must have been one block, weighing not less than thirteen tons. In the fosse itself will be seen a mass of stone which has not been dislodged from its bed; on its upper

---

*Chipchase Castle presents several features of architectural interest. At its western extremity is a square pele house, or castle, dating from the fourteenth century. Machicolations surround its summit. Some foolish proprietor of modern date has thought to make this fine old building beautiful, by inserting in it blank sash windows all properly glazed. At the other end is a handsome Jacobean building, erected by Cuthbert Heron in 1621. In the Library of the Castle is a black oak mantel piece, on which is carved with great skill a scene representing "The March of Time." The whole range of buildings has recently been put into good order by its present owner, Hugh Taylor, Esq.

surface may be noticed a number of holes intended for the insertion of wedges. For some reason the wedges were not inserted or not driven home, and the mass of rock remains unmoved to this day. It will be observed that the wedge holes are all inserted in the thin veins of quartz which intersect the basalt, and which, when the wedges were driven in, would aid the cleavage. Perhaps wooden wedges were used. in which case they would be expanded by having water poured upon them. The etching here inserted represents the western portion of the north fosse, looking eastwards.

South of the plantation, on the summit of the hill, and nearly opposite the *castellum*, is another temporary camp. Its entrenchments, its gateways, and traverses are all visible.

Proceeding onwards, we advance towards the farm-house of Carrawburgh. The farm-house on our right hand is called Teppermoor. Just after passing a small quarry on our left, we have on our right the remains of another mile-castle, and shortly afterwards encounter the station of PROCOLITIA. Immediately before coming to the camp, however, we notice a pump. The history of it is this. A few summers ago a severe drought prevailed, and the farmer had to drive his cattle twice a day a considerable distance to water. He felt sure that this ought not to be the case. He knew that the Romans never planted a station where a good supply of water could not always be obtained. He carefully examined the surface in the vicinity of the station, and fancying that in this spot the grass seemed fresher than in other places he broke the surface. His antiquarian knowledge was rewarded by finding here a well cased with Roman masonry, and containing plenty of water. He afterwards put a pump into it to be used when occasion required.

Carrawburgh.

The site of this station is all desolation, but the aspect of its herbage, especially in winter, indicates the usual richness of a Roman camp. It is about three miles and a half from CILURNUM, and it contains an area of about three acres and a half. It was garrisoned by the first cohort of Batavians. This fact is brought out in the mutilated stone, shown in the woodcut, which was found here; in one of the lines COH . I . BATAVORVM is quite distinct. The date of this inscription is A.D. 237, when Maximinus was emperor, and Perpetuus and Cornelianus were consuls. The Batavians, and their neighbours in the next station the Tungrians, seem to have come to Britain in the time of Vespasian, for Tacitus tells us that Agricola commenced the battle of the Grampians by ordering three Batavian and two Tungrian cohorts to charge the enemy sword in hand. The ramparts of this station are distinct, and, if freed from rubbish, would be found to stand several feet high. The position of the east, south, and west gateways are clearly discernible. The southern guard chamber of the west gateway has recently been laid bare. A barrack-room attached to the western rampart of the station may be seen a little to the south of this gateway. When the room was excavated a centurial stone was found built into the upper course of its front wall. It bears the inscription —Ɔ THRVPO ‖ NIANA ‖ P XXIIII.—"The Thruponian century [built] twenty-four feet." However desirable it might be to leave the stone on the spot where Roman artificers had placed it seventeen centuries ago, the cupidity of curiosity-mongers (not antiquaries) was feared, and the inscription has been removed to Chesters.   The great Wall has coalesced with the north rampart of the station.   Outside the western wall are distinct marks of suburban buildings.

A natural valley, in which a strong stream of water formally flowed, gave strength to the fortification on this side. In Horsley's day a well was noticed here, cased with masonry. "The people," he says, "called it a cold bath, and rightly judged it to be Roman."

In recent years however a change has come over the scene.   In consequence of the workings of a lead mine in the valley below the station the waters which supplied the well, the overflowings of which constituted the stream that bounded the station on its western side, were cut off.   The surface of the well became grass-grown, and it was lost to sight, and almost to memory, when some lead miners thinking to strike upon a vein of ore began their operations here.   Coming in contact with the upper courses of the stone framework of the well, they rightly thought that further search in that spot was vain, and went elsewhere.   Mr. Clayton, hearing that the well described by Horsley and others had been hit upon, thought it desirable that it should at once be properly explored, and gave directions accordingly.   Covering the mouth of the well were some large stones, which had probably been taken from the upper courses of its containing walls and thrown, for the purpose of concealment, upon the mass of treasure of which the well had been made the recipient.   On the removal of these stones, and some of them were so large as to require to be broken before this could be done, a mass of coins, chiefly of the lower empire, met the gaze of the excavators.   Then carved stones, altars, coins, vases, Roman pearls, old shoes, fibulæ, and other Roman remains were met with in an indis-

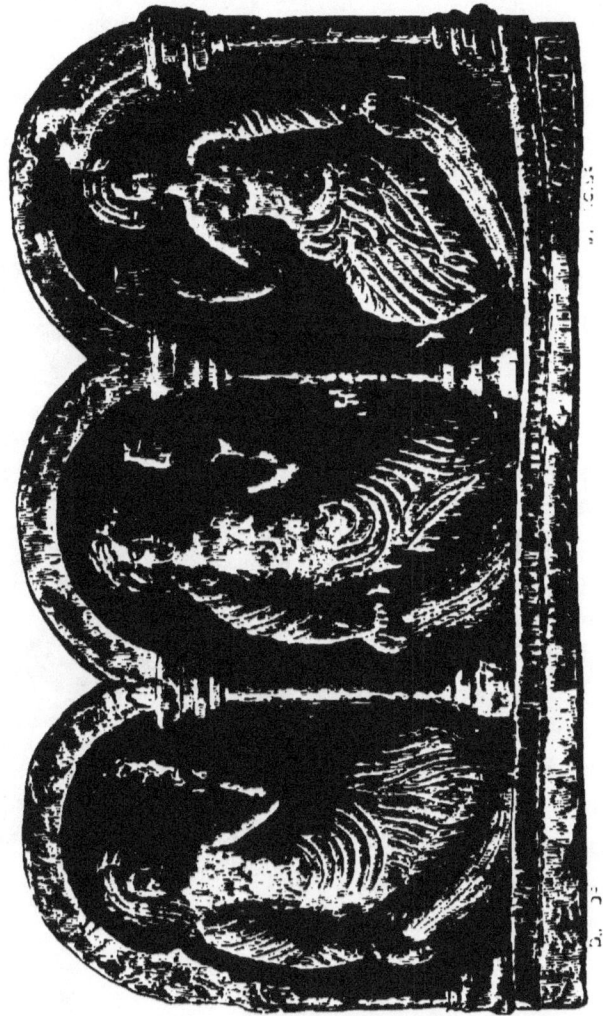

criminate mass. There can be little doubt that in a moment of panic the treasure chest of the station and the contents of the chapel which had been built over the well, some slight remains of the foundations of which may yet be noticed, had been thrown into the gulf for security. The writer happened to accompany Mr. Clayton to the spot the day after the work of excavation had commenced. Before they reached the place they were informed that "three beautiful ladies" had been discovered. On coming to the well they found lying upon its edge the sculptured stone figured on the previous page, which represents three water nymphs—the ladies in waiting probably of the goddess of the fountain. The fountain, which was probably a health resort, was presided over by a deity hitherto unknown in either Greek, Roman, or Celtic mythology —the goddess Coventina, to whom the traveller has been already introduced. As he may like to know the character of the altars dedicated to her worship, a woodcut of one of them is here given. A carving representing the goddess has already appeared, p. 117.

DIE COVE	"To the goddess
NTINE A	Coventina ;
VRELIVS	Aurelius
GROTVS	Grotus
GERMAN	a German."

An extraordinary number of coins were found in the well.

amounting to upwards of sixteen thousand, four of them being gold, the rest silver and bronze, ranging from the time of Marc Antony to that of Gratian. One singular circumstance may here be noticed. Amongst the coins were a very large number of the second-brass coin of Antoninus Pius, the reverse of which is shown in the woodcut. The writer counted 318 of them ; there were doubtless many more. This coin was struck in the fourth consulship of the Emperor, A.D. 145, to commemorate the exploits of Lollius Urbicus in Britain (see

 page 7), a period in which the country was reduced to its lowest state of depression. Britain, personified as a disconsolate female, sits upon a rock. She has no helmet upon her head, no sword or spear in her hand. Her head droops, her banner is lowered, her shield is idly cast away. The legend is BRITANNIA. To circulate this coin in Britain was to add insult to injury.

The well may be seen just inside the field dyke on the west of the station. It is usually half full or more of water, owing to the surface drainage.

Before bidding a final adieu to this well the reader may be interested in Wallis' account of it. (*Northumberland*, Vol. I., p. 23.) "Many springs and rivers were consecrated by the Romans for their religious rites, for their lustrations at funerals and sacrifices, and before they entered their *Sacraria* or temples. Of this kind was their *Fons Blandusiæ*, and their *Flumen Clitumni*. And of this kind, probably, is their well here at their station of Carrawbrough, called the Roman well. It is between two sloping fields, on the west side of the station, just under it, to the south of their famous Wall, about 400 or 500 yards from the twenty-fifth mile-stone on the military road; square and faced with freestone, hewn-work; and has either had a dome over it, or been walled round; the stones now lying about it, nearly covered with water from the conduit's being stopt, and demolished by the carelessness or ignorance of a plowman, as I am informed; it is full up to the brim and overflowing in the hottest summer; and by that man's indiscretion, he that would satisfy his curiosity to see it must risque the wetting his feet, especially in winter or in a rainy season."

Pressing onwards, we come to the farm house of Carraw, formerly a rural retreat of the Priors of Hexham. We soon pass the site of another *castellum*. To the south of the Wall in this vicinity is an earthen camp, shown upon the Map, which commands an extensive prospect; it is called Brown Dykes. On the top of the next hill the works approach very close to each other; the Vallum proceeds onwards in a straight line, but the Wall swerves towards it for the double purpose (apparently) of avoiding a bog on the north, and securing the crown of the hill. The mounds of the Vallum and the fosse of the Wall are here very grand.

Another mile-castle is passed on our right hand. The visitor will do well to examine it. It was partially excavated last autumn. Its northern wall and gateway are grandly developed; the fosse too is remarkably bold. The southern portion of it, that within the stone dyke which here divides two estates (the northern belonging to Mr. Clayton, the other to the Duke of Northumberland), has been miserably robbed.

Proceeding onwards, we have the cottage of Shield-on-the-Wall on our left. The sheet of water below is an artificial accumulation, for the purpose of supplying the

Settlingstones lead mines. The bold basaltic ridge along which the Wall runs in the central part of its course now comes strongly into view. Four great mountain waves are before us—the escarpments of the strata—which seem to chase each other to the north. We now, to adopt the language of Hutton, "quit the beautiful scenes of culti- vation, and enter upon the rude of nature and the wreck of antiquity."

After passing the twenty-seventh mile-stone, the modern military road takes to the south of both Wall and Vallum. The Wall and Vallum also part company, the Wall taking to the heights, and adhering most tenaciously to every projecting headland; the Vallum, on the other hand, running along the "tail" of the hill. Their respective distance is continually varying. Taking the Wall as our companion, we will soon reach Sewingshields.

On the ascent to Sewingshields farm house the Wall has been rooted up within a recent period to furnish building stones for the enlargement of the house, and the construction of fences. When Dr. Lingard passed this way, in 1807, he found the Wall five feet high. The fosse as it begins to ascend the hill is good, but, on reaching a mile-castle, which we soon do, it altogether dies away, the height of the cliff rendering it unnecessary. The mile-castle is replaced by a modern wall and the interior planted with trees. On the moor, opposite to it (south of the modern road), may be seen another of those temporary camps, of which we have already had some examples. It may be well for the traveller who keeps by the road to examine it, and notice the traverses in front of its gates.

North of the Wall two works of interest were until

recently to be traced. One of them (opposite the mile-castle) had all the appearance of an ancient British camp; within its area were some of those rounded enclosures which are indicative of the dwellings of our rude ancestors. To the west of this encampment, and in a direction nearly north-east from the farm house, is the site of Sewingshields Castle, referred to by Sir Walter Scott, in the sixth canto of "Harold the Dauntless," under the denomination of the Castle of the Seven Shields. Too truly he says :—

> . . . . "No towers are seen
> On the wild heath, but those that Fancy builds,
> And, save a fosse that tracks the moor with green,
> Is nought remains to tell of what may there have been."

When Dr. Lingard was here, its walls were five feet high. A former farm tenant, Mr. Errington, removed the vaults of the castle, and its whole area is now subjected to the plough.

But though the walls of the castle have been uprooted, the following tradition relating to it will not readily perish :—

"Immemorial tradition has asserted that King Arthur, his queen Guenever, his court of lords and ladies, and his hounds, were enchanted in some cave of the crags, or in a hall below the Castle of Sewingshields, and would continue entranced there till some one should first blow a bugle-horn that lay on a table near the entrance of the hall, and then with 'the sword of the stone' cut a garter also placed there beside it. But none had ever heard where the entrance to this enchanted hall was, till the farmer at Sewingshields, about fifty years since, was sitting knitting on the ruins of the castle, and his clew fell, and ran downwards through a rush of briars and nettles, as he supposed, into a deep subterranean passage. Full in the faith that the entrance into King Arthur's hall was now discovered, he cleared the briary portal of its weeds and rubbish, and entering a vaulted passage, followed, in his darkling way, the thread of his clew. The floor was infested with toads and lizards ; and the dark wings of bats, disturbed by his unhallowed intrusion, flitted fearfully around him. At length his sinking courage was strengthened by a dim, distant light, which, as he advanced, grew gradually brighter, till, all at once, he entered a vast and vaulted hall, in the centre of which, a fire without fuel, from a broad crevice in the floor, blazed with a high and lambent flame, that showed all the carved walls and fretted roof, and the monarch and his queen and court, reposing around in a theatre of thrones and costly couches. On the floor, beyond the fire, lay the faithful and deep-toned pack of thirty couple of hounds; and on a table before it, the spell-dissolving horn, sword, and garter. The shepherd reverently, but firmly, grasped the sword, and as he drew it leisurely from its rusty scabbard, the eyes of the monarch and his courtiers began to open, and they rose till they sat upright. He cut the garter; and as the sword was being slowly sheathed, the spell assumed its ancient power, and they all gradually sunk to rest; but not before the monarch had lifted up his eyes and hands, and exclaimed :

> O woe betide that evil day
> On which this witless wight was born,
> Who drew the sword—the garter cut,
> But never blew the bugle-horn.

Terror brought on loss of memory, and the shepherd was unable to give any correct account of his adventure, or to find again the entrance to the en-chanted hall."—*Hodgson's Northumberland*, II., iii., 287.

One other local tradition of this renowned king the traveller may be pleased to hear, as he may personally verify it. To the north, and a little to the west, of Sewingshields, two strata of sandstone crop out to the day; the highest points of each ledge are called the King's and Queen's Crag, from the following legend :—

"King Arthur, seated on the farthest rock, was talking with his queen, who, meanwhile, was engaged in arranging her 'back hair.' Some expres-sion of the queen's having offended his majesty, he seized a rock which lay near him, and, with an exertion of strength for which the Picts were proverbial, threw it at her, a distance of about a quarter of a mile! The queen, with great dexterity, caught it upon her comb, and thus warded off the blow; the stone fell about midway between them, where it lies to this very day, with the marks of the comb upon it, to attest the truth of the story. The stone probably weighs about twenty tons!"

The farm house of Sewingshields is entirely built out of the stones of the Wall. Its occupant, Mr. Thompson, will doubtless kindly satisfy the inquiries of the peripatetic antiquary, and may possibly gratify him with a tune on the Northumberland bagpipes, on which instrument he is a skilful  performer. A centurial stone, shown in the woodcut, is built up in one of the farm buildings here. It may probably be read —The century of Gellius Philippus [erected this part of the Wall.]

From Sewingshields to Carvoran the Roman military way, which accompanied the Wall throughout its entire length, is, with but few intermissions, to be seen. It is always to the south of the Wall, but does not keep parallel with it ; it selects the easiest gradients. When we view the mural ridge from the tail of the hill we can generally detect the course of the road by the peculiar tint of its herbage.

We now pursue our course westwards. For a little distance we go through a young plantation. The basaltic columns soon attract attention. There used to be one that was dignified with the name of King Arthur's Chair, but it was purposely dislodged by a mischief-loving countryman. Every thunder-storm throws down some. We soon come to Cat's Gate, a narrow chasm in the rocks, by which, according to tradition, the Scots crept under the Wall; it has an artificial appearance. A mile-castle is next reached. It has been much robbed lately for the repairs of the farm house. The walk along these basaltic heights is most exhilarating when the day is bright. Broomlee Lake, to the north of the

Wall, now comes boldly into view. According to tradition, a box of treasure lies sunk in it.—*(Richardson's Table Book. Legendary Division*, Vol. III., p. 100.) The small sheet of water to the south of the turnpike road is Grindon Lough. It has recently been to a considerable extent drained, damaging the landscape, but the ground gained is valueless, in consequence of its consisting merely of gravel.

Busy Gap, one of the widest of the gaps or breaks in the basaltic chain over which the Wall runs, is the next point to be reached. Before descending into it, it will be well, from the elevated position where we now are, to pay some attention to the Black Dike, an ancient cutting belonging to these parts. It consists simply of a ditch with the earth taken out of it thrown on the east side. In the old maps of Northumberland it is represented as extending from the north-west extremity of Northumberland to the Tyne at Water House, near Bardon Mill; it reappears at Morley, and is said to go by Allenheads, into the county of Durham. We see from the height on which we stand a plantation on the other side of the valley, to the south of us, called the "Black Dike Planting." The fosse, even at this distance, may be discerned on the west side of it. The point where the Dike crossed the Wall has long been a matter of speculation. It probably crossed at the opening, west of Busy Gap, and then, as the Wall here is running in a northerly direction, it took the course which the Wall now does as far as the foot of the Sewingshields Crags; it then made off to the northern wastes, passing the Queen's and King's Crag. The Wall has destroyed all trace of it where the course of the two structures coincided, but there are some remains of it north of Sewingshields Crag. The stone dike which forms the western boundary of the Sewingshields property probably represents its course. (*MacLauchlan's Memoir*, pp. 37*n*, 42.)

We now descend into Busy Gap, which is shown in the woodcut. It is supposed to have got its name from the fact of its being the pass most frequented by the freebooters of the Middle Ages. In consequence of its width, the Roman engineers have defended it with peculiar care. In addition to the fosse on the north of the Wall, which here reappears, a triangular rampart beyond it embraces the valley, and still further strengthens the fortification. On the western acclivity of the gap is a wicket gate through which a "drove road" passes to the north.

This part of the country long retained the disorganization produced by the incessant wars between England and Scotland. A "Busy Gap rogue," was a well-known name of reproach. When Camden and Cotton visited the Wall in 1599, they durst not venture into these parts. "From thence,"

[Carvoran] Camden says, "the Wall goeth forward more aslope by Iverton, Forsten, and Chester-in-the-Wall [House-steads], near to Busy Gap,—a place infamous for thieving and robbing; where stood some castles (chesters they called them), as I heard, but I could not with safety take the full survey of it, for the rank robbers thereabouts."

Matters are vastly different now; a more orderly, upright, and intelligent community than that of North Tyne and Redewater does not exist.

Resuming our march, the site of a mile-castle is soon reached; it stands on ground which slopes at the rate of one in five. We next encounter two narrow, but rather steep gaps, in rapid succession, which do not seem to have obtained names. Advancing a little further, we come to the valley permeated by the Knag Burn, which forms the eastern defence of the famous station of BORCOVICUS.

The Vallum in some parts of the course we have just

traversed is in excellent preservation.   The sketch on the previous page was taken in this vicinity by the late Mr. Fairholt.

Thus far we have kept company with the Wall.   In order to notice some objects that lie near the road, we will for the moment return to the point where it and the Wall parted company.   Proceeding on our way we have on our right the School House in which the intellect of the neighbourhood is cultivated.   A little further forward on our left hand, at the bottom of a rising knoll, may be observed traces of some "drifts," from which the Romans have probably taken the coal which they undoubtedly used in the neighbouring station of BORCOVICUS.   As we proceed, we will next notice an outcrop of limestone rock, which has been largely quarried by the Romans.

The farm house of Moss Kennel on the south of the military road is now reached, and after it, also on our left hand, a house called Beggar Bog; opposite to it is a small chapel in which divine service is occasionally held.   In advance of us, to the south of the road, and immediately opposite BORCOVICUS, may be noticed a barrow, the grave, doubtless, of some chieftain of the ancient British period. There is another in the valley to the south of it.

We now resume our position on the heights to the east of the Knag Burn.   It will be well for the traveller to notice, before descending into the valley, the platform on which the station stands.   It is strong on its northern, southern, and eastern sides, and yet is not unduly exposed.   The Wall which crosses the valley runs up to the station and joins it at its north-east angle.   It has been brought into its present state by placing the fallen stones on the courses which remained in position.

A Roman villa of considerable size and pretensions once

stood on a shelf of the rock, on the east side of the Knag Burn, opposite the middle of the station. It was warmed by hypocausts; and soot was found in the flues. Though removed many years ago, to supply stones for the neighbouring fences, an occasional fragment of tile or tufa marks the spot where it stood. Nearer the Wall is a powerful spring carefully cased with Roman masonry. It was discovered in the summer of 1844. It is fenced with iron railings to keep the cattle from it.

In the bottom of the valley is a passage through the Wall, which was discovered in 1856; it is thus described by Mr. Clayton:* "In the valley of Knag Burn, 371 feet east of the station of BORCOVICUS, has recently been discovered and explored an unexpected passage through the Roman Wall. It has been closed by double gates, similar to those of the stations; and there is a guard-room on each side. The middle of the gateway guarding the south of the passage is eleven feet three inches. The width of the gateway guarding the north of the passage is ten feet six inches. In the middle there is an upright stone, such as we find in the gateways of the stations, and in the streets of Pompeii. The pathways are on each side of this stone, and the thresholds have been much worn by the feet of the passenger. The two guard-chambers are of nearly equal dimensions . . . . During these excavations have been found coins of Claudius Gothicus and Constantius, a broken altar, and the usual relics of Roman occupation, fragments of Samian ware and Andernach mill-stones."† The object of this gateway has been to give access

* "Proceedings" of the Society of Antiquaries of Newcastle for 1856, p. 186

† Mill-stones from the quarries of Andernach on the Rhine are frequently met with in all the stations. The stone is a hard volcanic tufa, and being porous, acts vigorously on the grain.

to a place of entertainment—an amphitheatre on a small scale—which is on the north side of the Wall. The woodcut represents it. It is 100 feet across and about ten feet deep. It has no doubt been furnished with wooden seats. The path leading from the gateway to the entrance into the amphitheatre may be traced. Nettles may usually be seen growing in the bottom of it—a sure proof of human presence. Has the arena been soaked with human blood? Amphitheatres, similar

in construction to this, though larger, have been found at Silchester, Dorchester, Banbury, Cirencester, and other places. Even when on a campaign in an enemy's country, amphitheatres were erected for the amusement of the soldiery. Two appear in the delineations given on Trajan's column at Rome of the Dacian campaigns. Time must often have hung heavily upon the hands of the Tungrian cohort at BORCOVICUS; what more natural than that they should catch a couple of natives, and set them to slaughter each other for their pleasure? As the pilgrim sits here, and ruminates upon the past and the present of the history of Rome and Britain, he may find food for thought in the following statement of Dion Cassius:—"Plautius, for having ably managed and concluded the Britannic War, was highly commended by Claudius, and obtained a triumph. And in the gladiatorial combat many freed men, as well as the British captives, fought, numbers of whom he destroyed in this kind of spectacle, and gloried in it."

Housesteads.

The Knag Burn passes under the Wall in the way that, probably, it used to do in Roman times.* Between the burn and the station are traces of suburban dwellings; and the old Roman road may be seen winding up to the eastern gateway. The manner in which the Wall unites with the north-east angle of the station should be observed. Both its eastern and western angles are rounded in the same manner as the angles of the south rampart. It is evident that the station was rendered complete in itself before the contiguous portions of Wall were commenced. When the builders were safe within strong stone walls they then reared the great Barrier to the right and left of them. The Wall, at its junction, has eight courses of stones in position.

The eastern wall of the station has been cleared of the rubbish which long encumbered it, and is in a good state of preservation. Its masonry differs but little, if at all, from that of the great Wall. It is five feet thick.

We now enter this city of the dead. All is silent; but dead indeed to all human sympathies must the soul of that

* An arch would have admitted of the passage of an enemy.

man be who, in each broken column, each turf-covered
mound, each deserted hall, does not recognise a voice telling
him, trumpet-tongued, of the rise and fall of empires—of the
doom and ultimate destiny of man!

Housesteads is nearly five miles from the last station,
Carrawburgh, and it contains an area of nearly five acres. Its
form is the usual one of a parallelogram, rounded at the
corners, but its greatest length is from east to west. It is
planted on a shelf of basalt, the rock in many places protruding through the superincumbent soil. It slopes gently
to the south.

If the traveller be not familiar with the usual arrangements of a Roman camp, he had better, before beginning a
particular survey, advance to the centre of the station, and
make himself acquainted with its plan. One main street,
called the *via principalis*, crosses the station from the eastern
gate to the western; and another of similar width runs at
right angles to it from the northern to the southern gate.
The gate nearest the enemy (in this instance the north) was
called the prætorian gate, the one in the opposite rampart
the decuman. The street leading from the prætorian gate
bore its name. In the case before us, this street is to the east
of the central line. Not far from the point where these two
main streets intersect each other, the visitor will find the
solid base of a column, which, if the city had been a mediæval
one, would be pronounced to be the pedestal of the market-
cross. All the other streets of the station are exceedingly
narrow, and lie parallel with the main ones. In this way the
whole interior of the camp is divided into parallelograms of
greater or less size.

Having taken this general survey, we will now return to

the east gate. Like all the other gates of the stations, it has been a double one, each portal having folding doors. One of its portals has, at some period before the abandonment of the station by the Romans, been built up. All the other gates have been contracted in a similar manner. This was probably done towards the close of the period of the Roman occupation of Britain. There are guard-chambers on each side of the gate. On the closing up of the southern section of the gateway, the guard-chamber belonging to it was converted into a dwelling room. When this chamber was excavated in 1833, nearly a cart-load of coals was found in it. The holes in which the pivots of the doors moved will be noticed. The stone against which the gates struck when they were closed remains. We might suppose that this stone would be an obstruction to carriages entering the city. No doubt, however, the kind of chariot used was the *biga*—requiring two horses; in that case, the horses would pass on each side of the stone. The horses, too, would probably be small. In the middle of some of the narrow streets of Pompeii, boldly projecting stepping stones occur, which have been placed there for the convenience of foot passengers. These do not seem to have interfered with the transit of wheeled vehicles, as the ruts in the streets show. Here, too, as well as at Pompeii, the Roman chariots have left their marks behind them. A rut about eight inches deep appears in the stone threshold of the gateway, on each side of the central stone, evidently caused by the action of wheels. The grooves which are shown in the accompanying cut on the following page are a little more than four feet six inches and a half apart.* The

* The groove on the right hand is less perfect now than when this wood-ut was prepared, part of the stone having been broken off.

wheel marks in Pompeii are at exactly this distance from one another, and this is the gauge of our English railways.

On entering the station, we will keep close to the east wall, and proceed northwards. On the inside of the walls of the station, barracks for the soldiers have no doubt been built, having roofs leaning against the station walls. As, however, these were less carefully constructed than the outside walls, and as they were not "tied" into the main structure, they have, in many instances, disappeared. In this

and other stations we have abundant traces of them. Going forward, we see a solid platform of masonry about twenty feet square. Has a catapult been planted here for throwing large stones against the enemy? Lying on the spot was found a conical-shaped stone, such as may have been used for such a purpose. Lying near the north wall of the station, which has been increased to nearly twice its original thickness, as if to form a solid bed for a catapult or ballista, several of these conical-shaped stones were found. Stones of similar form have been found in other stations. Their occurrence cannot have been accidental. The rudely-formed chamber on the top of this platform is no doubt of late construction. In passing the north-east corner, its nicely-rounded form will be noticed. Going forward a little, by the side of the north wall, a mass of ruins is seen, which, when first excavated, bore marks of fire.

We now pass through the field-gate to examine the outside of the north rampart wall and the north gateway. It presents one of the finest pieces of masonry on the line of the Wall. The large square blocks forming its base have been skilfully and securely laid. Their joints are as close as ever. An inclined roadway led up to this gate, but it was removed at the time of the discovery of the gateway, in order to display its masonry. This gateway, like all the rest at Housesteads, is double. The pillars which, on its outer and inner margin divided it, are both standing. The innermost one has a considerable elevation. The east portal of this gateway has been walled up at a comparatively early period. This may be inferred from the fact that, whereas the angles of the stones forming the basement of the western portal have been much worn by the tread of feet, those of the eastern portal are not injured. The western portal, too, bears marks of change. Its present threshold is about three feet higher than its original one. The station having been devastated by a temporarily triumphant foe, has been re-occupied by the Roman troops, without giving themselves time to remove the ruins of their former habitations. Clambering into the portal, its interior arrangements may be viewed. One of the pivot-holes of the gate still retains traces of the oxide of iron—the pivot having been shod with iron. The guard-chambers on both sides are in good condition.

In the formation of that on the west side a portion of an altar that had been dedicated to Jupiter has been used; the letters I. O. M.—*Jovi optimo maximo*—may still be seen upon it.*
Before leaving this gate, let the antiquary once more look at its wide portals and massive masonry, and ask himself if appearances warrant the supposition that the Wall was built when the Roman Empire was in the throes of dissolution, and when the natives of the island were, as Gildas describes them, "a useless and panic-struck company, equally slow to fight, and ill adapted to run away." Putting out of consideration the strength of the masonry, do these bold apertures indicate any dread of a northern foe? A few yards to the east of us, as we have seen, is the opening at the Knag Burn, and at the next mile-castle, not a quarter of a mile to the west of us, we shall meet with another. Surely the Wall must have been built long before the days of Arcadius, and it can never have been intended as a mere fence to ward off the aggression of the Picts and Scots.

On the inner side of the gateway to the right, a large stone trough is seen. The stones comprising it are not in their original position, as will at once be seen by a little examination. Some of them are grooved, in order to make a tight joint. The stones are much worn, as if by the sharpening of knives. This trough evidently belongs to a late period of the

---

* So the author wrote in his first edition. Not long afterwards the stone was found to be missing, having been stolen by some modern heathen. In the place where Roman hands had placed it it yielded decided evidence of the prevalence of a new faith at the time that the existing guard-chamber was built. The chief idol of the Roman pantheon had been found out to be nothing. In due time the conscience of the thief seems to have been smitten, for the stone was eventually, by unknown hands, conveyed to Chesters, though in an injured condition. The person who took it had evidently broken it down to render it of portable size, and in doing so had cracked it across its face.

occupation of the station. It is difficult to conjecture its purpose. Has it been used in the preparation of the winter's store of provisions for the garrison? One of the labourers* employed in the excavations here displayed the usual prejudices of a Northumbrian borderer, by giving it as his opinion "that the Romans used it for washing their Scotch prisoners in." Near to this was a circular hearth, formed of three courses of Roman tiles. When discovered it was covered with coal ashes and the scoriæ of iron. It was probably a smithy. The action of the weather and the tread of oxen have nearly destroyed it. The north wall, to the west of this, may next be examined. A second wall, of inferior masonry, has been built inside the first, and the space between them filled up with clay. This gives the wall a considerably increased thickness. It was in this vicinity that some of the stones which may have been intended for the service of the ballista were lying. Proceeding along the wall to the north-west corner of the station, we meet with another chamber, the door of which has been built up.

Let the student now return to the vicinity of the north gate, and examine the buildings to the south of it. Not far from the gate, and on the west side of the street extending from the prætorian to the decuman gate, is a large apartment, seventy-eight feet long and eighteen feet wide. On the south of this is another not quite so long. Its floor is probably supported upon pillars. At the west end of it is a kiln for drying corn, which probably belongs to the moss-trooping times. The steps by which the apartment is reached at the other end are evidently of a late date, and may also be referred to the "troublesome times." This building is strengthened

* Anthony Place who did much good service in displaying the Wall. At a good old age he bade farewell to all sublunary things.

K

by buttresses. Crossing the prætorian street, we find a very large building, extending nearly to the east rampart, and bounded at its lower margin by the *via principalis*. It is 147 feet long and thirty feet wide. It is strengthened by numerous buttresses. The masonry of it is different from that of the other buildings that we have seen. Its stones are longer, and they have the feathered tooling that we noticed in the facing-stones of the abutment of the bridge over the North Tyne. We can scarcely resist the opinion that it belongs to a different period from the other buildings. It may have been one of Severus's restorations. At its eastern extremity are several small rooms: one of them has been heated by underground flues; in another is a cistern or bath, four feet long and three broad, which, when discovered, was coated with cement. Some of these large buildings were no doubt the halls in which the public business of the district was transacted, and others were used as the residences of the prefect and his chief officers.

Proceeding once more to the intersection of the main streets, we make our way to the southern gate. We soon come to a considerable mass of building on our right hand. Part of it was excavated in 1858, an enormous mass of debris having been removed. It is not easy to assign a use to each apartment. One of them, when first opened, strongly resembled (though on a small scale) an Italian kitchen; there were marks of fire on its raised hearth. In this part of the camp the ordinary soldiers would dwell. No remains sufficiently perfect exist to give us a complete idea of a Roman house in these military cities. Judging from the remains which do exist, they seem to have been of a dark and gloomy character. Excepting in the newly excavated buildings at Chesters (p.

100), no windows have been found; but in most of the stations window glass is met with in the debris. Probably a framework of timber usually intervened between the upper part of the walls of a house and the roof, and here windows were inserted, as well as apertures for the admission of air. Rome, prior to the great fire in Nero's reign, seems to have been built in this manner. The upper stories of the houses of Pompeii were of wood; these for the most part have perished, but the stairs leading up to them in many cases remain, thus proving their original existence.

We now reach the south gateway, which was partially excavated by the Rev. John Hodgson. It forms an interesting study. Here all the main features characterizing the other gateways will be recognized. It is of the same massive character; it has a guard-chamber on each side, and the pivot-holes in which the gates rotated are seen. When excavated, the eastern portion of the gateway was found to have been walled up. This must have been done before the houses in front of it were built, the foundations of which are now to be seen. The entrance into the guard-chamber has been closed, and amongst the materials used in doing this the fragment of a circular shaft will be noticed. But this is not the only instance which we have here of the adaptation of former materials to present purposes. Centuries after the abandonment of the station by the Romans, some mosstrooper seems to have chosen this spot for his habitation. He had little difficulty in converting the guard-chamber and contiguous buildings into chambers suited to his own purposes. The "byre" in which he folded his cattle at night, the kiln in which he dried his unripened grain, and the lower part of the flight of steps by which he ascended to the little

fortress that was his own habitation, may all, though perhaps
with difficulty, be distinguished.

Stone slabs with a circular headway
are often seen lying beside the gates
of the stations. They have probably
formed the top of the doorway leading
into the guard-chambers. In the span-
dril of a fragment of one, at the south
gateway here, is an ornament resembling
a Maltese cross, and in its centre there
has been a small St. Andrew's cross,
though it is now much obliterated.
The cross is not necessarily a Christian
symbol. It is met with in all its forms in heathen lands in
every age. In ancient Egyptian pictures it assumes the form
of the Greek letter *tau*. In several altars, addressed to false
gods, found on the line of the Wall, it occurs in the form called
Gammadion. We shall meet with one of these at Birdoswald.
Even in the form called the Constantinian monogram it is
in some mosaics associated with heathen deities It is supposed
to have been an emblem of vitality. The early Christians
regarded it with dislike. Eventually, though not until after
the lapse of two or three centuries, it was adopted as the
symbol of the Christian faith.

The south wall of the station is in a good state of preservation ; it stands ten or twelve courses high. The woodcut
on the next page represents the south-west angle of the
station ; it will be noticed that it has been repaired in Roman
times with stones of a different character from those used
in its original construction.

Proceeding along the west wall of the station, we have the opportunity of contemplating a noble piece of Roman masonry, eleven courses high. The west gate—the *porta*

principalis dextra—is in a state of greater perfection than any of the rest. The woodcut exhibits the plan of it. As usual it had been contracted to half its width; but, to expose an

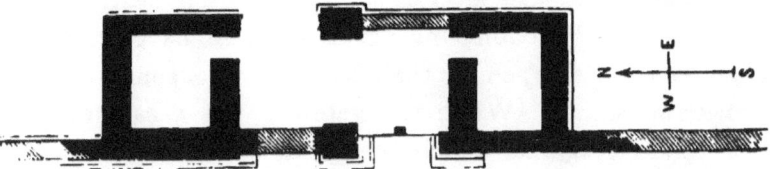

intruding foe to greater difficulty, the passage was rendered diagonal by closing up the northern portion of the outside gate and the southern portion of the inside gate. The inner

of these interpolated walls is nearly all removed ; the other
was standing when the gate was excavated and the woodcut
here given prepared, but it has since fallen—its masonry
having been of an inferior character. The woodcut shows
the gate as it appeared from the outside. As is uniformly the
case in all the gateways, the masonry is strong and massive,
the stones being larger and better dressed than those of the
other parts of the ramparts. The threshold has been worn by

the tread of feet. In several places there are indications that
the soldiers, whilst loitering about the gate, have employed
themselves in sharpening their knives or weapons upon the
projecting stones. When the gateway was excavated, the
central stone against which the gates struck, was found in
the position shown in the drawing. The guard-chambers
are in an encouraging state of preservation, as the woodcut
on the opposite page, which represents the gate as seen from
the inside of the camp, shows. When these chambers were

excavated, they were covered up to the top of the walls with earth, in which was a large quantity of bones and other animal matter. They have been warmed by flues going round the walls.

South of the gateway are some minor buildings closely connected with the rampart, which were excavated in 1858. The lowest chamber is of the ordinary size, and, when discovered, was paved with tiles. A walk by the side of the south rampart brings us once more to the south gateway.

In front of the station are several objects of interest. The farm house which stood near the south gateway has been removed, and a new one built in a more convenient situation. The well which supplied the house was supposed by tourists to be Roman. It is about fifteen feet deep, and is cased with Roman stones, excepting the last yard, which is sunk into the whin rock. The late Mrs. Routledge told the writer that she used to be a frequent visitor at Housesteads when her grandfather, Mr. William Magnay, resided there, and that *he* sunk the well in front of the house for his own convenience. Others have since confirmed this statement. The traveller, if he be from the south country, will by this time have found out that the pronunciation of the inhabitants of Northumberland is different from that of those born within the sound of Bow bell, and will be able to appreciate the following incident:—Two antiquaries arrived at Housesteads. The weather was unfavourable, and by the time they had completed a survey of the station they were drenched to the skin. Cold and weary, they called at the herd's house for information as to their sleeping quarters. Before leaving, they were asked in the Northumberland guttural if they would like a glass of *Roman* water. One of the shivering antiquaries, thinking that a little *Rum* and water in present circumstances might be highly beneficial, gratefully accepted the offer. What was his horror to see the hind take a bucket, and repair to the supposed Roman well! To the credit of the strangers, they both quaffed the cooling fluid with a good grace, and pronounced it excellent. (*Tour along the Roman Wall*, by James Wardell.)

The Tungrian cohort had, however, no lack of water. There is a spring to the north of the crags which they seem to have enclosed with masonry; the remains of a well, as has already been noticed, have been found near the spot where the Knag Burn passes under the Wall, and there is a very abundant runner of excellent water at the bottom of the slope in front of the station. The spring yielding this runner was not discovered until the summer of 1844, up to which time it had been concealed by loose stones and herbage. The spring may now be seen enclosed by four upright flag-stones, and these are surrounded by walls of masonry forming an oblong building, circular at its northern end but rectangular at the other. These arrangements date, doubtless, from the Roman era.

The whole of the bank in front of the station is covered with the foundations of streets and houses. To the west of these are long terraced lines, which have no doubt been devoted to cultivation, after a mode still practised in Italy and other continental countries. The plain below the station, extending towards the east, was drained some years ago. It seems to have been the burial-ground of the camp. In cutting the drains, numerous human remains were found. Two stones that have formed portions of circular columns of great magnitude are lying in this valley. They have probably rolled down from the station above.

A ridge, caused by the protuberance of the sandstone rock, rises gently out of the plain at our feet. It is called Chapel Hill. Some considerable temple is supposed to have stood upon it. Many altars have been found here. One of them is represented in the woodcut. It may be translated:—"To Jupiter, the best and greatest, and the deities of Augustus, the first cohort of Tungrians (a milliary one), commanded by Quintus Verius Superstis Præfect [erected this]." This altar is now in the Museum of the Society of Antiquaries of New-castle. Towards the close of the year 1883, two large altars, dedicated to Mars Thingsus, and two female deities named *Beda* and *Fimmilena*, together with an arch-shaped sculptured stone, were found at the bottom of Chapel Hill, on its northern side. The altars are larger than usual, and the inscriptions on them have excited the interest of the best antiquaries of Europe, but they are too elaborate for insertion

here. They are fully explained in the *Archæologia Æliana*, Vol. X., pp. 148–172. The altars have been removed to Chesters. See p. 106.

The spring, noticed on the previous page, is just to the north of the spot where these altars were found.

A little to the west of Chapel Hill is the site of a semi-subterranean cave, dedicated to the worship of Mithras, which was discovered in 1822. It is described with considerable minuteness by Mr. Hodgson, in the *Archæologia Æliana*, O.S., Vol. I., p. 263, &c. The worship of Mithras—the Sun or the Persian Apollo—was introduced from the East into Europe about the time of Julius Cæsar. The mysteries connected with it are supposed to have involved the sacrifice of human victims and

various other abominations. Edicts were issued for its suppression by Hadrian and others, but in vain. Amongst the
altars found in the cave here, was one bearing the names of
Gallus and Volusianus, who were consuls in the year 252.
There was also found the tablet, given on the opposite page,
which represents Mithras himself coming out of an egg and
surrounded by an oval belt, containing the signs of the Zodiac.
The site of the temple is now nearly obliterated. There can
be little doubt that when the mythology of Greece and Rome
had lost hold of the sympathies of the community, the worship
of Mithras was pressed upon the attention of mankind, in
opposition to the verities of Christianity.

It may be well also to mention that the worship of the
Deœ Matres—the good mothers—whose name it was not
lucky to mention, was much in vogue with the Romans of a
later age, especially with the Gothic portion of the Roman

community. Several statues of them have been found here; two of these, shown in the woodcuts on the previous page, are now preserved in the Museum of the Newcastle Society of Antiquaries. These figures usually occur in triplets. As already remarked, nothing on the line of the Wall that was capable of destruction has escaped the effects of Caledonian vengeance, and these sculptures show it.

Naturally enough, Victory was a favourite goddess with

the Romans. The statue shown was found in this station, and is now at Newcastle. With outstretched wings she careers over the round globe; her garments fly behind her. See a similar figure, p. 112.

Only one more allusion to the antiquities of this station can be indulged in. In a paper read by Mr. Clayton before the Society of Antiquaries of Newcastle in 1853 (*Archæologia Æliana*, Vol. IV., p. 274, O.S.,) the following facts appeared.

In clearing the ground in front of the south gateway of the station, a gold signet ring, a gold pendant for the ear, and

a coin of Commodus, apparently fresh from the mint, were found lying together, a little beneath the surface of the ground. They are all figured here, of the actual size, from the skilful pencil of the late Mr. Fairholt. The ear-drop is of the purest gold, and is of the same pattern as several other gold ornaments in the Museum at Lyons.

The stone of the ring is an artifical one, and has the figure of Mercury engraved upon it; the circular part is somewhat flattened by the pressure to which it has been exposed. The coin has on the reverse a figure of Providence, and is dated the third consul-ship of the Emperor, which corresponds with the year A.D. 181.

It was about this period that the terrible disasters, recorded by Dion Cassius, and which are referred to in the introductory chapter of this work (p. 7.) took place. The inference is not improbable, that these ornaments were worn by the Roman tribune and his lady, who were slain when making their escape from the south gate of the city at the time of the general devastation.

Mr. MacLauchlan has laid down a Roman road, extending from Housesteads, in a south-easterly direction, to the "Stanegate" or "Causeway" at Grindon Hill (*Memoir*, p. 40). The writer had no difficulty in tracing it as Mr. MacLauchlan has described it, from the vicinity of the Moss Kennel farm house to Grindon Shield.   Horsley was of opinion that

another branch road went in a south-westerly direction to join the "Stanegate" near Chesterholm.   The writer has sometimes thought that he saw traces of this road, particularly at a place south of the present turnpike road, opposite the thirtieth mile-stone.   After considerable examination, however, Mr. MacLauchlan could not satisfy himself as to its existence, and therefore does not insert it.

On leaving the station, the visitor will notice the junction of the Wall with the north-west angle of the station. Here, as we saw was the case on the eastern side, the station is independent of the Wall. Some repairs have been made in this corner, and longitudinal stones with the feathered "broaching" introduced. The woodcut opposite represents it. The remains of suburban buildings will be observed outside the west gate of the station.

We now proceed on our journey westward. Those to whom it is an object to avoid fatigue will best consult their ease by proceeding along the Roman military way, which will be easily found. All the field-gates are placed upon it. The gentle pilgrim does not need to be reminded how needful it is in a pastoral country to close the gates after him. This military way was in use as a public road not very long ago. The family of Wright were hereditary carriers between Newcastle and Carlisle for more than 100 years, and so continued till driven off the road by the railway. The representative of the family at the time the first edition of this book was prepared, was tenant of the Housesteads farm. He stated that the tradition in the family was, that the traffic from east to west was originally conducted on pack-horses, and that the carriers, in the central part of their journey between Newcastle and Carlisle, were accustomed to resort to the Roman way. In certain parts of their journey they had to camp out all night, and one of their camping places was opposite "Twice-brewed Ale," a carriers' inn contemporaneous with the turnpike road, which is now abandoned as a place of public entertainment.

The walk along the cliffs is exceedingly beautiful, and the Wall for the most part is in excellent condition all the way to Hot Bank. The traveller will notice, too, that it differs in width in different places, as is shown by the offsets and insets which occasionally occur. No doubt different gangs of workmen wrought simultaneously on different parts of the line, and the superintendent of each was allowed to exercise, within certain limits, his own judgment as to the width of the Wall. On the north face of the Wall the line is continuous.

At the distance of two furlongs from Housesteads, and seven from the last that we noticed, above Moss Kennel, is another mile-castle. It is plain from this and other examples, that the position of the mile-castles was not influenced by the contiguity of a station. At the time of the publication of the second edition of *The Roman Wall*, this mile-castle was covered with turf. It was thus spoken of:—"Its ruins are sufficiently conspicuous to invite the use of the pickaxe and spade." This attention it shortly afterwards received, by Mr. Clayton's direction, and it forms an interesting object of study. The castle has adapted itself to the rocky site on which it has been placed, which is very uneven—dipping chiefly to the north. The great Wall forms the north wall of the castle, and stands fourteen courses, or nine feet six inches high. This is the finest specimen remaining on the whole line. The castle itself measures, on the inside, fifty-seven feet seven inches from west to east, and forty-nine feet seven inches from north to south. The thickness of the east and west walls of the castle is nine feet. The thickness of the Wall at the north gateway—and it always assumes additional width at the gateways—is not less than ten feet. The southern angles of the castle are rounded exteriorly, but are square in the inside. It will be noticed, that in building the walls of the castle, occasional courses of sandstone slate have

been used for bonding, very much in the way that tiles are
in the Roman structures of southern Britain. An inspection
of the south-east corner will show that this angle has been
built before the contiguous parts, and that it formed a sort of
buttress for the adjacent walls to rest against. The same
arrangement will be noticed on both sides of the jambs of
the north gateway. The north gateway may now attract
our attention. It is obviously of two periods. The original
portal is of most substantial masonry, and has an opening ten
feet wide. It has been spanned by an arch. The springers
of the arch are in position, and several of the arch-stones lie
upon the ground. Unfortunately one of these was broken up
before its use was known, or the whole arch might have
been restored. Each stone has a *luis* hole in it, which is
so placed as to facilitate the bringing of the inner edge of the
stone into its proper place in the arch. The height of the gate,
from the floor to the impost of the arch, is a little under six
feet. At some period subsequent to its original construction,
the width of this gateway has been reduced to three feet nine
inches. The floor of this new gateway is three feet six inches
above the sill of the original. In order to understand these
arrangements, we must now revert to the facts which were
revealed at the time of the excavation. On digging down to
the foundations of the *castellum*, on the inside of the north
wall, a number of masons' chippings were met with, and a
mason's chisel. Upon the chippings, in the neighbourhood
of the walls, had been laid a flooring of rough flags. These
flags, however, were much broken, and some of the fragments
were forced into an almost vertical position, all indicating
that the walls of the building had been forcibly thrown down.
Immediately above the flags was found a quantity of finely

L

comminuted charcoal, as if the sheds or barrack-rooms, which probably were placed against the main walls of the building, had been destroyed by fire.   The ashes were not found in the centre of the area.   At this level were discovered an axe and a knife, resembling those carved on altars.   Above the mass of stones, mortar, and rubbish, a second floor and a second series of buildings connected with the main walls were found. It is thus evident that the building had more than once suffered from the devastations of the enemy, and that each time when the repairs were effected a large part of the ruined matter had been allowed to remain (see p. 87).   The north door had probably been diminished in size late in the era of Roman occupation.   To show the height of the second floor, the part in front of the north gateway has been left unexcavated.

The south gateway is in a ruinous state, but it has evidently been diminished in width as well as the other. The masonry of the repairs is quite Roman in its character. In conducting the excavations, numerous fragments of Samian ware were found.   A fragment of a vase had the word DEDICO scratched upon it.   Some roofing-tiles and slates were found, as well as some coins of Hadrian and Antoninus Pius.   The most valuable relic, however, was a portion of a slab containing a record of the second legion, and of Hadrian's legate, Aulus Platorius Nepos (see p. 114).   When complete, it was no doubt the same as those found in the next two *castella* to which reference will immediately be made.   This stone, which had formed part of the flooring of the renovated structure, is much worn.   On the inside of the east wall of the *castellum*, near the south-east angle, is a small recess, which, when first opened, was black with soot and charcoal-dust.   It has no doubt been a fire-place, but it has no chimney.

The hill rising from the opening, which we meet with on the west side of this mile-castle, is called Cuddy's Crag. The next opening is called the Rapishaw Gap. The view here given is from the western side of this gap, looking eastward.

Our course now lies over an eminence, which leads us down to Hot Bank. The woodcut on the next page shows us the general aspect of the Wall in this part of its course. The view from the summit is very extensive and fine. All the four loughs—Broomlee, Greenlee, Crag Lough, and Grindon, are in sight. Not far from the western margin of Greenlee, is Bonnyrig, a shooting-box belonging to Sir Edward Blackett, Bart. The aspect of the crags in this vicinity will be viewed with interest. Beyond the waste to the north-east are the Simonside Hills, and beyond them is the Cheviot range. The heather-clad hill immediately to the south of us is Borcum, now called Barcombe, from which the Romans

procured much of their stone, and from which the name of the
station of BORCOVICUS is no doubt derived. The defile leading
by its western flank to the South Tyne will be noticed, and
the propriety of guarding it by a stationary camp perceived.
The platform of the station of VINDOLANA may be distinguished by its peculiarly verdant surface. On the south side
of the Tyne, Langley Castle may be noticed—near the angle
of a large plantation; beyond it are the chimneys of the

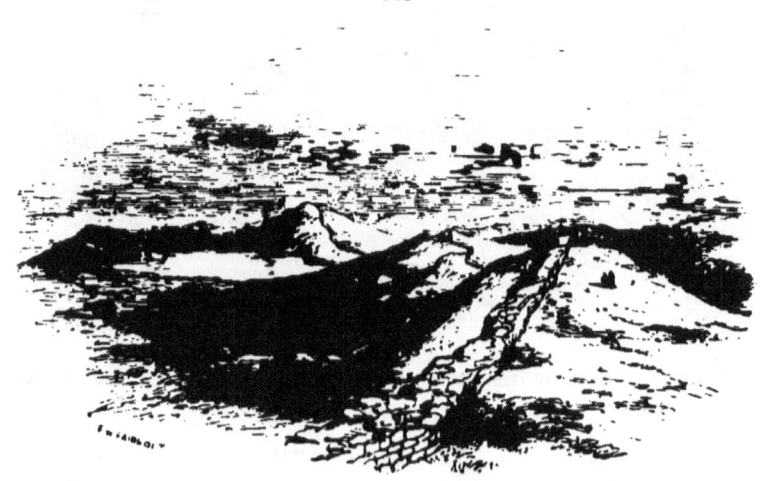

smelt-mills. The valley of the river Allen is seen joining
that of the Tyne; and near the confluence of the two rivers,
may be discerned the ruins of Staward Peel. In the distance,
to the south-west of us, are the lofty summits of Cross-fell,
Skiddaw, and Saddleback.

The farm house of Bradley stands on the tail of the crag
on which we now are. Built up in the doorway of the old
kitchen, was one-half of the Hadrian slab, which will pre-

sently be noticed; it had, no doubt, been brought at an early period from the neighbouring mile-castle of Milking Gap. On the other side of the modern military road stands a farm house, dignified by the name of Bradley Hall. It was once a place of importance, and even now the foundations of considerable buildings may be traced. It appears that Edward I. rested here for a few days in September, 1306, on his last journey to Scotland. The king's health was evidently breaking up at the time. He made his journey from

Newcastle to Lanercost, where he spent the winter, in short stages. The route which he pursued—Newburgh, Bradley, Henshaw, Haltwhistle, Melkridge, Blenkinsop, and Thirlwall —would almost induce us to suppose that he had availed himself on his journey of the roads constructed by the Romans in connection with the Wall. *(Arch. Inst. Journal,* Vol. XIV., p. 268.)

Passing onward, Crag Lough comes fully into view. It adds greatly to the beauty of this wild and interesting region.

The water-hen builds extensively amongst the reeds at its western extremity; and flocks of wild ducks are often seen skimming its surface. We now descend into the valley of the Milking Gap. There are distinct traces of a mile-castle in the defile. In its ruins was found the inscribed stone shown here;* the left hand portion of which is now at Durham, the right at Matfen Hall (p. 59). The reading and translation of this important inscription has already been given. The Wall having descended into the bottom of the defile, bends at a sharp angle

to take the ascent of the opposite hill. Its course is well marked by the fosse which accompanied it on its north side. The farm house of Hot Bank is a sunny spot in the memory of many pilgrims—not a few having here received much kind attention at the hands of Mr. Clayton, to whom the farm belongs, and his tenant. But changes come over all things. The farmer is no longer personally resident at Hot Bank. Notwithstanding, the visitor is requested to insert his name in the book that is preserved here, in which many travellers along the line of the Wall have left a proof of their interest in the great historical structure.

* A stone similar to this, but unbroken, is shown on p. 114. It was procured from the Castle Nick mile-castle.

Chesterholm.

We may now forsake the Wall for a little, in order to pay a visit to the station of VINDOLANA, the modern Chesterholm. It is about a mile due south from Hot Bank. A bridle road by the side of the burn running out of Crag Lough takes us down to the military road. Before crossing the Vallum, some circles and other enclosures, formed of whinstones, are seen on the right hand. They are probably relics of ancient British camps. The Vallum makes two rapid curves in this neighbourhood, assuming something like the form of the letter S, apparently to avoid the contiguous marsh; this is best seen from the heights. Crossing the turnpike road, we pass two old cottages, and a recently built farm house, called High Shields, and then descend into the valley. It is not improbable that the road we tread upon is the remains of a Roman one. Before coming to the station, a large barrow— possibly the burial-place of some British chief—may be noticed. On the south side of it is a Roman mile-stone, standing in its original position. This mile-stone stands upon a line of road called the Stanegate, (see p. 30), which extended from CILURNUM to MAGNA, and which probably went further in both directions. The position of both of these stations, and that also of VINDOLANA, warrant the supposition that they were planted by Agricola. The road which connected them would not be altogether disused after the Wall was built. Another mile-stone stood, some years ago, to the west of this, but it was broken up for gate-posts. This, Horsley tells us, had on it the remarkable inscription, in large coarse letters, BONO REIPVBLICAE NATO, which was intended as a compliment to the emperor then reigning. The farm house near the mile-stone is called Coadley-gate.

The station stands advantageously. Though it occupies an elevated platform, it is sheltered by an amphitheatre of hills, and is naturally protected on every side but the west. The walls, ditches, and gateways, though in a dilapidated condition, may be easily made out.   It has an area of three acres and a quarter.   To the west of the station are the ruins, now nearly obliterated, of an extensive building, which has been furnished with hypocausts.   The pillars long retained the marks of fire and soot, which gave rise to the popular belief that a colony of fairies had here established themselves, and that this was their kitchen.   To the west of this ruin is a series of gutter-stones (some of which have been laid bare), by means of which water has been brought from a neighbouring spring.

The ornamental cottage in the valley was built by the late Rev. Anthony Hedley, an earnest and able antiquary, as a residence for himself.   He got a death-chill whilst watching the digging up of some urns in the station.   With the exception of the quoins and lintels, it is constructed of stones chiselled by Roman hands.   Some valuable antiquities were discovered here by Mr. Hedley, most of which have been removed to Chesters.   One of them, an altar to Jupiter, has been already described (see p. 107).   Another, which also is at Chesters, is figured in the accompanying woodcut.   The Notitia places the prefect of the fourth cohort of Gauls at VINDOLANA.   As this and the altar already given were erected by prefects of this cohort we may fairly conclude that Chesterholm was the VINDOLANA of the Romans.   On each side of the *focus** on the top of the altar is a volute which probably represents the fagot for burning the offering.   On

* *Focus*, the hearth or place where the offering was burnt.

the sides of the altar are representations of the implements used in sacrifice. On the one side are an axe, a knife, and the victim itself—an ox; on the other the jug for holding the

wine and the patera or ladle for laying the offering on the focus. The inscription and its translation are as follows:—

GENIO	To the Genius
PRAETORI[I]	of the Prætorium
SACRVM PI	sacred. Pi-
TVANIVS SE	tuanius Se-
CVNDVS PRAE	cundus the Pre-
FECTVS COH[ORTIS] IV	fect of the fourth cohort
GALLOR[VM]	of Gauls [erected this]

In the walls of the covered passage leading from the kitchen of the cottage to the burn-side, several Roman stones have been built up. Amongst them is one in which the

FIG. 1.   FIG. 4.

pivot of one of the gates has been inserted; several coping-stones (Fig. 1); a fragment of an inscription to Hadrian (Fig. 2); a stone recording the name of the 20th legion, which was styled the Valerian and the Victorious, and whose badge was

FIG. 2.   FIG. 3.

a boar (Fig. 3); with several others. In the front wall of the house is a triangular stone (Fig. 4), on which are carved a cockatrice, a globe, a crescent, a cross, and, at the top, a small circular knob, which Hodgson terms "The umbilicated moon." The sculpture is supposed to have reference to the mysteries of Mithraic worship. It was found in the farm house of Low Foggerish. Here also is a figure of Mercury, which is shown in the wood-cut; and one or two other fragmentary inscriptions.

The stream which flows out of Crag Lake is joined near the mile-stone by another from Winshields, when the united rivulet takes the name of the Chineley Burn, and runs into the South Tyne at Bardon Mill.

Should it be a clear day and the traveller has time, he will do well to ascend the hill of Barcombe. From the top, an excellent view is obtained of the line of mural fortification. Some of the Roman quarries will be noticed. In one of them near "the Long-stone," a small copper vessel was found in 1835, carefully depos-ited beneath the stone-chippings. The woodcut shows the form of this bronze purse; which was no doubt worn upon the arm. It contained sixty-

three coins, which seem to have been wrapped up in a piece of leather; part of which remained. Three of the coins are of gold; the rest are silver denarii. The gold coins belong to the reigns of Claudius, Nero, and Vespasian. Of the silver coins, nine are consular; the others are imperial, extending from the time of Nero to that of Hadrian. No less than seventeen of them are coins of Trajan; four belong to the time of Hadrian. As the coins of Trajan are more numerous than those of any other, and as his coins and those of Hadrian are in excellent preservation, the conclusion is natural that this deposit of coins was made early in Hadrian's reign. This in-

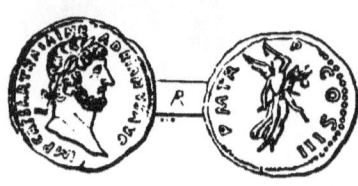

ference strongly favours the idea that Hadrian did not content himself with casting up an earthen mound, but that he wrought quarries and built the Wall. In order to show the excellent preservation of the coins of Hadrian, a drawing of one of them is here introduced. This collection of coins, together with the curious bronze purse figured on the previous page, is now in the possession of Mr. Clayton, of Chesters.

This hill-top has another object of interest for the antiquary. A little to the east of the Long-stone, and on a platform which, though it is a little below the summit, commands a view of the mural ridge from Sewingshields to the Nine Nicks of Thirlwall, is an ancient camp, of the kind usually ascribed to the aboriginal Britons. Its ramparts, which are tolerably complete, will be descried with interest. On its northern edge are a series of circular cavities, probably the lower portions of concealed huts. From these hiding-places the occupants have no doubt often watched their enemy.

Bardon Mill, one of the stations of the Newcastle and Carlisle Railway, is to the south of Chesterholm.

On the other side of the river in this vicinity is the mediæval stronghold of Willimontswyke, which is believed to have been the birth-place of Nicholas Ridley, the martyr.

Returning to Milking Gap, we resume our companionship with the Wall. The cliffs along which we walk, and the lake below, are interesting objects of contemplation. A number of goats, in a half-wild state, used to frequent these crags, adding to their romantic aspect ; but they have recently been destroyed.

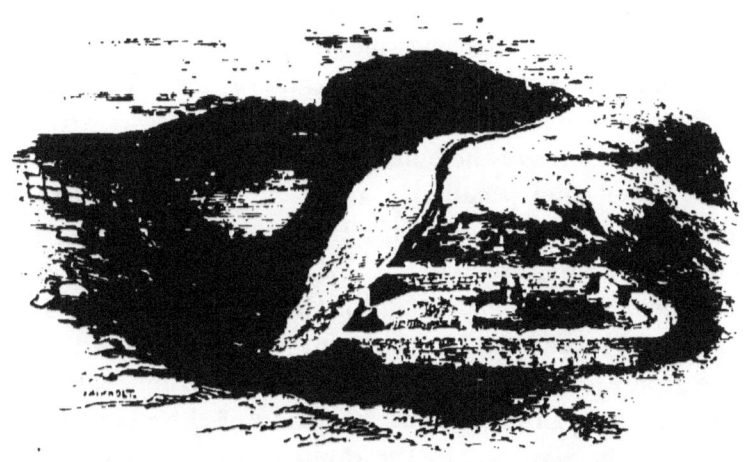

Pursuing our course westward, we soon arrive at a conspicuous gap on the Steel Rig grounds. The Wall on its eastern declivity may be studied to great advantage. Owing to the rapid dip of the hill, the stones are laid parallel to the horizon. The mode of forming the interior of the Wall will be noticed. After placing a course of rubble-stones, in a slanting position, a layer of mortar has been laid upon the top of them, and then another course of stones. The Wall soon ascends a hill to the west of the Steel Rig, and after turning sharply to the north, almost immediately descends again into the gap called the Castle Nick. This name is no doubt derived from the *castellum* here, and which was, in 1854, freed from its encumbering rubbish by Mr. Clayton. The woodcut shews its present appearance, as viewed from the west. Crag Lough and Hot Bank are seen in the distance. The walls of this mile-castle, which are seven feet thick, are in excellent preservation, having six or seven courses of stone standing. The castle measures fifty feet from east to west, and sixty-two feet from north to south, inside measurement. The gateways do not present the usual massive masonry; they have doubtless been altered since their original construction. The rubbish which encumbered the site impressed the excavators with the idea that the walls of the building had been purposely thrown down. The chief peculiarity about this castle is, that the foundations of the interior apartments of the building still remain, on its western side. These erections have been quite independent of the main walls of the castle, and have been more rudely constructed. In front of this mile-castle are some groups of boulder stones which have possibly been used by the ancient Britons in the formation of their habitations. Here, too, the structure of the Roman military way may be studied to advantage. The important slab given in page 114, bearing an inscription to Hadrian was, there is reason to believe, derived from this castle. It was long in the possession of Mr. Lowes, of Ridley Hall, who was at the time of its discovery the owner of the Castle Nick.* It is now in the museum of the Society of Antiquaries of Newcastle.

A little further on, another depression in the mural ridge, called the Cats' Stairs, is reached. The view here given is

* *Archæologia Æliana*, Vol. IV., p. 273, O.S.

taken from the north side of it. Should the pilgrim wish to have a view of the crags along which the Wall runs, he would do well to go down the Cats' Stairs, and walk along the plain to the north of the Wall as far as the next gap, which is the great defile at Peel Crag, where the basaltic columns rise in pillared majesty.

As the gap at Peel Crag is wider than usual, special precautions have been taken to defend it. On both sides of the pass the Wall bends sharply to the south: this has the double effect of narrowing the gorge, and exposing an enemy to a flanking fire within half a bowshot on both sides. It is not unlikely that the low ground north of the Wall was a swamp in the days of the Romans. The road which passes through the defile leads to Kielder, and so into Scotland; in its progress northwards it soon degenerates into a mere track.

In the valley by the side of the military road is a farm house which once was an inn known as "The Twice-brewed."

Before the construction of the Newcastle and Carlisle railway, it was much frequented by the carriers who conducted the traffic between the eastern and western sides of the Island. As many as twenty men and fifty horses used to be put up here on a carriers' night. It is now a lonely farm house. Hutton lodged here for a night, and he gives us an amusing account of the proceedings of his fellow travellers, the carriers. He says he had great difficulty in getting a separate bed — having no wish to share a couch with one or more carters; and when he saw them at supper, he came to the conclusion that there were no barricades in their throats, and that eating was the chief end of man. A little to the westward of this, we come to a small inn now having the name of "Twice-brewed," where simple refreshments can be obtained.

We now return to the Wall. On the western side of Peel Crag, sheltered by a few trees, there formerly stood the farm house of Steel Rig. It is now removed. Here the Wall loses the basaltic ridge, and runs along a stratum of sandstone. The Wall at first is in bad condition, but the fosse, with a rampart on its outer margin, is boldly developed. The crags shortly reappear, and the ditch again ceases. Before reaching the top of Winshields—just where the fosse ceases—a mile-castle is met with; it is about eight furlongs from that at Castle Nick. Winshields is 1230 feet above the level of the sea. This is the highest point of the Wall. The prospect from this elevation is very extensive in every direction. On a clear day the vessels navigating the Solway can easily be descried. Burnswark and Criffell, well-known heights in Dumfries-shire, come into view.

Proceeding onwards from this point, we find the Wall in an encouraging state of preservation. A little friendly help has been used to make the facing-stones on each side equal the height of the core of the interior. "At about a furlong west of the top of Winshields, and about eighty yards south of the Wall, is a sheltered spot, called Green Slack, in which are some foundations, apparently sites of ancient [British] residences; thence crossing a deep valley, called Lodham Slack, where the Wall requires its ditch again, we gain a summit, where are traces of [ancient British] encampments, close to the Wall." *(MacLauchlan's Memoir*, p. 44.) A gentle descent now brings us to a spot called Shield-on-the-Wall—where once was a thatched cottage, now removed. It represented the site of a mile-castle, and was composed of its materials. Haltwhistle is, as the crow flies, two miles-and-a-half distant from this point.

Nearly due south from Shield-on-the-Wall, is a large stone lying on the edge of the south agger of the Vallum, which Mr. MacLauchlan thinks "has the appearance of having been a cromlech, one of the supporters being still under it in a broken state." *(Memoir*, p. 44.)

We next come to a gap of bold proportions, having the ominous name of Bogle Hole. The next gap is Caw Gap. A cattle shed, formed out of a ruined cottage, stands in it. The extreme jealousy with which the Romans defended an exposed situation is well shown here; the fosse which guards the pass through the low ground is discontinued on the western side as soon as the crag attains a sufficient elevation, but when again the ground droops, though only for the space of a few yards, it reappears for that short distance. A road passes through this gap, north and south. Northwards is a solitary house, called Burn Deviot, which was long the resort of smugglers and sheep stealers. Lights, as the shepherds

M

believe, are still to be seen at night flickering about the
windows—the spirits of those who have been murdered in it.
After passing Caw Gap, the Wall is for some distance nearly
uprooted.   To the south of us two large stones are seen
standing.   They are called "The Mare and Foal."   In
Armstrong's Map of Northumberland three are marked.
They are probably remains of a Druidical circle.   Proceeding
onwards, we come to a part of the Wall where it diminishes
in thickness one foot at a single step.   The cliffs once more
begin to assume a high elevation and to present the columnar
form; the Vallum is well developed.   Passing Bloody Gap,
and another gap called Thorny Doors, we find the Wall once
more in an excellent state of preservation, and it continues
so for a considerable distance.   The farm house to the north
is called Cawfields.   In the next gap, named by the peripatetic
party of 1849 the Pilgrims' Gap, is a mile-castle of great
interest.   It was excavated by Mr. Clayton in 1848, and
was the first of these structures to be exposed by this gentleman for the benefit of the modern antiquary.*   It measures
sixty-three feet from east to west, and forty-nine from north
to south, inside measurement.   Its walls have seven or eight
courses of stone standing, and they are eight feet thick.   The
massive masonry of both northern and southern gates may be
studied with advantage.   They have an opening ten feet wide.
The pivot-holes of the gates remain.   At each side of the
entrance there is a recess in the wall for receiving the gate
when thrown back.   Two inscribed stones were found in this
castle.   One of them is an old monumental stone, which has
evidently been converted into a hearth-stone.   What remains
of the inscription has been thus expanded :—D[IS] M[ANIBUS].

* *Archæologia Æliana*, Vol. IV., p. 54, O.S.

DAGVALD[VS] MIL[ES] PAN[NONLÆ] VIXIT AN[NOS] . .
PVSINNA [SVA CONIV]X TIT[VLVM] [POSVIT.] "To the divine
shades—Pusinna erected this tablet to the memory of her
husband, Dagvaldus, a soldier of Pannonia, he lived . .
years." The other is a fragment of an inscription to Hadrian, in all respects similar
to the important one already referred to in
p. 114. It is here shown. South of this
castle, on the Roman military way, two
mile-stones were recently found; on one of
them was inscribed the name of Hadrian,
the other bore an inscription to Severus
Alexander. South of the Vallum was

found, some years ago, an altar to Apollo. These objects are
preserved at Chesters. *(See Arch. Æliana, IX., 211.)*

A road leads from the vicinity of the mile-castle to the
town of Haltwhistle, in the sheltered valley of the South Tyne,
whither, should the shades of evening be approaching, the
way-worn antiquary may be glad to bend his steps. Just
before reaching the modern military road, a Roman camp
will be observed. On the sides which are most exposed,
double and triple lines of earth-works have been raised. It
has no' doubt been occupied during the construction of the
Wall. A quarry by the burn-side was used by the Romans.
Mr. Clayton, in 1847, discovered on the face of it the letters
LEG. VI. V.; but the inscription soon afterwards was obliterated by the quarrymen.

Rejoining the Wall at Cawfields mile-castle and proceeding
on our course we soon reach Haltwhistle Burn. It is derived
from the overflowings of Greenlee Lough. Between its
source and the Wall, it is called Caw Burn.

Westward of the Burn-head farm house the fosse is boldly developed, but the Wall is traceable only in the ruins of its foundation. "About mid-way between the water and the station of Æsica are traces of a building about the size of the mile-castles, but, unlike them, it is partly within and partly without the Wall. Its distance from the last is only about four furlongs." (*MacLauchlan's Memoir*, p. 44.) Hence it remains a question whether it be a mile-castle or not. Under any circumstances, it is in bad condition.

Great Chesters.

ÆSICA, or Great Chesters, is the tenth stationary camp on the line of the Wall. It incloses an area of about three acres.

The second cohort of the Astures was stationed here. The stamp on this fragment of a roofing-tile, as well as some lapidary inscriptions, confirm the *Notitia* in this respect. In Gordon's day some of the walls of the station were standing twelve or thirteen feet high; at present all that can be said is, that the ramparts and fosse are clearly defined. Two or more ramparts of earth seem to have given additional security to the western side, which is naturally the weakest. The southern gateway may be traced; it is nearer the eastern than the western side. The east gate may be discerned, but no satisfactory traces of the west remain. In the centre of the camp is a vaulted chamber, which reminds us of a somewhat similar structure in CILURNUM. At present it is in a ruinous and neglected state. To the south and east of the station are traces of suburban buildings. At some distance down the hill are the remains of a hypocaust; time and the tread of cattle have damaged it much of late years. An ancient road leads from the southern gateway of the station to the "Stanegate." In the flat ground south of the station, and in the near neighbourhood of the Vallum, are traces of some barrows and some circular and quadrilateral enclosures. In this vicinity stood Walltown Mill, where the burying-ground of the station seems to have been. Brand observed here several remarkable barrows, which are now scarcely visible. He was shown some of the graves which had been opened.

The peculiar feature of this station is the water-course, which is to be found to the north of it. Dr. Lingard knew of it; in his MS. notes he says:—"The water for the station was brought by a winding aqueduct, still visible, from the head of Haltwhistle Burn; it winds five miles." But from Dr. Lingard's time to the publication of *The Roman Wall*, it seems to have been lost sight of. The water-course consists of a channel three or four feet deep, and proportionately wide, cut in the sides of the numerous little hills which stud the plain north of the Wall. In order to preserve the water-level, a most circuitous course is taken, but so effectually is this done, that only once has it been necessary to resort to a bridge or embankment. This bridge is now gone, but the place has the name of Benks Bridge. The whole length of the aqueduct is six miles; the distance in a straight line is little more than two miles and a quarter. By this means the water of the Caw Burn was brought within a short distance of the station. Within about 350 yards of the station the aqueduct is lost sight of. Owing to the nature of the level, the water could only be brought over this part of its course by means of an artificial embankment; this, if ever it existed, is now entirely removed. It may surprise the reader to find the means of supplying so important an element as water placed on the north of the Wall. The truth is, that the Romans by no means gave up the district beyond the Wall to the enemy. An aqueduct within sight of Æsica was perfectly safe when the forces of Rome were vigorously handled. An accurate plan of this remarkable aqueduct, from a survey specially made, is given in the first edition of the author's book on *The Roman Wall.*

Shortly after leaving Æsica, the crags again appear, and the Wall ascends the heights. For some distance little more than the foundation courses remain in position. The fosse, which at first is distinct, is soon discontinued. Soon after passing Cockmount Hill farm house, we meet with a long and very encouraging tract of the Wall. Its north face exhibits six and seven courses of facing-stones, and in some places as many as nine; the south face is broken. Before coming to Allalee farm house, the ruins of a mile-castle, very distinctly marked, are met with, at the distance of seven furlongs and a quarter from Æsica. Opposite the farm house the Wall is reduced to a pitiable condition, and it continues so until after passing Walltown. Two centurial stones have been built into the front wall of the farm house; they are both much weathered. One seems to read ⊃ VALERI[I] VERI; the other, ⊃ MARIDI. About three furlongs beyond the mile-castle we reach Muckle-bank Crag, the highest of the Nine Nicks of Thirlwall. It is 860 feet above the sea. The view is very extensive. In addition to the objects already named, the viaduct of the Alston railway forms a pleasing feature in the landscape. The defile of Walltown Crags is a wide one. The fosse of the Wall is, as is usual in similar situations, strong.

At Walltown several objects attract our attention. Nearest to the Wall is a spring, surrounded by masonry, now much disordered, called the King's Well; the present inhabitants call it King Arthur's Well. Other accounts are given of it. Hutchinson says:—"Travellers are shown a well among the cliffs, where it is said Paulinus baptized King Egbert; but it is more probable it was Edwin, King of Northumberland." The well has no doubt been a place of historical interest and importance, but, unhappily, modern drainage is robbing it of its treasures. Another interesting circumstance is connected with this locality. In the crevices of the whin rock near the house chives grow abundantly. The general opinion is, that we are indebted for these plants to the Romans, who were much addicted to the use of these and kindred savoury vegetables. Most of the early writers refer to this subject; let the reader take a passage from Camden:—"The fabulous tales of the common people concerning this Wall, I doe wittingly and willingly overpasse. Yet this one thing which I was enformed of by men of good credit, I will not conceale from the reader. There continueth a settled perswasion among a great part of the people thereabout, and the same received by tradition, that the Roman soldiers of the marches did plant here every where in old time for their use certaine medicinable hearbs, for to cure wounds: whence is it that some emperick practitioners of chirurgery in Scotland, flock hither every year in the beginning of summer, to gather such simples and wound-herbes; the vertue whereof they highly commend as found by long experience, and to be of singular efficacy." *(Phil. Holland's Transl.,* p. 795.) Another point of interest here is the site of the Tower of Walltown, the inheritance of John Ridley, the brother of the martyr. The present farm house is a modern erection. Only a fragment of the old castellated building remained in Wallis's time; even this is now gone. Mr. MacLauchlan discerned "Faint traces of Tower" to the north-west of the present house. The old village of Walltown, which hung on the sunny slope near the Tower, has also passed away. (See *Hodgson's North.,* II., iii., p. 324.) To the east of Walltown House, on a small hill covered with fir trees, is an ancient camp, which reminds us of that on Castle Hill, Haltwhistle.

Leaving the valley, we climb a steep ascent, which soon brings us to the site of another mile-castle. Hutton says, "I found the ascent so difficult that I was sometimes obliged to crawl on all fours." This is a most interesting and peculiar part of the line. The mural ridge, divided by frequent breaks into as many isolated peaks, gives rise to the denomination of the Nine Nicks of Thirlwall. The Wall climbs and descends the little hills unflinchingly, and adapts itself with strange pertinacity to the ragged edges of the basaltic line. Its northern face occasionally shows a well-preserved specimen of the structure. The general aspect of the country is well shown in the etching on the opposite page; in the foreground may be noticed a considerable fragment of the Wall, while in

the distance may be discerned all the prominent heights traversed by it in its tortuous course from Sewingshields to this point. The highest crag near the centre of the picture is Muckle Bank, and the highest on the right hand side is Winshields.

Sir Walter Scott, who was familiar with this part of the Wall, probably here penned the lines :—

"TO A LADY WITH FLOWERS FROM THE ROMAN
WALL.

" Take these flowers, which purple waving,
    On the ruined rampart grew,
Where, the sons of freedom braving
    Rome's imperial standards flew.

" Warriors from the breach of danger
    Pluck no longer laurels there :
They but yield the passing stranger
    Wild-flower wreaths for beauty's hair."

The lady to whom these lines were addressed was doubtless the personage who in due time became Lady Scott.

At length the cliffs, which extend in a nearly unbroken series from Sewingshields to Carvoran, sink into a plain, and the fertility and beauty of a well-cultivated country re-appear.

Within the last few months the Nine Nicks of Thirlwall have become specially interesting to the students of the Roman Wall. In the autumn of 1883 a turret was discovered and laid bare on the westernmost height of these crags. It was, like the others we have seen, let into the Wall to the extent of between two and three feet. Its interior area was thirteen feet by about twelve. The Wall which formed the north wall of the turret was nine courses of stones high. Its north-west corner was damaged when the writer's attention was first called to it; the quarrymen having removed the foundation of this part of it, some stones had fallen. The etching over leaf shows the character of the structure as it was when the attention of antiquaries was first drawn to it. As the quarry is an extensive one it was understood that the turret would be spared, and that other portions of the cliff would be submitted to the operations of the miner. Not so, however; this priceless memorial of our country's early history has been utterly destroyed. The discovery of this turret led to the inquiry as to whether there might not be some others to the east of it. Mr. Clayton sent his chief explorator Tailford to examine the cliff. He found two others. Seeing, however, the fate of this one, it will be well to let them enjoy the protection of the soil which now covers them, until England becomes an educated nation.

Carvoran.

Carvoran is the MAGNA of the *Notitia*, where the second cohort of the Dalmatians was stationed. An inscription found near Thirlwall Castle corroborates this statement.* The station is a little more than two miles and a half from Great Chesters, and it contains an area of three acres and a half. Its position is particularly strong. It is to the south both of Vallum and Wall, having probably been erected before them, by Agricola, in order to command the valley of the Tipalt. The numerous sharp turns which the Vallum makes to avoid the bog on the north of the station, are inimical to Horsley's idea that the north agger of the Vallum was Agricola's military way. The interior of the station has, in recent times, been subjected to the plough; before this its ruins were stately. Stukeley says, "There were vestiges of houses and buildings all over, within

* It is No. 316 in the *Lapidarium Septentrionale.*

TURRET NEAR CARVORAN

and without." The outline of the station, which is to the west of the farm house, may, though with difficulty, be made out; some portions of the north rampart remain, and the north fosse is distinct. Numerous memorials of Roman days are to be seen in the farm house, on the garden wall, and other parts of the premises. In the house are two small altars inscribed to the local god BELATVCADER; one of which is here shown. The Stanegate, or direct Roman way, came in front of the station, and the Maiden Way,  after traversing the wastes of Stanemoor and Alston, came up to its south-east angle. With Mr. MacLauchlan's Survey in hand, the course óf these roads may yet be traced.

The north fosse between Carvoran and Thirlwall Castle, is particularly well developed; the lines of the Vallum, running parallel with the Wall, may also be traced in their course to the little river Tipalt. In an outhouse at Holmhead a Roman inscribed stone is inserted. It may puzzle the uninitiated, in consequence of its being placed upside down. It reads CIVITAS DVMNONI. The woodcut shows it. The Dumnonii were a British tribe occupying Devon-shire, Cornwall, and part of Somer-setshire. The castle of Thirlwall has some interesting features. The woodcut on the following page represents its general aspect as it was a few years ago. It is entirely built of Wall stones.

It is generally stated that Thirlwall derives its name from

the fact that here the Caledonians first *thirled* or threw down
the *Wall*. *Thirl-ian* is an Anglo-Saxon word, signifying to
penetrate. Whatever truth there may be in this etymology,
it is certain that this is the weakest part of the Wall.

Not far from Thirlwall Castle is the village of Glenwhelt.
This name has a thoroughly Celtic sound. Mr. MacLauchlan
says:—"It is possibly British, from *Glynn*, a valley; and
whelt, darkness; an appropriate name, from the precipitous
nature of the ground." (*Memoir*, p. 49.) In a stone fence
near what was the inn of the village, is a much weathered bust
that no doubt once adorned the Roman camp.

The railway station of Greenhead is close to Glenwhelt.

VI.—FROM THE TIPALT TO THE EDEN.

No traces of the Wall and Vallum remain in the flat
between Thirlwall Castle and the railway, but both appear on
the bank to the left of the railway.

Before pursuing his journey further, the traveller, if he
have time at his command, had better examine a camp and

the military way (Stanegate), which he will find to the south
of the lines, and very near the railway station. "The form
of the camp is a rectangular parallelogram, having its east
and west sides about 165 yards, and its north and south 88,
giving an area of about three acres. It appears to have been
an earthwork only, now nearly destroyed, except the east
part of the north front; its entrances, and the whole outline,

however, are visible. Each of the gates has had a straight
traverse in front, together with that peculiar semicircular
flexure of the rampart opposite the gateway, so frequently
noticed in camps on the line of the Watling Street, and
supposed by some persons to have been used by Agricola."*
(*MacLauchlan's Memoir*, p. 49.) The Stanegate is on the

* This peculiar traverse is believed to be characteristic of the camps of
the Ninth Legion.

north side of this camp. There is another smaller camp, of
similar construction, about five furlongs to the west of this.
These are the only two camps noticed by Mr. MacLauchlan
on the line of the Wall, having the peculiar defence of
gateway referred to. Besides these two, there are other three
camps, of the ordinary construction, lying to the south of the
Wall, between the Tipalt and the Irthing. "We have thus,"
says Mr. MacLauchlan, "five camps between Carvoran and
Birdoswald, at a mean distance from each other of about
half a mile; occupying every prominent height on the south
of the Wall, at a mean distance from it of about two furlongs
and a half. We may fairly consider them as a third line of
defence, along that part of the barrier where the natural
defences of the ground were the weakest." (*Memoir*, p. 52.)

We now hurry on. Wallend is soon reached. The
earthworks are for a short distance in excellent preservation.
Between Wallend and Chapel House, the fosse of the Wall is
of unusually large dimensions. Its north bank is in some
places fifteen and in others nearly twenty feet high. A view
of it is given on the preceding page.

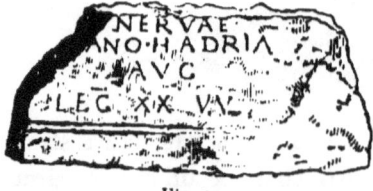

Fig. 1.

Fig. 2.

Before coming to Chapel House, the traces of a mile-castle
were formerly visible—the plough has now obliterated them.
Foultown is a farm house contiguous to Chapel House. Built
up in a stable at Chapel House, the stone here represented (Fig.
1) was found. It is a dedication, on the part of the twentieth

legion, to the Emperor Hadrian. At the village of Gap, the Vallum, which is very distinct, stands considerably above the Wall. In the gable end of an outhouse here, in the lowest course but one, and at an angle of the building, a centurial stone is to be seen (upside down). The woodcut (Fig. 2) shows it. It may be read, "The century of Claudius Avidius of the second (?) cohort."

Gap is the watershed of this part of the island; on the east of it the waters run into the Tyne, on the west into

the Irthing. The fosse of the Wall is grandly developed between Gap and the railway station. The summit of Rose Hill has been removed to afford a site for the railway station. Dr. Lingard, in his MS. notes (1807), has the following notice of it:—"A sugarloaf hill, 200 yards from the Wall, called Rose Hill. It has a platform on the top twelve yards in diameter, with a ditch round it. Here was a figure of flying Victory." This sculptured stone is now at Rockliffe; a wood-cut of it is here introduced, from the pencil of Mr. Fairholt.

Gilsland Spa, a sulphur spring, is about a mile and a half distant from Rose Hill. The Romans would not neglect these medicinal waters. Is Gilsland the BANNA of the Romans? Here is a hostel at which excellent entertainment may, if needful, be obtained.

A little to the north of the railway station is Mumps Ha', formerly the residence of the Meg Merrilees of Sir Walter Scott. It is the house round which the road bends at a right angle before we reach the bridge over the Irthing. The building has been modernised, though it still retains some of its ancient features. It is an "ale house" no longer. The woodcut represents the back of the building before it was

altered. "Meg" was buried in Over Denton churchyard. Her tombstone, which lies on the ground near that of her daughter, Margaret Teasdale, also of Mumps Hall, bears the following inscription :—"Mumps Hall. Here lies the body of Margaret Carrick, yᵉ wife of Tho. Carrick, who departed this life yᵉ 4 of Decem., 1717, in the 100 year of her age."

The present writer, in his visits to Bewcastle to see the Roman camp, the castle, and the Runic cross, has occasionally traversed the wastes which lie between Gilsland Spa and that place. In doing so he has in due course come upon the Maiden Way, which Dandy Dinmont and Brown found to be so advantageous.

Taking the Wall in the vicinity of the railway station we soon come to the Poltross Burn, the boundary line between Northumberland and Cumberland. The gorge in which the stream flows is deep and well wooded. No remains of a

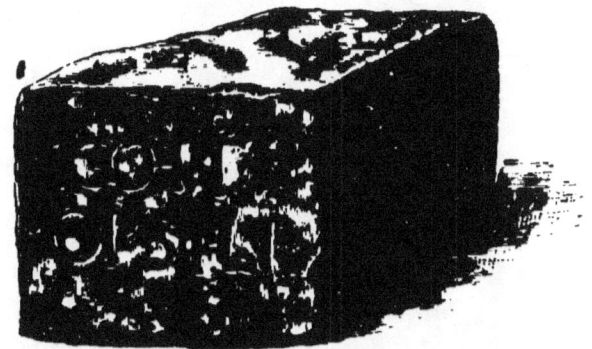

bridge appear. On the top of the western bank we meet with the marked vestiges of a mile-castle, known in the neighbourhood under the denomination of the King's Stables. It is seven furlongs and a quarter from the last, near Chapel House. The Wall now crosses the railway, and it is seen two or three courses high, stretching westwards towards Willow-ford. The north fosse is strongly developed.

In the Vicarage grounds, the residence of the Rev. A. Wright, the Vicar of Over Denton, a gentleman well acquainted with the antiquities of this neighbourhood, and who is exceedingly willing to impart his knowledge to any earnest inquirer, we meet with an interesting portion of Wall. He has carefully excavated it in the vicinity of his parsonage, and in doing so discovered the centurial stone inscribed—

COH I [ɔ] OPSILI—Of the first cohort, the century of Opsilius. The woodcut on the previous page shows it. Here also are to be seen two Roman altars which from time immemorial formed part of the altar steps in the old Norman Church at Over Denton. One of them is uninscribed; the other, which is represented in the woodcut, has evidently been dedicated I. O. M.—To Jupiter, the best and greatest. It will be observed, however, that the greater part of the inscription is obliterated, and the altar worn down by the stone having been made use of for the sharpening of knives or weapons. If this was done, as there can be little doubt was the case in Roman times, it is further negative proof of the influence of Christianity at this early era.

Before we reach the river Irthing the fosse of the Wall is well developed. We now encounter the farm-house of Willowford, in the garden wall of which is a centurial stone, having the inscription ↄ COCCEI REGVLI—the century of Cocceius Regulus.

On the flat ground bordering upon the river the Wall cannot be distinctly traced; the hedge, amongst the roots of which are a number of Wall stones, probably indicates its course. How the Wall crossed the river, and ascended the cliff which bounds its western bank, no remains are left to show. Camden says, "The Picts' Wall passed over the river Irthing by an arched bridge;"* but he gives no authority for the statement. John Armstrong of the Crooks, Gilsland, told the present writer that, being employed in 1836 to build Willowford farm house, he got stones from the Wall. At about 60 yards from the eastern bank of the river, as it now is, he came in contact with the "land-breast" (abutment) of the bridge, which, as he says, had evidently crossed the river. The stones were large and had the *luis* hole in them; there were three or four courses of them. The "land-breast" might be about 20 feet long. He said the stone had been brought from Lodge's Quarry, Low Row. From this account it would seem that the bridge was of the same character as the one over the North Tyne at Chesters. Horsley says, "The bank of the river Irthing on the west side is very steep and high, but it seems to have become more so of late years from the falling away of the sandy bank."† The river has probably worked westwards and undermined the bank, which would not be so steep when the Romans carried, as they probably did, their Wall up it. On the very edge of the cliff, on the western

* *Holland's Camden*, p. 785. † *Britannia Romana*, p. 152.

side of the Irthing, the Wall is seen standing of the height of seven courses on its south side.   Here also we meet with a mile-castle.

Birdoswald.

We now approach Birdoswald, the AMBOGLANNA of the Romans, and the twelfth station on the line.   Its position is remarkably strong.   In addition to the bold cliffs which guard it on the south, and at the foot of which the Irthing flows, a bold chasm on its northern boundary admits of the flow of the superfluous waters of the Midgeholm Bog into the Irthing.   Its western side is its weakest.   On the edge of this northern chasm, approaching the station, are some artificial lines of defence.   It has been suggested that these are the remains of a Saxon or Danish fortress.   Two small hills in this vicinity have the appearance of barrows; they are probably, however, the result of diluvial action.

Birdoswald is nearly three miles and a quarter from Carvoran.   It is the largest station on the line, having an area of five acres and a half, which is about a quarter of an acre more than Chesters, and half an acre more than Housesteads.   It possesses, like Chesters, the peculiarity of having two gates in both its eastern and western ramparts.   Most of the camps of the Wall have a southern exposure; in this, the southern margin is slightly elevated above the rest of the ground; the northern half of the station is nearly level.   A very great number of inscriptions have been found in the station, most of which confirm the *Notitia* statement that the first cohort of Dacians, styled the Ælian, was quartered here.   One of them, which is here drawn, was found by Mr. Glasford Potter in excavating the upper gateway in the eastern rampart.   The inscription may be translated:—" The first

cohort of the Dacians (styled the Ælian), commanded by
Marcus Claudius Menander the Tribune, [erected this] by

direction of Modius Julius, Imperial Legate, and Proprætor."
On one side of the slab is a palm branch, the emblem
of victory; on the
other is a sword of
peculiar form.   A
reference   to   the
Trajan   column   at
Rome shows us that
the Dacians used a
curved sword.   An
example   is   here
given.   Hence it
would almost ap-
pear that the Ro-
mans, in adopting
the services of the

various nations whom they subdued, encouraged them to use the accoutrements and arms with which they were most familiar. They avoided the imprudence of putting into their hands the superior weapons which they themselves used. During the Indian mutiny the British suffered from the consequences of an opposite policy.

The walls of the station are in a good state of preservation, the southern rampart especially, which shows eight

courses of facing-stones. The walls are five feet thick. The moat which surrounded the walls may also be satisfactorily traced. On the east side of the station are extensive and strong marks of suburban dwellings.

Although the Wall adapts itself to the north rampart of the fort, the station is entirely independent of the Wall (as is shown in the woodcut),* and must have been built

* Since this cut was prepared, that portion of the Wall which adjoined the station has been removed, to allow of a new entrance to the house.

before it. Probably, as has been already observed, the first
step taken in the construction of the Barrier, in every case,
was the erection of the stationary camps.

The north gateway has been destroyed, but the foundation of one of its jambs may sometimes be seen in the road
in front of the station. A heap of ruins in the shrubbery
marks the site of the most northerly of the west gates. The
other gateway on this side is shown in the woodcut. It is a

single gateway. Marks of ruts appear in its threshold; the
pivot-holes remain.

The south gateway is a double one, and is a very noble
specimen of Roman masonry. The plan of it is similar to
that of the gateways at Housesteads, though its masonry is
not so massive. Each portal is eleven feet wide, and has
been spanned by an arch. The pivot-holes are to be seen.
The west portal of this gate has, at some period before the

abandonment of the station, been closed, and converted into
a dwelling-house; the stones with which it was floored
remain.   As usual, this gateway has two guard-chambers;
the eastern one has not been excavated; the other, though
excavated, has again become encumbered with its own ruins.
Adjoining the west guard-chamber is another apartment;
in one angle is a circular depression, bearing marks of fire.
The south-west angle of the station contains several buildings,
which, if excavated, would no doubt display points of considerable interest.

Both of the gateways on the eastern side have been
excavated.* The lower one is much twisted and broken by
the yielding of its foundations. The other gateway is in an
excellent state of preservation. The accompanying sketch,
which has necessarily been drawn to a minute scale, shows it.

* The gateways and other portions of this station were excavated in 1852
by Mr. H. Norman; the proprietor of the camp, Mr. W. S. Potter and Mr.
H. Glasford Potter. The latter gentleman described the more important of
the excavations in the last quarto volume of the Transactions of the Society
of Antiquaries of Newcastle-upon-Tyne.

This gateway is a double one, and is provided with guard-chambers on each side. The plan of it nearly resembles that of the gateways at Housesteads. As usual, one of the portals (the north) had been closed with large stones. Some traces of a second floor will be noticed, raised about a foot above the original one. This is in consistency with the signs of hasty reparation which we have met with throughout the line. The pivot-holes remain, and in the threshold of the northern

portal is a large stone, against which the leaves of the gate closed. Several circular door-heads were found in the vicinity of this and the other gateways. The accompanying woodcut, showing the entrance into the northern guard-chamber, indicates the use to which they were applied. These door-heads are always found thrown down and often broken.

The whole interior of the camp is marked with the lines of streets and the ruins of buildings. Near the lower gateway in the east wall three chambers, of nine or ten feet square each, have been laid bare. One of them is furnished with a hypocaust. Being exposed to the tread of cattle they have become a mass of confusion. Here was found the figure represented on the following page, the body of which is now in the farm house; the head, which had been discovered thirty years previously, is in the Museum at Newcastle.   This figure is one of those usually represented

in triplets and called *deæ matres*.   Her hair is neatly dressed.

In 1859 Mr. Norman, in levelling the broken ground in front of the farm house to form a new garden, came upon a very perfect specimen of a Roman building of large dimensions. A wall, three feet six inches thick, was found, extending ninety-two feet from east to west. This wall has not been excavated to the bottom; but it has been proved to be upwards of eight feet in height. It is supported by eight buttresses. In the middle of the space between each buttress is a long slit or loop-hole. These perforations are supposed to be connected with the flues used in warming the building. Immediately in front of this wall is another of similar thickness. Three other walls were found to the north of the main one. Until the entire building be laid bare (of which there is no immediate prospect), it will be difficult to form a correct idea of its arrangements and uses. Many roofing-slates were found amongst the rubbish, some of them perforated with nail-holes. A few coins were discovered, belonging to the reigns of Vespasian, Domitian, Hadrian, Antoninus Pius, Marcus Aurelius, and Diocletian.

Some excavations were made here, at the expense of the Archæological Institute, when it met in Carlisle in 1859. A spot near the centre of the station, which always had a damp appearance, was cut down upon. The remains of a tank or reservoir for supplying the station with water was found. Some arrangements for filtering the water, by making it pass through a mass of charcoal, were noticed. These arrangements are now much obscured. Shortly after this the late Mr. Parker, of Brampton, discovered that this cistern was fed by a spring on the west side of the station. The water-course conducting the water to the tank was formed of flat stones set up on end, covered over by a third on the top; the whole was sunk in the ground. The writer was shown it at a distance of about 300 yards from the station; the water was then flowing in it.

Several inscribed stones remain here. A broken and defaced altar lies in the station. It has been described both

by Gordon and Horsley. It seems to be a dedication to the standards (SIGNIS) of the cohort. An altar to Fortune was found on rebuilding the farm house; it has been ruthlessly treated in order to fit it for use as a building-stone. Another rudely-carved altar, once built into the farm house, is dedicated to Jupiter, the best and greatest, by the first cohort of Dacians, which at this time, besides the epithet of Ælian, derived from Hadrian, seems to have had that of Tetrician derived from the Emperor Tetricus. (*Horsley, Cumb.*, VII.) There is here also another altar (shown in the accompanying woodcut), dedicated to Jupiter, having on the capital above the dedi-

catory letters (I. O. M.) a series of crosses, one of them being of that peculiar form called "gammadion." A stone broken across the middle has on it the inscription—LEG. VI. VIC. FIDELIS, intimating that the sixth legion, styled the victorious and faithful, took part in the erection of the building in which it was inserted. Here also are several stones, on which are inscribed the names of the centuries engaged in erection of the Wall in this vicinity. One of them imports that the troop (of a hundred men) had been commanded by CONCAONUS CANDIDUS(?); another bears the inscription CENTURIA HORTENSIANA; and a third commemorates the century of PROBIANUS, belonging to the fourth cohort. At the foot of the cliff on which the station stands, is the farm house of Underheugh. Here is a stone trough formed out of an altar dedicated to Jupiter.

Before taking leave of the station, we must notice the prospect both to the south and the north of us. The Earl of Carlisle, in his *Diary in Turkish and Greek Waters*, p. 87, says :—"Strikingly, and to any one who has coasted the uniform shore of the Hellespont, and crossed the tame low plain of the Troad, unexpectedly lovely is this site of Troy, if Troy it was. I could give any Cumberland borderer the best notion of it, by telling him that it wonderfully resembles the view from the point just outside the Roman camp at Birdoswald : both have that series of steep conical hills, with rock enough for wildness and verdure enough for softness; both have that bright trail of a river creeping in and out with the most continuous indentations : the Simois has, in summer at least, more silvery shades of sand." The view to which his lordship refers (as he informed the writer) is that which is obtained by a spectator who stands upon the edge of the cliff beside the south rampart of the station.

We now take our stand on the road skirting the north wall of the station. Looking towards the north-west, we see (as shown in the woodcut here given) a tower-like object; it is a fragment of the walls of Triermain Castle, a building celebrated by Scott, in his "Bridal of Triermain," and by Coleridge, in "Christabel." But more to our present purpose;—the Maiden Way, which came up to the south rampart of Carvoran, seems to have proceeded northwards from this station right over the hills before us, past Bewcastle, and so into Scotland. On the top of a distant hill, called Gillalees Beacon, nearly due north, a small cairn-like object may be discerned, in favourable states of the atmosphere;

this is the ruin of a Roman watch-tower by the side of the Maiden Way. Between Birdoswald and the King-water, the traces of the road are somewhat dubious; but after crossing this river and coming to Ash Fell, a strip of the Way is met with in a nearly perfect state. Having once fallen in with the road, the antiquary may, without much difficulty, trace it nearly to Bewcastle. Beyond this its course is dubious.

We now follow the Wall westward from Birdoswald. The Wall for a short distance is in a good state of preservation. It is seven feet six inches thick. Its south front is the best. Some portions of it, however, are beginning to exhibit signs of decrepitude and decay. On the south side of the Wall, in the second field from the station, are the feeble remains of a turret. When the first edition of this book was published they were the only traces of a turret visible on the whole line of the Wall. Hodgson writing of it says:—"In 1833 I saw a turret opened about 300 yards west of Birdoswald, the walls of which were standing to the height of six courses of stones, and 34 inches thick; the doorway on the south; and the internal area 13 feet square; all of it in 1837 was taken away." At the distance of little more than half a mile from the station we come to the site of another mile-castle. The fosse of the Wall and the earthworks of the Vallum here form interesting objects of study; they are very bold. In this part of its course the Vallum is strengthened on its northern side by a second ditch. This additional defence begins to appear shortly after we leave Birdoswald, and it terminates abruptly at the next mile-castle, that of Wallbours. Over Denton is a little to the south of this spot. Canon Shipman, in rebuilding the rectory a few years ago, discovered a large quantity of Roman remains, pottery, coins, &c. There must have been a camp or Roman settlement of some kind here.

After passing a cottage called Apple Trees, now in ruins, the Wall and Vallum draw towards each other, until, on the top of the next summit, where the Wallbours mile-castle stands, they are in tolerably close proximity. After this they run parallel to each other for some distance.

Arriving at a lodge on the traveller's left hand, a path

leads to Coome Crag, a red freestone quarry, which has been extensively wrought by the Romans.* The workmen have left some inscriptions on the face of the rock, amongst which may perhaps be discerned the names SECVRVS, IVSTVS, MATH-RIANVS. One of these is shown in the woodcut. At the foot

of the cliff is an inscription which reads FAVST. ET RVF. COS. Faustinus and Rufus were consuls A.D. 210. Curiously enough, whilst the rock in the immediate vicinity of this inscription is covered with a smoke-coloured lichen, the letters themselves are covered with a white lichen; this renders them distinct.

Nothing will occur to arrest attention until we arrive at Banks Head. Here were formerly the remains of a mile-castle; but the traveller will have some difficulty in detecting them now. A limestone quarry has greatly interfered with it. In 1808 two altars to the local deity Cocidius, which are now at Lanercost, were discovered at Banks Head.

The Wall next goes over a small hill called Pike. Here was discovered in 1862, a broken slab, bearing the name of Antoninus Pius. When the road was lowered some years

* The wayfarer will do well to inspect it. Independent of the antiquarian interest of the spot, its picturesqueness will well repay a visit. It may be prudent to obtain the assistance of some one in the lodge to enable him the more readily to find the inscriptions. Unfortunately many of the markings in the rocks were some time ago covered with white paint with the view of preserving them (!); this destroyed their antique appearance; the paint is happily now disappearing.

ago a turret was found on the summit of Pike Hill. The next group of houses is called Banks, or Banks Hill. The view from this point of the fertile plains below is exceedingly striking. Some of the stones of the Wall are to be seen in the road near here.

Before coming to the brook called Banks Burn, a piece of the core of the Wall is seen. Ascending the hill on the western side of the brook, in a garden, is a fragment of the Wall, which stands nine feet ten inches high. It is, however, divested of its facing-stones. Hutton, speaking of the Wall here (Hare Hill) says :—"I viewed this relic with admiration. I saw no part higher." Just beyond this piece of Wall is the still distinguishable site of a mile-castle.

Lanercost and Naworth.

At this point of our progress the antiquary may be disposed to forsake the Wall for a while, to view two

relics of the mediæval period of great interest—Lanercost Priory and Naworth Castle. Before reaching Lanercost, a rock inscription, shown in the woodcut, may be seen on the face of a limestone quarry, overhanging Banks Burn.

Divested of its ligatures, it reads :—I. BRVTVS DEC. AL. PET.
—Junius Brutus, a decurion of the ala Petriana.   Lanercost
Priory was founded by Robert de Vallibus, Lord of Gilsland,
and intended for the comfort of the canons regular of the
order of St. Austin.   The church was consecrated in the
year 1169.   In 1296 the monastery suffered from an invasion
of the Scottish forces.   During the winter of 1306 and 1307
King Edward I. resided with his queen in the monastery.
On the suppression of the monasteries, the priory and adjacent
lands were granted to a branch of the Dacre family.   In
consequence of the failure of male issue, in 1716 the lands
reverted to the crown.   They were long held on lease by the
Earls of Carlisle, but they now belong to the family by purchase.   Of the priory church the only portion which is in
repair is the nave, and this is used as a parish church.   It has
recently been renovated.   The choir and transepts are roofless.
Here are several large tombs.   One is the resting place of
Humfrey Dacre and Mabell his wife; the latter dying in
1509.   Another is attributed to Sir Humfrey's son Thomas.
the second Lord Dacre, who married Elizabeth, the heiress of
Greystock, and who died in 1525.   Another records the
death, in 1716, of the last male heir of the Dacres of
Lanercost.

Several of the monastic buildings remain.   The site of the
cloisters is an open space used as a garden.   The refectory
was on the south side of the cloisters, parallel with the church.
Its walls are thrown down, but the vaulted cellars, upon
which the refectory was usually placed, remain.   At the west
end of the vault is a door-way, which led up to the refectory.
The dormitory was on the west side of the cloisters ; it is often
taken for the refectory, in consequence of a large fire-place
having been inserted in it by Christopher Dacre of Lanercost,

son of Thomas Dacre, the grantee. It is marked "C. D. 1586." At the angle formed by the union of the dormitory and refectory was the prior's own mansion. It is now deserted.

The priory church and monastic buildings are almost entirely composed of Roman stones. These may have been procured from the Wall; but the mind can scarcely divest itself of the idea that there must have been a station here. The ground does not possess the elevation which the sites of Roman stations usually exhibit; but if, as appears to be the case, the river was here in Roman times crossed by a bridge, it may have been thought necessary to plant a station on the spot to guard the passage. CILURNUM which guarded the passage over the North Tyne does not occupy an elevated position. A horse regiment was stationed both at CILURNUM and PETRIANA. There are some indications of ramparts and of a north gateway in the priory-green.

There are some Roman inscribed and sculptured stones here. In the west wall of the cloister-garth is one, which may be translated—The century of Cassius Priscus. In the headway of the clerestory, in the south-east angle of the choir, is an altar, which was first described in the *Gentleman's Magazine*, for 1744. The inscription on it may be translated—"To Jupiter, the best and greatest; the first cohort of the Dacians, styled the Ælian, commanded by Julius Saturninus the tribune [dedicates this.]" In the vault are several interesting antiquities. One of them, an altar (here shown) dedicated by the hunters of BANNA to the holy god Silvanus, is curious, as indicating the mode in which the officers of the Roman

army sought to relieve the tedium of their leisure hours. It is as yet an unsolved question where BANNA was; it must have been in this neighbourhood. Has it been Gilsland? The Romans greatly prized medicinal waters and would not overlook the healing fountains of this locality. The next altar is one of those found in the Banks Head mile-castle (p. 208); it reads—"To the god Cocidius, the soldiers of the legion styled the Valerian and the Victorious dedicated this altar, in discharge of a vow to an object most worthy of it in the consulship of Aper and Rufinus." It is shown above. This gives us the date of about A.D. 153. The boar at the foot is the emblem of the twentieth legion. On another stone (here shown) is a somewhat spirited representation of Jupiter and Hercules. A metal thunderbolt (probably gilt) was no doubt inserted in the hole in the right hand of Jupiter. There are, besides, some large altars, either partially obliterated or uninscribed. One of them has been dedicated to

Jupiter, the letters I. O. M. being plain, but the rest obliterated.

A little below the present bridge, and immediately opposite the priory, are the remains of a Roman bridge. In the river the wooden frame-work on which one of the piers has been founded is visible when the water is low. Another pier, which has been deserted by the river, and is deprived of its facing-stones, is ten feet high. About forty feet beyond this are the remains of what appears to have been the land abutment, on the north side of the river. There are some traces of a road on the south side of the Irthing.

Ascending the rising ground south of the river, we soon come to Naworth Castle. The great hall of the fortress is redolent of heraldic pomp—the Greystock dolphin, the Howard calf, and the Dacre bull and griffin being made use of to support the banners of the house. The private apartments of Lord William, and the careful manner in which he guarded the approach to them, are worthy of observation.

South of Naworth Castle, and near the railway, is an ancient earthwork, probably British. "It has two encircling ramparts." (*MacLauchlan, Memoir*, p. 60.)

The Naworth station of the Newcastle and Carlisle Railway is close at hand.

We now rejoin the Wall at Hare Hill. About two hundred yards west of this point a break in the Wall occurs, in which a turret or small quadrangular building has been situated. This building projects beyond the Wall, northwards, rather less than three feet. It is constructed of smaller stones than the Wall; the workmanship of it is excellent. It measures fourteen feet six inches (inside measurement) from east to west. When first noticed, it was full of black ashes; the discoverers took it to be a smithy. Altogether it is a peculiar building; though it has some of the features of a turret, it

seems to have been built independently of the Wall.* At
Money Holes attempts have been made to discover treasure;
no doubt in vain. Through the priory-woods, to the south
of us, the works of the Vallum proceed undauntedly on their
onward course, and are in good condition. The fact that the
Vallum goes along the southern slope of the hill, leaving the
summit to the Wall, bears upon the question of the contemporaneous or successive construction of the works.

At Craggle Hill the north fosse is very bold. At Hayton
Gate a drove road, closed half a century ago, crossed the Wall.

A very little west of Randelands we meet with the feeble
traces of a mile-castle. After crossing the rivulet called
Burtholme Beck, a piece of the Wall is seen, which stands
nearly seven feet high; its facing stones are gone, but the
rough pebbly mortar possesses its original tenacity. As is
often the case, the ruin is tufted with hazel bushes, oak saplings,
and alders. Beyond this point a second ditch and rampart,
outside the Wall, seem, for a short distance, to have been
added to the usual lines of fortification. As the traveller

---

* This excavation has since the publication of the first edition of this
work been covered up to prevent the sheep falling into it, and the surface is
now grass-grown. A thorn tree is close to the spot where it is.

proceeds onwards let him occasionally look back upon the ground which he has traversed in order to observe the boldness with which the fosse of the Wall climbs the hills he has just passed. The Wall runs by the north of Howgill, Low Wall, and Dovecote on its way to the King-water. In the wall of an outhouse at Howgill is a rude inscription (shown in the woodcut on the opposite page) mentioned by Horsley and all subsequent antiquaries, which seems to record the achievements of a British tribe, the Catuvellauni. Tacitus tells us that Agricola took southern Britons with him to the battle of the Grampians; Hadrian and Severus may have been similarly accompanied in their expeditions.

Nearly due north of Low Wall are slight indications of a mile-castle. The prickly enclosures of the fields may prevent all but very zealous antiquaries keeping very close companionship with the Wall for a little distance; those who take the road by Dovecote will be brought back to their old friend before crossing the King-water.

It may be well to remind the reader before proceeding further that the river Gelt, on whose rocky banks the Roman quarrymen have left lettered memorials of their toil, is about four miles to the south of this place. The most famous of these inscriptions has been given at page 33. The woodcut on the next page represents Pigeon Crag, which is about half a mile higher up the river, and on the opposite side of it from the "Written Rock of Gelt." The inscription on the Pigeon Crag is of too fragmentary a nature to yield us definite information. The woodcut, however, gives us a general notion of the scenery of the place.

Westward of the King-water, the village of Walton is reached; many of the stones of the Wall may be detected in

its cottages.   The Vallum is here indistinct, and some distance
from the Wall.   At the entrance of the village faint traces of
a mile-castle are to be observed.   On the green to the west

of the church, Horsley saw traces of an earthen camp, which
was probably occupied by the troops, when building the Wall.
At Sandysike farm house, besides the foundations of the Wall,

two sculptured Roman stones are to be seen, which doubtless are parts of altars—one bears a thunderbolt, the other a wheel. We now descend into the valley of the Cambeck, having the north fosse for our guide. The next mile-castle must have stood either on the west side of the Cambeck-water or at Cambeck Hill; most likely the latter; all traces of it are obliterated.

Castlesteads.

To reach the Castlesteads station, it is best to turn off at Sandysike. The station stands to the south both of Wall and Vallum. Its situation is strong. On the north the ground falls precipitously towards the river Cambeck; on the south and west it slopes gently towards the Irthing. The station contains an area of two acres and three quarters. It is distant from the station of Birdoswald about seven miles—an unusually long distance.

If this be the station which, according to the *Notitia*, immediately follows AMBOGLANNA, and of this, independent of the excessive distance, there is some doubt (see p. 211), it is the PETRIANA of the *Notitia*, the headquarters of the *ala Petriana*. The area of this camp seems to be too small for the accommodation of a cavalry regiment, which, at one time at least, was a thousand strong. No inscriptions have been found in any of the stations of the Wall westward of AMBOGLANNA enabling us to identify them with the stations of the *Notitia*. This circumstance is the more to be lamented, inasmuch as antiquaries are not agreed as to which of the camps they meet with in their course westwards are stations *per lineam Valli*. But for this we might have given each succeeding station the name which follows next in order

in the *Notitia*.   We will not attempt therefore to give the
stations west of AMBOGLANNA their Roman designations.   An
inscribed stone may one day turn up which will relieve us
from our present difficulties.

As the site of the station has long been used as a garden,
its exact outline is considerably obscured.   The traces of the
ditch are visible, particularly on the west front.   Professor
Carlisle gives us an account of the digging up of this station
(in 1791), in the *Archæologia*, Vol. XI., and of the overthrow

of the Wall in its vicinity. His account of the Wall will remind the reader of what he saw at Steel Rig. "As the remains of the Vallum itself [Murus] for near half a mile were entirely dug up, Mr. Johnson, to whom the estate belongs, had an opportunity of examining the construction of this curious remnant of Roman industry with the greatest accuracy. Of this he gave me the following account:—"The breadth of the foundation was eight feet; the Wall, where entire, was faced with large stones on both sides, and the space between them filled with rubbish-stone to the depth of a foot; then a strong cement of lime and sand, about four inches thick; over that a foot of rubbish, and then a cover of cement as before; these layers were succeeded by others of rubbish and cement alternately, till the interstice between the facing-stones was filled up to the top, and thus the whole became one solid cemented mass."

Several valuable altars and other antiquities have been found in the station, most of which are carefully preserved on the spot by the present proprietor, George John Johnson, Esq. The most remarkable of these is the altar to Jupiter, a representation of which is given on the opposite page. It has been translated:—"To Jupiter, the best and greatest; the second cohort of Tungrians, a miliary regiment, having a proportionate supply of horse, and consisting of Roman citizens, commanded by Albus Severus, prefect of the Tungrians, erected this, the work being superintended by Victor

Severus, the princeps." Here is a figure of Fortune; and here is a priest vested in his cope, and holding an incense-box in his hand. The are both shown in the woodcuts on the previous page. The altar inscribed DISCIPVLINAE AVGVSTI is peculiar. The piety, the chastity, the courage, and other moral qualities of the emperors, were often deified; but it was not usual to rear altars to their administrative properties. But on the reverse of several of the coins of Hadrian we have the legend DISCIPLINA AVG., as in the two examples here introduced, with a suitable device.

There can be little doubt that the Augustus referred to on this altar is Hadrian. He maintained a strict discipline.

We now rejoin the Wall on the west bank of the Cambeck, and will follow it without interruption to Stanwix. Having done this, we will return and view the camps that have been noticed south of both lines of the Barrier.

It will be observed how deeply the fosse of the Wall has been cut into the red sandstone rock forming the western bank of the stream. The fosse of the Vallum is also discernible a little lower down. Cambeck Hill farm house is passed. The farm buildings at Beck are partially constructed of Roman stones. Looking westward from Beck the fosse of the Wall and Vallum are grandly seen.

Headswood, as its name implies, occupies a commanding situation. The ditch, both of Wall and Vallum, are seen as you approach it. There are some works here on the north side of the fosse. Mr. MacLauchlan thinks that they may perhaps be the remains of one of those camps with a round elevated part, which are thought to have a Saxon or Danish origin. (*Memoir*, p. 70.) About two hundred yards west of the Newtown of Irthington, we meet with evident traces of a mile-castle. We next come to White Flat, where the rubble of the foundation of the Wall is very discernible, and the ditch very deep. The visitor who wishes to keep by the Wall will avoid the cart-road which takes to Irthington, and follow the footpath which runs through the fields. Westward of White Flat the works are feeble, but we soon meet with a long strip of the Wall, in an encouraging state; it is planted with oak trees; the north fosse shows nobly. We now pass Hurtleton, leaving it a little to the south. Here the Wall and Vallum are but thirty-five yards apart; the fosse of each is distinct. Both works now bend northwards. About midway between this point and Old Wall a mile-castle stood;

the traces of it are now very faint. In the buildings at Old
Wall many Roman stones will be noticed; in a stable is a
centurial stone, here shown, bearing an inscription that may

 be thus translated:—"The century of
Julius Tertullianus, belonging to the
second legion, styled the August."
The Wall is here entirely uprooted,
many hundred cartloads of stone
having been removed within living
memory; but the fosse of the Wall is visible between the roadway and the houses. From this point westward the works may
be traced for some distance with satisfaction, an ancient drove-
road running upon the site of the Wall. At the end of this
lane, tall hedges and cultivated fields interfere materially with
the pilgrim's progress. At a spot called High Strand there
ought to be a mile-castle; tradition says that there once was
one here.

Bleatarn is a place of considerable interest. The Wall
runs a little to the north of the farm house; the Vallum is
immediately south of it. Between the Wall and the Vallum,
and westward of the farm house, is a large tumulus, which has
been diminished in height within the last few years.

Before coming to Wallhead there ought, judging by the
distance, to be a mile-castle. About six hundred yards before
we reach Walby there are faint signs of a mile-castle, being
seven furlongs and a half from the last; they are where the
road turns sharply to the north. At Walby there are some
pools in the north fosse. Here the Wall bends strongly to
the south. At Wall Foot there has probably been a mile-
castle. "The place for the next mile-castle would fall opposite
to Drawdikes Castle." (*Memoir*, p. 73.) Immediately in front

of Drawdikes Castle the lines of the Vallum are clearly discernible, though the mounds have been lowered of late, to make the place more sightly. The three busts on the top of Drawdikes Castle are said to have come from the Wall; and yet, with strange perversity, they are believed to represent the devil and two local celebrities, one of them a modern lawyer. On close inspection they will be found to have nothing Roman about them. Built into the wall at the back of the house is a monumental stone, which, according to Horsley, was brought from Stanwix. The inscription may be read:—"To the Divine Manes of Marcius Trojanus son of (?) Augustinus; his most loving wife, Ælia Ammillusima (?) caused this tomb to be erected."

The Wall now makes straight for Stanwix. As we approach this place, the advantageous nature of its position, as a Roman station, is seen. A fine elevated platform is observed, having the church at its eastern boundary. The ground falls from it on every side except the west, and here the river, with its wide and precipitous valley, is close at hand. Between Tarraby and Stanwix a broad footpath running through fields and market gardens, occupies the site of the Wall. The north fosse used to be boldly developed, but it has been much filled up within living memory.

Stanwix.

The church and church-yard of Stanwix occupy the site of the station which guarded the northern bank of the Eden.

The station is upwards of eight miles from that at Castlesteads. The outlines of it are not well defined, but Mr. MacLauchlan, from the information which he was able to obtain, came to the conclusion that it contained an area of two acres and a half. No inscriptions have been found here to inform us what troops were in garrison in Roman times. The sculptured stone shown in the woodcut was found in the wall of the parish church about the year 1790. It is evidently a funereal stone, the greater part of the inscription having been broken off. It is now at Nether Hall. In pulling down the

old church, to make way for the present structure, a figure
of Victory was found, which is now at Newcastle.   The
Romans were ad-
dicted to the use of
the bagpipes. Nero
was an excellent
performer.   The
figure of a piper,
now in the Carlisle
museum, was found
at Stanwix.   Hut-
ton thus notices
it :—"I observed a
stone in the street,
converted into a
horse-block, three
steps high, with the
figure of a man in
a recess eighteen
inches in height, in
a Roman dress, and
in great preserva-
tion.   I wondered
the boys had not
pelted him out of
the world."   The
woodcut represents
the more important
part of the stone.
Between the station

and the northern margin of the river Eden the fosse of the

Wall may be discerned descending the bank in the vicinity of the Hyssop Holme Well. Here for the present we must leave the important structure.

Brampton, Irthington, and Watch Cross.

The distance between Castlesteads and Stanwix renders the probality great that there was some Roman stronghold between them. Two places have been thought likely— Brampton Park and Watch Cross, both of them to the south of both Wall and Vallum. As they can be visited better from the line of the road between Brampton and Carlisle than from that of the Wall, we have reserved a notice of them to this place. We will now commence our subsidiary exploration at Brampton. This little manufacturing town was once upon the main line of road between Newcastle and Carlisle. The natural route for the railway was along the valley in which it lies. So violent, however, was the opposition of the inhabitants (yielding to ill advice), that the railway company were constrained, at a greatly increased cost, to take their line up the southern ridge of the valley. Brampton suffers accordingly. The only ancient feature belonging to Brampton is the Mote, at the east end of the town. It consists of a natural elevation, which has no doubt been, at different periods, applied to defensive purposes. The small platform at the top was formerly "defended by a breastwork;" lower down a rampart and fosse still appear. This hill-post may have given origin to the town. About a mile and a half west of Brampton is the old church of Brampton, of which only the chancel remains. It is composed of Roman stones. In some excavations made about twenty years ago, traces of a Roman road were found, and some coins and pottery. On a gentle eminence, to the south of the old church, are the fast-fading remnants of a Roman station. A century ago the site was covered with brushwood, and by this means escaped the attention of Horsley. The late Mr. Robert Bell, of the Nook, Irthington—a warm hearted and intelligent antiquary—had, in early life, assisted in carting away the stones of its ramparts. His subsequent observations, communicated to Mr. Hodgson, Mr. MacLauchlan, Mr. Roach Smith, and the writer, render it clear that the Romans had a camp here. Mr. MacLauchlan estimates its area at an acre and a half. It is about a mile and a half from the station at Castlesteads. A large jar full of Roman coins was found near this place in 1826. The coins were of a late date, extending from the time of Decius to that of Florianus. In the meadow below this camp are several remarkable barrows. They probably belong to the Romano-British period ; but the spade and pickaxe alone can decide the point.

Irthington, a village that lies to the west of the Irthing, and is situated about midway between the river and the Wall, has two objects of interest for the antiquary. A castle stood here in Norman, and perhaps, also, in Saxon times. Nothing is left but the mound, off which probably a stronghold, most likely of timber, was reared. The church, a Transition-Norman building, is worth attention. It was restored a few years ago. The old structure consisted entirely of Roman stones. This church has doubtless often been the scene of fierce Border encounters before the union of the kingdoms. The columns were marked by fire, and numerous skeletons, lying in disorder, were found within the area.

East of the Glebe farm at Irthington are extensive remains of ancient quarries.

Nearly due south from Bleatarn, and close to the turn-pike-road leading from Brampton to Carlisle, is the site of Watch Cross, another Roman camp. The boundaries of the station are now scarcely discernible, and all traces of building are entirely removed. It has contained an area of an acre and a half. (*MacLauchlan*, p. 72.) Horsley considered it to be ABALLABA, the station following PETRIANA in the *Notitia*. Little can be gleaned by a visit to it. We now return to the Eden at Stanwix.

Carlisle.

After crossing the river at Stanwix, the Wall, instead of proceeding straight to Carlisle Castle, kept a course more to the west, and, passing over the flat ground between the castle and the river,* made for a spot near the engine-house at Newtown, which was used in supplying the canal between Carlisle and Port Carlisle (now converted into a railway) with water. (*MacLauchlan, Memoir*, p. 75.) The Vallum is supposed to have passed on the south side of the castle. (*Memoir*, p. 77.)

All antiquaries agree that Carlisle is the LUGUVALLIUM of the Romans; but it does not occur in the list given in the *Notitia*. Up to a comparatively recent period, the Roman features of this city were very marked. Stukeley, writing in 1725, says :—" Fragments of squared stones appear in every quarter of the city, and several square wells of Roman workmanship. At the present day, whenever an excavation is made, articles of Roman make are turned up." During the formation of the city sewers in 1854, Samian ware, coins, and various bronze articles were found in great quantities. The

* In making, in 1854, the great sewer which drains Carlisle the Wall was here cut upon three feet below the surface of the ground.

cut represents a "Judæa Capta" of Vespasian, which was found on this occasion. It is striking to turn up in British soil, deposited in Roman times, such testimonies of the fulfilment of prophecy. (*Deut.* xxviii., 49.) In the City Museum in Finkle Street, Carlisle, may be seen an interesting collection of antiquities, chiefly derived from the neighbourhood. One of the latest acquisitions is a tombstone which was found in the western suburbs of the city. The deceased lady, sitting in her chair, holds in her hand a fan of a form still in use in the island of Malta and elsewhere.

Her left hand is lovingly placed upon the shoulder of her child who strokes the back of a dove upon her lap. At the top of the slab are two lions with a human head in their claws and a sphynx also holding a human head. These figures allude to the destruction of human life and the riddle (as it appeared to the heathen) of death. The lower part of the inscription, which we doubt not gave the name of the lady, is lost.

The castle and the cathedral will repay the attention of the mediæval antiquary. Carlisle being situated so near the borders of Scotland, its castle was a building of great importance. William Rufus visited Carlisle in 1092, and took

measures for rearing a fortress here. The general figure of
this keep, and of the encircling walls, are probably identical
with those planned by Rufus. The foundations are, for the
most part, composed of Roman stones.

The Cathedral of Carlisle is an interesting building. The
nave, the south transept, portions of the north transept, and
the lower part of the tower are the earliest parts; they belong
to a church commenced by Walter, a Norman follower of the
Conqueror, in 1092, and completed in 1101 by Henry I.
These parts are of the simplest and most massive type of
Norman architecture. No portions of the Norman choir
remain. The present choir was probably commenced by
Bishop Silvester de Everdon, who came to the diocese
in 1245, when the Early-English style had developed itself.
Bishop Welton (1352-1362), and his successor, Thomas de
Appleby, seem to have carried on the work vigorously,
and to have completed the choir, including the wooden roof,
before the death of Edward III. By this time the decorated
style of architecture had become established in England, and
was of course followed by these builders. The great east
window, if it be not the very finest "decorated" window in
existence, is rivalled only by the west window at York.

VII.—FROM THE RIVER EDEN TO THE SOLWAY FIRTH.

Westward of Carlisle the Wall is not easily traced.
Having attained the high ground just beyond the North
British Railway sheds, it runs along the southern bank of
the river as far as Grinsdale. Slight traces of it may be seen
at the distance of about fifty yards from the river, which has
served as its northern fosse. Hence, to Kirkandrews, it still

adheres to the cliffs, though the river runs deviously in the flats to the north. The Vallum, instead of following closely the variations of the high ground, runs in a straight line past Mill-beck to Kirkandrews. The churchyard at Kirkandrews is a mass of stones; it has probably been the site of a mile-castle. In a garden attached to the house of Mrs. Norman, in the village of Kirkandrews, is preserved an altar which was found at Kirksteads, about a mile south of the Wall. Its base has been removed and its capital cut down to fit it for use as a building stone. What remains of the inscription may be translated—"Lucius Junius Victorinus Flavius Cælianus Imperial Legate, (belonging) to the sixth legion, (styled) the victorious, the dutiful,

and the faithful, (erected this altar) on account of achievements prosperously performed beyond the Wall." It is shown in the woodcut. It is interesting to notice the fact as recorded by the Romans themselves that the land to the north of the Wall was not given up to the enemy.

In crossing the beck, before approaching Beaumont, the

fosse of the Wall is well developed.   The church at Beaumont
stands upon an eminence, formerly occupied in all probability
by a mile-castle.   It is remarkable how many churches stand
upon the line of the Wall, having, in the first instance, derived
their structure from the ruins of Hadrian's work.   In a wall at
Beaumont is the larger part of a somewhat ornamental
inscription commemorating the doings of the fifth cohort of
the twentieth legion, which was surnamed the Valerian and
Victorious.   It was fished out of the Eden in a salmon net
more than half a century ago.

The Wall, which had pursued a north-west direction to
reach Beaumont, now resumes its westerly course, and may
be traced all the way to Burgh-upon-Sands, and thence to
Dykesfield, selecting with care every eminence it meets.   The
Vallum pursues a nearly direct course from Kirkandrews to
the same point.   A little to the west of Monk Hill it crosses
the turnpike road, and keeps on the north side of it nearly
all the way to Burgh-upon-Sands.

Burgh-upon-Sands.

Here we have another station of about three acres in
extent.   It is about five miles and a half from Stanwix.   The
outlines of the station are not well defined.   It has, no doubt,
extended a little to the north of the present road, and has
had the Wall for its northern rampart.   The church is
within its eastern boundary ; a road running north and south
probably indicates its western rampart.   The Vallum has, as
usual, come up to its southern rampart.   In the churchyard
frequent indications of Roman occupation are turned up.

The church at Burgh-upon-Sands, of the construction of
which the woodcut opposite gives a general idea, is a good

specimen of the fortified border churches. The tower at the west end has evidently been a place of refuge. Its walls are seven feet thick. The church has recently been restored.

To the north of the village is Burgh Marsh, on which Edward I. and his army were encamped, waiting for a

favourable opportunity to cross the Solway, when death

seized the monarch, on the 7th July, 1307. The monument represented on the previous page marks the spot where his tent was pitched at the time.

On the northern bank of the Solway is a beacon called the Tower of Repentance. It was erected by a conscience-stricken marauder, who, on a stormy passage from the English to the other side of the Firth, threw his prisoners overboard in preference to the cattle which he had stolen.

From Burgh the Wall passes by West-end farm house to Watch Hill; an accumulation of small stones renders it probable that a mile-castle stood here. It then makes straight for the edge of the marsh at Dykesfield. The Vallum is traceable at intervals throughout this distance. It is seen

for the last time about fifty yards north of the public road, south of Watch Hill. It will be remembered that at the eastern extremity of the Wall there is no Vallum; it begins at Newcastle, and here at the west end it seems to terminate at Dykesfield. At Dykesfield there used to be a broken altar to the mother goddesses, found on the spot,* and at Longburgh is a small altar to Belatucader, also found in the neighbourhood.

* The writer did not see it on his last visit.

Although the Wall, when last seen both at Dykesfield and Drumburgh, seems to be making straight for the opposite side of the marsh, there can be little doubt that it skirted its southern margin, going round by Bowstead Hill and Easton. No traces of it now remain.

At Drumburgh is a station, the smallest on the line, containing an area of only three-quarters of an acre. It is four miles and a quarter from Burgh. South of the station

is a well, said to be Roman, from which the water is now drawn by a pump. The castle here, of which there are considerable remains, is a fine specimen of the fortified manor-house of the olden time. Leland, writing of it in 1539, says :—"At Drumburygh, the Lord Dacre's father builded upon old ruines a pretty pyle for defence of the country. The stones of the Pict Wall were pulled down to build it."

In cutting the canal (now the railway), in the vicinity of Glasson, a prostrate forest of considerable extent was met with. "Although the precise period when this forest fell is not ascertainable, there is positive proof that it must have been prior to the building of the Wall, because the foundations of the Wall passed obliquely over it, and lay three or four feet above the level of the trees." Much of the timber was sound; some of it was used in forming the jetty at Port Carlisle. The President's chair of the Society of Antiquaries of Newcastle-upon-Tyne is made of it.

The Wall, after leaving Drumburgh, bends to the north of Glasson, keeping to the south of the road, and having reached the shore, runs along it past Westfield and Kirkland to Port Carlisle. Occasionally traces of it are faintly discernible. The mound called Fisher's Cross would be an admirable site for a mile-castle, and may have been one. Over the door of the

 Packet Hotel at Port Carlisle is the fragment of an altar, having on it the letters MATRIBVS SVIS, a dedication, doubtless, to the *Deæ Matres*. The site of the Wall may be traced from this point nearly all the way to Bowness. Besides its foundation, the north fosse occasionally appears. The Wall here, when first seen by the writer, was several feet high; gunpowder was used in bringing it down. On the right hand, close by the shore, is another barrow-like object, called Knock's Cross. "As old as Knock's Cross" is a local proverb. "The water-course to a mill [now disused], leading straight to the entrance to Bowness, probably occupies the site of the fosse of the Wall." (*Memoir*, p. 87.)

The station of Bowness is well situated. It stands upon

a **bow-shaped** promontory, round which the waters of the Solway bend, and are then lost in the Irish Channel. Its platform is slightly elevated above the general level of the surrounding country. The station is not made out without difficulty. Its northern wall has stood upon the ridge overlooking the estuary. An ancient mound, still known to a few as the Rampire, or Rampart Head, is just outside its eastern rampart. Its western rampart is easily detected, its fosse being well marked; and its south-west angle may, though with difficulty, be traced. Although the form of the ground might lead to a different conclusion, the church is to the south of the station, and is not included in its area. The greatest length of the station is from east to west. It contains an area of five acres and a half. Its distance from Drumburgh is nearly three miles and three-quarters. Over a stable door, about the middle of the town, is the small altar here engraved. It is a dedication to Jupiter for the welfare of the Emperors Gallus and Volusianus, and was erected by Sulpicius Secundianus, tribune of the — cohort. At Wallsend we found that the eastern wall of the station was continued down the hill to a point below low water mark in the river Tyne; a similar arrangement prevailed here. Mr. MacLauchlan says, "Beyond Bowness we find no satisfactory account of the continuance of the Wall, though the old in-

habitants point out at about 250 yards from the north-west angle of the station, a spot where a quantity of stone was dug out of the beach many years since, for building purposes, and the line of it was followed for some distance under the sand, without arriving at the end of it. The direction of these remains, as pointed out by the old people, would fall in with a continuation of the north front for about 100 yards, thence down a natural ridge, well suited to a line of defence, and on the south of the school house, into the water."

At first sight Camden thought that the Solway was a sufficient defence, and that the Wall need not have been taken thus far; his words are (as rendered by Holland):—"I marvailed at first, why they built here so great fortifications, considering that for eight miles or thereabout, there lieth opposite a very great frith and arme of the sea; but now I understand that every ebbe the water is so low, that the Borderers and beast-stealers may easily wade over."

Although a little to the east of the station, the Solway is early fordable at low water, no one in the memory of the inhabitants of the place has forded the estuary westward of the town. This circumstance would render Bowness a fit place at which to terminate the Wall of Hadrian.

The present repose of Bowness seems to contrast strangely with the bustle which must have reigned in it, when so large a station was fully occupied by Roman troops. The little town is, however, the resort, during the summer season, of families from neighbouring places, for the purpose of sea bathing.

If the pilgrim who has followed the Wall from its eastern to its western extremity has enjoyed favourable weather, he will doubtless regret the termination of his labours.

One consolation remains to him. The Wall was supported, both on its northern and southern margin, by stations of considerable importance, and to these he may now direct his attention.

DM REGINA LIBERTA ET CONIVGE
BARATES PALMYRENVS NATIONE
CATVALLAVNA AN XXX

CHAPTER IV.

SUPPORTING STATIONS.

In order rightly to estimate the strength of the Roman Wall, we must take into account the stationary camps which existed both to the north and the south of it. Against these the wave of hostile aggression, in either direction, would, in the first instance, dash.

The estuary of the Tyne was strongly fortified. There is no doubt that there was a camp at Tynemouth, and another at the west end of North Shields. though no traces of them are now to be found. There were also two on the opposite side of the estuary—one on the Lawe, at the east end of South Shields, and another at Jarrow. The camp at South Shields has recently been to a considerable extent excavated, and some important Roman remains have been discovered. The most remarkable is a tombstone now preserved in the Museum of the Free Library, on which is given the figure of a lady and a bilingual inscription. The first part of the inscription, which is in Latin. is to this effect :—" To the divine shades. To Regina, a freedwoman and [his] wife, Barates a Palmyrene [erected this monument. She was] by nation a Catuallaunian, [and lived] thirty years." Then follows a line in the Palmyrene language and character, which has been thus translated :—" Regina, freedwoman of Barate, alas !" The lady seems to be engaged in doing worsted work. See the woodcut opposite.

One other stone from South Shields may be noticed here as being the latest discovery in the mural region. It also is a funereal stone, and is in the possession of Mr. Robert Blair.

The inscription reads as follows, though in consequence of the

obliteration of two or three letters in it the last line must be
regarded as somewhat doubtful : —

D · M · VICTORIS NATIONE MAVRVM
ANNORVM · XX · LIBERTVS · NVMERIANI
[E]QITIS ALA · I ASTVRVM · QVI ♣
PIANTISSIME PR[OSE]QVTVS EST.

"To the Divine Shades of Victor. He was by nation a Moor,
he lived twenty years, and he was the freed man of Numerianus a horseman of the first ala of Asturians, who most
affectionately followed (his former servant to the grave)."

The remains of Bede's church and monastery render a
visit to Jarrow very interesting.

Chester-le-Street is about seven miles to the south of
Newcastle. Its name indicates its Roman origin. The
church, churchyard, and deanery gardens stand within the
station. Numerous Roman remains have been found here.

An important series of stations stand upon the Roman
road called Watling Street. BREMENIUM, the modern High
Rochester, is the most northerly. It is about twenty-two
miles north of the Wall. The ramparts, ditches, and gates of
the station are easily discernible. Some fine pieces of masonry
remain. Extensive excavations were made here in 1852 by
his Grace the Duke of Northumberland, and, more recently,
by the Society of Antiquaries of Newcastle. Important
discoveries were made, which are detailed in the *Arch. Æl.*,
N.S., Vol. I., p. 69, and in the *Lapidarium Septentrionale.*
Although the excavations are now filled in, there is much in
the station and its vicinity to gratify the antiquary. The
earthen camps at Chew Green, on the Scottish side of the
boundary-line, are very curious, and the Watling Street
between Chew Green and BREMENIUM is in a better state of
preservation than in any other part.

Otterburn and Elsdon are not far off. The Rectory at Elsdon, a fortified building of the fourteenth century, and the Moat Hill, an immense earth-work, probably of the early British period, but afterwards occupied by the Romans, are worthy of examination.

Following the Watling Street about seven miles southward, we come to HABITANCUM, the modern Risingham. The station is well defined. To the south of it is the rock on

which the figure of the famous Rob of Risingham was sculptured. The upper half of him has been blown off by gunpowder; the lower portion of his figure remains, as shown in the woodcut here introduced. Risingham is not far from the Woodburn station of the Wansbeck Valley Railway.

CORSTOPITUM, near Corbridge, is the next station on the Watling Street. Its form and extent give it the aspect of a city rather than a camp.

Ebchester is the next. All its ramparts may be traced. The parish church, built of Roman stones, stands within it. The turnpike road crosses the station, probably on the line of the *via principalis*.

Lanchester is next in order. Its remains are very encouraging, though they were more so a few years ago.

Binchester is still further south, on the same line of road. It is near Bishop Auckland. Within the station is the most perfect hypocaust in the North of England. Unhappily it is now closed.

Pierse Bridge is on the north bank of the river Tees. The station is well defined. To most of these places there is access by railway.

We now turn to the stations on the Maiden Way.

Bewcastle is difficult of access. A pedestrian can best reach it by taking his course across the moors, from Carvoran or from Gilsland; or it may be approached from Brampton. The turnpike road is somewhat circuitous. The camp occupies a platform slightly elevated above the rivulet Kirkbeck. It departs from the usual form of Roman camps, being six-sided. A ruined castle (Bueth's Castle) and the famous obelisk give additional interest to the place.

Whitley Castle is the modern name of another outpost, which is situated as far south of the Wall as Bewcastle is north of it. It is near Alston, to which there is a branch line from Haltwhistle, on the Newcastle and Carlisle Railway. The form of the station is peculiar, being that of a trapezoid. In addition to the ordinary walls, it is defended, on the western side, which is the most exposed, by seven earthen ramparts, and on the north by four. The Maiden Way passes by the east side of the station. In the farm house here, called the Castle Nook, is preserved an altar, which is carved on all four sides. The inscription has been nearly obliterated, but it has no doubt been dedicated to Apollo.

We now approach the western extremity of the line. Nearly due north from Carlisle, and not far from the Scottish frontier, is the station of Netherby. It is about a mile and a half from Longtown. The outline of the station is nearly obliterated. A number of very important inscribed and sculptured stones, derived from this station, are preserved in the Hall, the ancestral seat of the Grahams of Netherby.

Nearly due north from Bowness, and near Ecclefechan in Dumfriesshire, is the station of Middleby. Its ramparts and gateways are distinct. Some altars and other antiquities found in it are preserved at Hoddam Castle.

There are some important stations south of the Wall. About two miles south of Wigton, in Cumberland, is a large and well-defined station, called Old Carlisle.

On the cliffs overhanging the modern town of Maryport, are the manifest remains of a large Roman station. Its position gives it a commanding view of the Solway Firth and Irish Channel. The camp is a large one, and the lines of its ramparts are very boldly developed. The sill of the eastern gateway is deeply worn by the action of chariot-wheels. In the neighbouring mansion of Nether Hall, the seat of Mrs. Senhouse, is preserved a large and very important collection of inscriptions and other antiquities found in the station here.

At Moresby, within a short distance of Whitehaven, are the well-defined outlines of another Roman camp. It was partially excavated by Lord Lonsdale in 1860, but little of importance was found. The ramparts, and the walls of some buildings in the interior, were found standing about a yard high. A military way ran along the coast from this station, by Maryport, to the extremity of the Wall at Bowness.

One object of the camps on the Cumbrian coast, no doubt, was to exclude the "Scots," who at that time "poured out of Ireland."

At a very short notice the garrisons of an extensive frontier could be concentrated on any one point.

CHAPTER V.

THE BUILDER OF THE WALL.

WE may now discuss the question, "When was the Wall built and who was its builder?" or to put it differently, "Are the several parts of the Wall one work, or were they distinct structures, reared at different times, by different persons?"

Gildas, the earliest British historian, gives us the following account of its structure. After the departure of the Romans "The Britons, impatient at the assaults of the Scots and Picts, their hostilities and dreadful oppressions, send ambassadors to Rome with letters, entreating in piteous terms the assistance of an armed band to protect them, and offering loyal and ready submission to the authority of Rome, if only they would expel their invading foes. A legion is immediately sent, forgetting their past rebellion, and provided sufficiently with arms." We are further told that all of the Picts and Scots were driven beyond the Borders, and the humiliated natives rescued from the bloody slavery which awaited them. But this was not enough :—"By the advice of their protectors, they now built a wall across the island from one sea to the other, which, being manned by a proper force, might be a terror to the foes whom it was intended to repel and a protection to their friends whom it covered. But this wall being of turf instead of stone, was of no use to that foolish people, who had no head to guide them." On the departure of the Roman legion their former enemies descended upon them, spread slaughter on every side, and overran the whole country. "And now again they send suppliant ambassadors, with their garments rent and their heads covered with ashes, imploring assistance from the Romans." The Romans came once more to their help, and once more delivered them from their foes "and, because they thought this also of advantage to the people they were about to leave, they, with the help of the miserable natives, built a wall different from the former, by public and private contributions, and of the same structure as walls generally, extending in a straight line from sea to sea, between some cities, which, from fear of their enemies, had there by chance been built. They then give energetic counsel to the timorous natives, and . . . . then left the island never to return."

The Picts and Scots of course descended upon the country with greater boldness than before. "To oppose them there was placed on the heights a garrison equally slow to fight and ill adapted to run away . . . . Meanwhile the hooked weapons of their enemies were not idle, and our wretched countrymen were dragged from the wall and dashed against the ground. Such premature death, however, painful as it was, saved them from seeing the miserable sufferings of their brothers and children."

Gildas is a weak and wordy writer. Living as a monk at Bangor in the sixth century, he would have little opportunity of becoming acquainted with events which had occurred in the North of England in the second and third centuries, or even in the fifth.

Some writers have conceived that the Latin poet Claudian gives countenance to the view that the Wall was built after the departure of the Romans from Britain, and that it was erected by order of Stilicho, the prime minister of the emperor Honorius. The passage of Claudian which bears most strongly upon this subject is the following:—

> "Me quoque vicinis pereuntem gentibus, inquit,
> Munivit Stilicho, totam cum Scotus Iernen
> Movit, et infesto spumavit remige Tethys
> Illius effectum curis, ne tela timerem
> Scotica, ne Pictos tremerem, neu litore tuto
> Prospicerem dubiis venturum Saxona ventis."

Which literally translated will read thus:—"[Britannia] said, Stilicho defended me, also perishing from attack of the neighbouring nations, when the Scot put in motion the whole of Ierne, and the sea foamed with the hostile rower. It has been effected by the care of that general that I should not fear the weapons of the Scot, that I should not dread the Pict, nor look out from the secure shore for the Saxon ready to come with the veering winds."

Claudian is not a writer of authority. The great object of his verse is to flatter his patrons. "Hence it is impossible to feel any confidence in the fidelity of the narrator in regard to those incidents not elsewhere recorded."*

* Professor Ramsay, in *Smith's Dictionary of Greek and Roman Biography*, article *Claudianus*.

Bede follows Gildas in his account of the works:

Let us now look at the probabilities of the case. Is it likely that at the time when Rome was weakened by being divided into an eastern and western empire, at a time, too, when barbaric foes were making head against the rulers of both, Rome should be able once and again to despatch a legion to this distant part of the empire, in order to relieve the Britons from their distress?

Again, is it likely that a work of such extent as the Roman Wall, and involving such a vast amount of labour, could be so speedily executed as the words of Gildas would imply?

If a legion came to Britain in the fifth century, what legion was it? The second and the twentieth legions came into Britain in the time of Claudius, and the sixth in the time of Hadrian. The twentieth had been withdrawn from Britain before the compilation of the *Notitia*, near the beginning of the fifth century, and the other two retired not long afterwards on the final abandonment of the island. All of these troops have left inscriptions on the Wall, several of them dating from the time of Hadrian. How is it that we have no trace of any other legion than these? It is also an important fact none of the inscribed stones found in Britain give indications of a date so late as the time of Honorius. The latest inscription found in Britain, of which the date can be ascertained, belongs to the time of Crispus the son of Constantine the Great. Crispus was put to death A.D. 326.

We proceed to consider another theory. Horsley and some other writers think that the stations of the Wall were erected by Agricola, and that the north agger of the Vallum was also his work, it being the road by which intercourse was kept up from station to station. The ditch of the Vallum, and the aggers to the south of it, they ascribe to Hadrian ; the stone Wall, with its fosse and military way, they consider to be the work of Severus.

Let us look at the probabilities of this theory. It is certain that when Agricola advanced into Caledonia, with a view to the conquest of that country, he left several forts in his rear to prevent surprise, and to secure his retreat if necessary; but is it likely that he would build a chain of forts, four miles apart, all the way from the Tyne to the Solway? Not only would it be quite unnecessary, but he would not have time to do it in, for he seems only to have rested a single winter in the North of England.

Again, can any one who has seen the north agger of the Vallum, conceive that it has been intended for a military way? It is a mere mound of earth and stone, and is destitute of pavement. It is usually a little larger than the two southern mounds, but in no important particular does it differ from them. Further, it is a fact admitted on all hands, that all the lines of the Vallum—the north agger, the fosse, the two southern aggers run right across the country in lines perfectly parallel with each other. Now, is it likely that if these lines were constructed at different times by different engineers and for different purposes this would be the case? Most persons traversing the Vallum from end to end will come to the conclusion that its several parts are the work of one man, of one period, and for one object.

Let us next consider how far the theory is tenable that the Vallum, taken as a whole, was constructed by Hadrian, and that Severus built the stone Wall.

Severus, like Agricola, contemplated the conquest of Scotland. He would not build the Wall before he went upon his

northern expedition.   When he returned from his three
years' campaign, sick and sad, having lost fifty thousand men
in his enterprise, he would have neither the inclination to
enter upon so vast a work nor the power of doing so.   He
died shortly after his return at York, and his sons, Caracalla
and Geta, beat a hasty retreat to Rome.

Let us look at the works themselves, and consider their
testimony.   If the Vallum had been an independent fortification, erected with a view to operations against a northern foe,
it would have been drawn along the northern side of the
stations, or have been brought up to their northern ramparts;
the fact, however, is that it usually coalesces with their
southern ramparts, leaving the station itself, so far as it is
concerned, wholly exposed to the enemy.

Again, if the Vallum had been an independent fortification,
its track would have been along those portions of country
which would have enabled the military to operate with
greatest effect against a northern foe.   This is by no means
the case.   For miles together, the Vallum runs along low-
lying ground, which is commanded by considerable elevations
to the north of it.   Generally speaking, the Vallum occupies
ground which is best for a defence against a southern foe; the
Wall, that which is best against a northern.   This fact is
fully admitted by Horsley.   He says, "It must be owned that
the southern prospect of Hadrian's work [the Vallum] and
the defence on that side, is generally better than on the
north; whereas the northern prospect and defence have been
principally, or only taken care of in the Wall of Severus." *
We must therefore either come to the conclusion that Hadrian
reared not only the Vallum, as a means of preventing aggression

* Horsley's *Britannia*, p. 125.

on the part of the subdued but discontented Britons to the south
of his line of military organization, but the Wall also as a line
of operation against his fierce and avowed enemies on the
north; or that his engineers were great blunderers, and offended
against the primary rule of castrametation as laid down by
Vegetius, "That care should be taken to have no neighbouring hill higher than the fortification, which, being seized by
the enemy, might be of ill consequence."

Further, it is impossible to conceive that the stations of
BORCOVICUS, ÆSICA, and others, would have been placed where
they are, unless the Wall had been intended to traverse the
basaltic heights which it now does. The Wall and these
stations must have been virtually contemporaneous, and parts
of the same great design. These stations are where they are
in order to accommodate the troops who manned the Wall
in these parts.

The evidence of the coins found in the Barcombe quarry
(p. 171) is also in favour of the theory that Hadrian built the
Wall.

Lastly, the testimony of inscriptions is strongly in favour
of it. Several stones found upon the Wall mention the name
of Hadrian, none on the Wall itself bear the name of Severus.
The mile-castles are an integral part of the Wall. Now in
four of these mile-castles slabs have been found, bearing in bold
characters the name of Hadrian and his proprætor Aulus Platorius Nepos. (See pp. 114, 162, 166, 174, 179.) These mile-
castles are the one immediately west of Housesteads, that opposite Hotbank, the one at Castle-Nick, and that at Cawfields.
They all occur in the wild, central portion of the mural tract,
where the Wall and its buildings have been less interfered with
than elsewhere. The probability is that similar inscriptions

have been attached to all the mile-castles along the Wall. The name of Severus does not occur in any of them. It has been objected that these stones are for the most part in a broken condition, that they have been found among the debris on the floor of the buildings, and that they may have been brought from the Vallum as building stones. That they should be found in a fractured condition, and amongst the rubbish of the floor, is just what we would expect. Every station on the Wall, every castle, every turret, bears marks of having suffered more than once from the vengeance of a successful foe. It is most unlikely that these stones should have been brought from the Vallum, for the Vallum has no buildings specially connected with it ; and curiously enough it happens that the four mile-castles in which these stones have been found are further removed from the Vallum than is usually the case.

Justice to the memory of Horsley requires that we should state that all the inscriptions found upon the Wall bearing the name of Hadrian have been discovered since his day, with the exception of the fragment of one* which he had not the means of reading correctly.

If Hadrian built the Wall as well as the Vallum, it is quite evident that Severus, before setting out on his northern expedition, repaired the Wall, and saw that the stations were put into an efficient state of repair. We do not, as has been already stated, find his name on any inscriptions found upon the line of the Wall itself ; but we find it inscribed upon some quarries in Cumberland, and upon slabs found at Hexham, Risingham, and at Old Carlisle. An inscription found at Risingham, on the Watling Street, north of the Wall, is

---

* The left hand portion of the one found at Milking Gap.

suggestive. It is shown in the woodcut here given. It gives him the honour of restoring the gate of the station over which it was set, and the contiguous wall—PORTAM CUM MURIS VETVSTATE DILAPSIS . . . A SOLO REST*ituit*. This is probably the whole history of Severus' connection with the Wall; he repaired it and set it in order. As being the last person to have any dealings with it, it was called in the ages immediately subsequent to him, the Wall of Severus; just as the western world, which was discovered by Columbus, took the name of a subsequent adventurer Amerigo Vespucci.

The reader will naturally ask, What say the ancient writers upon the question at issue? If their statements are not entirely satisfactory, they are at all events not inimical to the view here taken that Hadrian built the Wall. Two historians of note flourished during the reign of Severus—Dion Cassius and Herodian—and they both treat of British affairs. Dion Cassius twice mentions the Wall. Speaking of the state of things in the time of Commodus, he says, "Some of the nations within that island, having passed over the Wall (τὸ τεῖχος) which divided them from the Roman station, . . .

committed much devastation," &c.   (*Monumenta Historica*,
p. lix.)   The other passage relates to the reign of Severus;
"Among the Britons, the two greatest tribes are the Caledonians and the Meatæ .... The Meatæ dwell close to the
Wall, which divides the island into two parts; the Caledonians
beyond them." (*Mon. Hist.* p. lx.).   Herodian flourished about
the year 238.   The only reference which he makes to the
Wall is the following—"His (Severus's) army having passed
beyond the rivers and fortresses which defended the Roman
territory, there were frequent attacks and skirmishes, and
retreats on the side of the barbarians."

These are the only passages that we have in the writings
of any contemporary author; they are consistent with the
idea that Hadrian built the Wall, but scarcely so with the
supposition that Severus did so.

Spartian is the next writer who mentions the subject.   He
is not an author of much credit; and as he did not flourish
till the close of the third century, his testimony is of the less
value.   Speaking of Hadrian, he says—"He sought Britain,
where he corrected many things, and first drew a Wall
(*murum duxit*) for eighty miles to separate the barbarians
and the Romans."   Writing of Severus, he says, "He secured
Britain which is the chief glory of his reign, having drawn
a Wall across the island (*muro per transversam insulam
ducto*); whence he also received the name of Britannicus.
(*Mon. Hist.* p. lxv.)   Once more he mentions the Wall in
connection with Severus—"After the Emperor had passed
the Wall or Vallum (*post murum aut vallum missum*), and
was returning to the nearest station," &c.   (*Mon. Hist.* p. lxv.)

Julius-Capitolinus, who flourished at the close of the third
century, in recording the erection of the Antonine Wall in

Scotland, says—"Antoninus carried on many wars by his legate; for he conquered even the Britons by his legate, Lollius Urbicus; having, after driving back the barbarians, constructed another wall composed of turf (*alio muro cespiticio ducto*.) (*Mon. Hist.* p. lxv.)

These are the chief passages bearing upon the subject, and all that our space will admit of.

These quotations are not in themselves decisive but none of them invalidate the testimony which the builders of the Wall themselves have given us in the tablets of stone found in the mile-castles. We must always bear in mind, too, that Hadrian was a great builder which Severus was not.

The first of modern writers to propound the view here advocated was Stukeley, the Antiquary. His testimony as given in his *Iter Boreale* is—"In my judgment the true intent both of Hadrian's Vallum and Severus's Wall was in effect to make a camp extending across the kingdom; consequently was fortified both ways, north and south." "Both works were made at the same time, and by the same persons." The Rev. John Hodgson in the last volume which he lived to write of his History of Northumberland enters at length upon the subject and successfully pleads the cause of Hadrian. The following calmly written sentence has great force, especially when we consider the great attention he had given the subject; and with it we conclude:—"In the progress of the preceding investigations, I have gradually and slowly come to the conviction, that the whole Barrier between the Tyne at SEGEDUNUM and the Solway at Bowness, and consisting of the Vallum and the Murus, with all the castella and towers of the latter, and many of the stations on their line, were planned and executed by Hadrian; and I have endeavoured to show that in this whole there is unity of design, and a fitness for the general purposes for which it was intended, which I think would not have been accomplished if part of the Vallum had been done by Agricola, the rest of it by Hadrian, and the Murus, with its castella, towers, and military way by Severus."

In taking leave of these two renowned men, Hadrian and Severus, who for a time held the world in their grasp, it may be allowable to advert to the testimony which they left behind them as to the unsatisfactory nature of their vast possessions and advantages. Hadrian, in his last sickness, is said to have addressed his soul in these words:—

> "Animula, vagula, blandula
> Hospes, comesque corporis
> Quæ nunc abibis in loca
> Pallidula, rigida, nudula?
> Nec ut soles dabis joca."

Lines which have been thus imitated by Prior—

> "Poor little, pretty, fluttering thing,
>   Must we no longer live together,
> And dost thou prune thy trembling wing,
>   To take thy flight thou know'st not whither.
> Thy humorous vein, thy pleasing folly,
>   Lies all neglected, all forgot;
> And pensive, wavering, melancholy,
>   Thou dread'st and hop'st thou know'st not what."

Severus' restless pursuit after happiness was equally vain. His dying words are said to have been "Omnia fui et nihil expedit:" "I have tried everything, and found nothing of any avail."

CHAPTER VI.

THE ANTIQUITIES FOUND ON THE WALL.

Many specimens have been given in the course of the preceding pages of the most important class of antiquities found upon the Wall—altars, dedicatory slabs, and centurial stones. Gold coins are extremely rare; many silver pieces have been found; the copper and brass coins that have been picked up are for the most part very highly corroded. Finger rings of gold, silver, bronze, iron, and jet are occasionally dug up. Many of them contain a jasper, carnelian, or artificial stone, on which some design is roughly but effectively cut. One of

the most recent acquisitions of this kind is one that was found in the station of CILURNUM. On the stone has been carved the representation of a chariot race in the Circus Maximus at Rome. It is remarkable what a number of objects the artist has been enabled to represent in so small a space, and so correctly. The woodcut on the following page is drawn to four times the size of the original. Fibulæ or brooches, generally of bronze, for the fastening of the woollen garments of the men, as well as women, are also found.

Another object of recent discovery shows that the Romans resident in Britain were not neglectful of the fine arts. The

R

woodcut represents a cameo, found at South Shields, and now
in possession of Mr. Robert Blair, of that town.   The stone is

Indian sardonyx of two layers, the upper opaque white, the

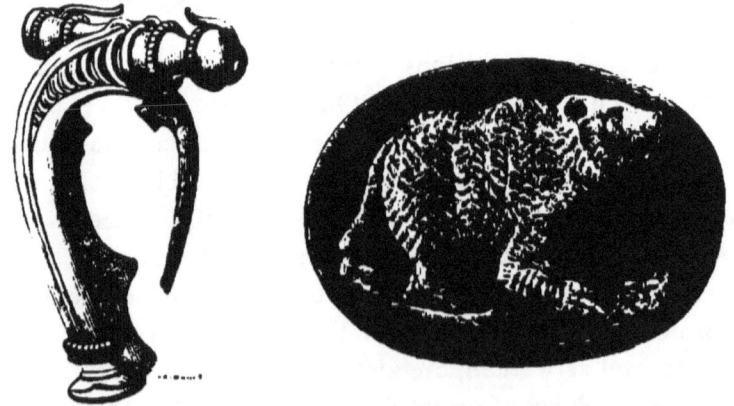

lower a rich translucent brown.   The subject is a bear.   The drawing opposite is of the size of the original. Cameos of this description were mounted in gold and silver, and served for the fastening the great military cloak upon the shoulder, in the manner of the modern solitaire.

If the object shown in the woodcut, which is here given of its full size, be as it appears, a vinegaret (Fig. 1), it proves

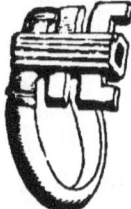

Fig. 1.   Fig. 2.

that the elegancies of life were not, even in those days ot fierce conflict, banished from the region of the Wall.   If modern locksmiths had but studied Roman antiquities, they would have found a royal road to some of their modern inventions.   Here is a key (Fig. 2) of elaborate form, intended to be worn as a ring upon the finger; it is from the museum at Chesters.

Pottery usually forms an abundant class of Roman relics in every camp that has been long occupied.   The Samian ware is very beautiful, and very characteristic.   It is sometimes embossed, as in the specimen here

given, but more frequently plain.   This species of "ware" has been imported from the continent.   Other kinds are common, and were probably of native manufacture. Amongst them may be noticed the *mortarium*, a strong shallow dish with a spout (of which there is a specimen in the centre of the next cut), which was used for gently bruising their food in, and was also occasionally thrust amongst the embers as a stew-pan. Fragments of wine amphoræ are not uncommon. Glass vessels are occasionally met with, but they are rare. Window glass, as has already been mentioned (p. 100), is also found.

The writer would now withdraw—hoping that the student, about to visit the Wall, for whose benefit he has penned these pages, may be strong of limb and stout of heart to undertake his task, that the sky may be propitious, that every step of his journey may yield him knowledge, stimulate the noblest aspirations of his soul, and fit him the better to fulfil those high duties for the discharge of which we have all been called into existence.

THE CHESTERS DIPLOMA.

APPENDIX I.

DIPLOMA OF CITIZENSHIP.

IN excavating the eastern guard-chamber of the southern gateway of the camp at CILURNUM, a small bronze tablet was found. (See p. 88.) The present writer coming up at the time of its discovery, it was put into his hands by the careful excavator, William Tailford. Although obscured with verdigris and mould, he discerned its real nature and importance. It is not every day that we enjoy the excitement of reading an important historical document which has been hid from human eyes for more than a thousand years. When cleaned by Mr. Ready, of the British Museum, it presented the appearance shown in the plate opposite,*

Roman citizenship was a privilege of great value. It rendered a man eligible for all public offices, whether civil, military, or sacred. It gave him the right of voting in the public assemblies, and of appealing from any decision of the magistrates to the supreme authority in the state. A citizen alone could hold property or make a will. He only could contract a lawful marriage. A Roman citizen could not be bound; he could not be scourged; and if guilty of a crime for which death was the penalty he could not be put to death by torture; he was beheaded.

The right of Roman citizenship was obtained by birth or by gift. In the reign of Claudius, chiefly through the agency of his wife, Messalina, it became purchasable. At first it was, as Dion Cassius tells, very dear.

When the privilege was conferred by the Emperor, the decree announcing the fact was engraved upon plates of

---

* This plate having been prepared by the photographic process, the letters, if somewhat less distinct than in the original document, are absolutely correct. In order to get it into the page it is shown a little smaller than it really is.

bronze, and affixed in some public place for the perusal of
all. Further, it is understood, that a copy of the decree, also
engraved upon bronze, was given to each individual to whom
the citizenship was granted, that he might the more readily
assert his claim. This copy was engraved upon two small
plates, which folded together and might be easily carried
upon the person. The decree was written both on the inside
and outside of the plates ; on the one side the lines ran along
the plates, on the other across them. The copy contained
the names of five or six witnesses, who certified as to its
correctness, and it stated where the original decree was displayed. These precautions rendered it an easy matter for a
man to establish his citizenship. Falsely to claim it was
death. When the Apostle Paul claimed to be a citizen his
word was not for one moment doubted.* These diplomas
are often called *Tabulæ honestæ missionis.*

The inscription on the Chesters diploma is as follows, the
words which are supplied being printed in italics :

INSIDE.

Imp · *Caes* · *divi* HAD*riani f* · *divi Trajani Part* · *n* ·
*divi Nervae pr*ON · T · A*elius Hadrianus An-*
TO*ninus aug* · PIVS *pont·max* · *tr·pot* · *viiii*
    IM*p* · *ii* · *c*OS IIii *p·p* ·
EQ · ET PED · *qui mil* · *in al* · *iii* · *et coh* · *xi q* · *a* · *aug* ·
GAL · PROC · ET I . . . . *et i Hisp* · *Astur* · *et i*
CELT · ET I HISP · ET *i Ael* · *Dacor* · *et i Ael* · *classica*
ET I FID · ET II GAL · *Et ii et vi Nervior* · *et iii*
BRAC · ET IIII LING · *et iiii Gallorum et sunt in*
BRITTAN · SVB PAPIR*io Aeliano quinque et vig* · *stip* ·
EMER · DIM · HON · MIS*sione quorum nomina subscripta*
SVNT C · R · QVI EORV*m non haberent dedit et*
CONVB. CVM VXORIB*us quae tunc habuissent*
CVM EST CIV. IIS D*ata aut cum iis quas postea*
duxissent dumtaxat singuli, &c.

* Acts xvi., 37, 38 ; xxii., 27, 28.

OUTSIDE.

Imp · CAESAR DIVI HADRIANI F · DIVI
Trajani PART · NEPOS DIVI NERVAE PRO
nep · T · *Ael*IVS HADRIANVS ANTONINVS
Aug · *pius* pONT · MAX · TR · POT · VIIII IMP · II COS · IIII
P · p · *equit* · *et* pEDIT · QVI MILITAVER · IN ALIS III
et cohort · *xi qu*AE APPELL · AVG · GALL · PROCVL · ET I
. . . . ET I HISP · ASTVR · ET I CELTIB ·
et i Hisp · *et i* AELIA DACOR · ET I AELIA
CLASSIC*a et i fid* · vARD · ET II GALLOR · ET II ET
VI NERVI*orum et iii Bra*C · ET IIII LING · ET IIII GALL ·
ET SVNT IN B*rittan*NIA SVB PAPIRIO AELI-
ANO QVINQ*ue et virgi*NTI STIPEND. EMERIT
is dimissis honesta missione quorum nomina
subscripta sunt &c.

Some portions of this inscription which are wanting on the one side of the plate are found on the other. We are thus able to make out the names of all the troops, with a single exception, to whom the important privilege of citizenship was by it given. Some phrases of a formal character which are also wanting may be supplied from other diplomas.

Making use of these means we get an inscription which may be thus rendered in English:—The emperor Caesar (of the deified Hadrian son, of the deified Trajan styled the Parthian grandson, of the deified Nerva great-grandson), Titus Aelius Hadrianus Antoninus august, pious, chief priest, possessing the tribunician power for the ninth time, declared imperator for the second time, consul for the fourth time, the father of his country, to the cavalry and infantry, in three alae and eleven cohorts, which are named the imperial horse regiment of Gauls styled the Proculeian, and . . . . and the first cavalry regiment of Celtiberians, and the first cohort of Spaniards and the first of the Dacians styled the Aelian, and the first of the Marines styled the Aelian, and the first of the Varduli styled the faithful, and the second of the Gauls, and the second and the sixth of the Nervii, and the third of the

Bracarians, and the fourth of the Lingones, and the fourth of the Gauls ; and are in Britain under Papirius Aelianus ; [to all of them] who having completed twenty-five campaigns and obtained an honourable discharge, whose names are given below, who do not already possess it, he has given the Roman citizenship and the right of lawful marriage with the wives they had when the citizenship was given, or with those they may afterwards take, provided one at a time.

The document dates from the year A.D. 146, when Antoninus Pius possessed the tribunician power for the ninth time, was imperator a second time and consul for the fourth time.

Our venerable friend, Mr. Clayton, rightly conceiving that the Chesters diploma was of national importance, has generously presented it to the British Museum, where, as already mentioned, the three others are preserved for the benefit of the zealous antiquary.

Three diplomas of citizenship had previously been found in England, and the fragment of a fourth. The earliest of these was found at Malpas, in Cheshire. It was issued by Trajan, and bears the date of A.D. 104. At Sydenham, in Kent, another has been discovered; it also was issued by Trajan, and bears the date of A.D. 106. The third was found at Riveling, near Stannington, in Yorkshire, and was issued by Hadrian, in the year A.D. 124. All of these are in the British Museum. Admirable chromo-lithographic plates of them, of the size of the original, are to be found in the *Lapidarium Septentrionale*. The fragment of a fourth, of the time of Antoninus Pius, A.D. 146, was found at Walcot, in Somersetshire. It is in the museum at Huntingdon, and is figured in the *Archæologia Æliana*, Vol. VIII., p. 219.

APPENDIX II.

EXCURSIONS.

It is difficult to plan excursions for travellers with whose physical powers you are unacquainted. The state of the weather, too, another matter of uncertainty, will, in most instances, have to be taken into account. Still a few suggestions may not be unacceptable.

A pilgrimage along the whole line of the Wall may be accomplished in about a week. The first day may be occupied in examining the Roman inscriptions in the Museum of the Society of Antiquaries of Newcastle, visiting the Old Castle, and doing that portion of the Wall that lies between Wallsend and Newcastle. On the second day, the stretch of Wall between Newcastle and Chollerford, about twenty-one miles, may be traversed. At Harlow Hill, ten miles out of Newcastle, simple refreshments may be obtained, and if need be a bed. If accompanied by an open carriage it may be resorted to occasionally with advantage. At the George Inn, Chollerford, accommodation of all kinds can be obtained ; here also carriages are kept.

Between Chollerford and Gilsland the great difficulty a tourist meets with is to find places where he can obtain food and rest; for these he will, for the most part, have to leave the Wall, and betake himself to the towns on the banks of the South Tyne. At Haydon Bridge he will find ample accommodation, at Bardon Mill one or two travellers can be housed, and at Haltwhistle there are several inns.

On the third day of his journey our traveller may, by dint of exertion, traverse the Wall from Chesters to Cawfields Mile-Castle, and then strike down to Haltwhistle for the night. He may, if he think proper, indulge in the use of wheels as far as Sewingshields, alighting at every point of interest.   In traversing the high grounds over which the Wall runs in the central part of its course, and giving due attention to the objects of interest you meet with, you cannot go at the rate of more than two miles an hour.

In estimating the distance of one point from another, it is convenient to note how many mile-castles lie between them; remembering that the *castella* are, for the most part, one Roman mile (about seven furlongs) from each other.

On the fourth day, the pilgrim rejoining the Wall at Cawfields may easily get to Gilsland by the evening.

Next day he ought to reach Carlisle.   In order to do this he will either have to leave a visit to Lancercost and Naworth to some future occasion, or have to avail himself of the aid of a wheeled vehicle.   In any case, the latter part of his journey will be a toilsome one, as the objects of special interest are but few.

At the close of the sixth day he will probably find himself standing upon the ramparts of the station at Bowness, gazing at the heights of Criffel on the other side of the Solway.

Many persons may wish to visit only the chief points of attraction on the Wall, and to spend a single day at a time in doing so.   For such persons the following hints may be of use.   The most interesting centres of observation are the camps of CILURNUM, Chesters; BORCOVICUS, Housesteads; and AMBOGLANNA, Birdoswald, and the neighbourhood of each.

———

1.—To see CILURNUM, Chesters, and neighbourhood, take the early North British train from Newcastle to Chollerford. From this point, walk along the eastern bank of the North Tyne to view the abutment of the bridge (p. 70); returning to the road, make up Brunton Bank to see the turret and fine piece of the Wall at Brunton (p. 69); then go to Chesters to examine the station there (p. 83).   Having done this, the traveller may be disposed to rest from his labours, and seek the refreshment of the inn.   If, however, he be disposed for further exertion, he can extend his walk westward, as far as the top of Limestone Bank, in the course of which the Vallum is seen to advantage: the turret and Wall on Black

Carts Farm (p. 120) may be examined, and the extraordinary excavations of the fosse of the Wall and Vallum on the top of Limestone Bank explored. Return to Chollerford for evening train. The distance of the top of Limestone Bank from Chesters is perhaps a little more than two-and-a-half Roman miles. The gradients are heavy.

2.—To visit BORCOVICUS, Housesteads. Go by the New-castle and Carlisle Railway to Haydon Bridge, then take the road which leads to the Wall at Sewingshields, a distance of about five miles, chiefly up hill. Then traverse the heights. in companionship with the Wall, to Housesteads. thence to Housesteads mile-castle, and on to Crag Lake beside Hot Bank. If tired, the tourist may then make for the railway at Bardon Mill, which is distant about three miles; visiting VINDOLANA on his way. A strong walker may, however. press on to the mile-castle at Cawfields, passing on his way Peel Crag and the heights of Winshields. At Cawfields he may make for the railway at Haltwhistle, distant about two miles.

3.—If a shorter excursion to Housesteads be desired, let the tourist alight at Bardon Mill, and then proceed to VINDO-LANA, the modern Chesterholm. After seeing the station, the inscribed stones about the house, and the mile-stone, let him then make for the military road, and go thence to Housesteads, which lies about half a mile to the east of the point where he joins the main road. If so disposed, he may on his way clamber up the eastern height of Barcombe, to examine the ancient British camp there (p. 172). Having examined the station, he may then, if he pleases, return to Bardon Mill; but it will be better for him to proceed a little more than a mile further along the Wall in a westerly direction, visiting the Housesteads mile-castle, and viewing the Northumberland lakes from the mural height nearest Hot Bank. Hot Bank is three miles from the railway station at Bardon Mill, to which he may then go.

4.—AMBOGLANNA, Birdoswald.   The objects of interest in this neighbourhood are very easily overtaken in a day. Besides the station and the Wall, they are Mumps Ha', Gilsland Spa, Lanercost Priory, and Naworth Castle.   If the visitor begins his investigations at Gilsland, he may, after tracing the Wall to Birdoswald, and examining the station there, follow the Wall as far as Hare Hill, and then make his way to Lanercost and Naworth.   There is an inn on the south side of the bridge at Lanercost, where refreshments may be obtained.   Close to Naworth is one of the stations of the Newcastle and Carlisle Railway.   If the traveller wishes to find himself at Gilsland at the close of his day's peregrinations, he can reverse the order of the proceedings here suggested.

After having made one or two excursions, the mural investigator will have gained sufficient experience to be his own guide, requiring no other assistance than that which this little work affords and the accompanying map.   The writer, therefore, thinks it needless to offer further suggestions.

INDEX.

FINIS.

www.ingramcontent.com/pod-product-compliance
Lightning Source LLC
Chambersburg PA
CBHW060541030726
47498CB00004B/1276